WITH A CASE OF MURDER, BLACKMAIL AND SCANDAL ON HIS HANDS, LT. GATES WAS TRYING TO KEEP HIS HEAD.

Advancing in hesitant hops and skips like a squirrel, the man yelled. "Hi! Lieutenant! Been looking all over for you. Wanted to tell you what I seen."

Frankie Gates fixed a saturnine eye on the shabby man. Conversation with a speck bum was the last thing he desired at that moment. "What's on your mind?"

Frainer fell in step with him. "I want to tell you what I seen last week in this empty old house where I was sleeping with Samantha. Nobody lives there. It's by the Fenway, Lieutenant—and we was sleeping there, me and Samantha. What I seen was a guy's head in the fireplace. Yeah, I woke up—and cripes, was it hot! I thought the thermostat was too high. Then I heard noises and saw lights, so I crawled down the hall and looked through the floor in one of the rooms, and I seen this husky bozo—and he was the one who threw the head in the fireplace. Wearing a hat."

"That right, Whitey?" said Gates. "What kind of hat was the head wearing? A derby?"

A CAN OF WORMS

BY RUSSELL H. GREENAN

OTHER BANTAM BOOKS BY RUSSELL GREENAN

IT HAPPENED IN BOSTON?

HEART OF GOLD

THE SECRET LIFE OF ALGERNON PENDLETON

A CAN OF WORMS

RUSSELL
H.
GREENAN

BANTAM BOOKS
TORONTO • NEW YORK • LONDON • SYDNEY • AUCKLAND

A CAN OF WORMS

A Bantam Book / July 1987

ISBN 0-553-26575-X

Published simultaneously in the United States and Canada

Bantam Books are published by Bantam Books, Inc. Its trademark, consisting of the words "Bantam Books" and the portrayal of a rooster, is registered in U.S. Patent and Trademark Office and in other countries. Marca Registrada. Bantam Books, Inc., 666 Fifth Avenue, New York, New York 10103.

PRINTED IN THE UNITED STATES OF AMERICA

O 0 9 8 7 6 5 4 3 2 1

For Althea and Ted Tyrer, and Elizabeth and Paul Greenan, and Ann Laura Greenan.

1

When Ludy Gilman dropped dead of a coronary thrombosis early one winter morning in the garish lobby of the Montevideo Motel on Route 3A outside Nashua, New Hampshire, the two maids who happened to be present at first thought he was just kidding around. Ludy liked nothing better than a little slapstick-pratfall comedy.

Only a moment earlier he had been telling a joke about a wealthy divorcee, who for her tenth husband wanted to marry "an innocent man, a pure man—in fact, a virgin." His fruity voice had bubbled with mirth as he described how the rich lady's agents finally discovered a handsome young candidate in the Outback of Australia who had never even *seen* a woman, and how this prodigy was transported to the United States and duly married to the divorcee several days later.

"So after the reception the bride and groom go to their hotel suite, and she ducks into the bathroom to put on her nightie," Ludy had said, grinning from ear to ear and waggling his eyebrows. "But when she comes back out she sees that her new husband has taken all the furniture and piled it against the walls—the chairs, the bed, the tables, everything. So naturally she gets excited and asks him why he did this. And the guy says, 'Well, my dear, I don't know much about ladies—but if they're anything like kangaroos, we'll need all the room we can get.' "

The two maids had laughed, of course. Nobody could tell a dirty story like Ludy Gilman. Seconds after he delivered the punch line, however, his jowly face suddenly went slack and he slumped to the nylon carpeted floor like a deflated balloon and, after a few feeble twitches, lay there perfectly still.

The older of the girls, Nathalie, a French-Canadian amazon from the St. Lawrence River town of Rimouski, was the first to realize the night manager's collapse hadn't been part of his comic routine. "*Malheur!* He's sick, the poor man," she blurted out. "A heart attack, *peut-être*! Phone the police, Arlene. Hurry! *Dépêche-toi,* Arlene! He is dying, maybe."

While not the brightest of women, Arlene was well accustomed to following Nathalie's orders. Within five minutes two New Hampshire state troopers arrived on the scene. An ambulance came shortly thereafter and efforts were made to resuscitate the stricken man, but without success. Ludy was as dead as a boiled dumpling. With his complexion chalky white and his lips a nice shade of lavender, he looked more the clown than ever.

Eventually the body was driven away. The troopers took down the girls' statements, uttered some words of comfort and reassurance, and departed.

While Arlene sobbed into a wad of pink Kleenex, Nathalie contemplated the faint impression in the nap of the electric-blue rug—the night manager's last at the Montevideo—and said in a tone of wonder, "So quick it happened. So sudden. Poor Ludy! He was not old, either. Only a touch of gray in his funny wavy hair. A crazy type, but I liked him—even if he was always pinching my *derrière*...and chasing after all the pretty young boys, too.

'*La vie est brève,*
Un peu d'amour,
Un peu de rève,
Et puis, Bonjour.' "

The brawny maid recited softly, as though to herself. "But now, Arlene, it is necessary to dry your tears and call up Mr. Ortega. Tell him the whole tragic *histoire*. He will have to employ another night clerk *tout de suite*. And do not leave the desk until Alfred arrives, eh? There will be guests checking out. Me, I am going to poor Ludy's cabin and search for the names of his relatives. They will need to be phoned. It is all so sad and cruel."

2

His crinkly hair windblown and his jowly face somber, Harold Gilman said, "I haven't seen much of him the last couple of years—my law practice and political commitments keep me busy as hell—but we used to be very close, Ludwig and me."

"Family ties are the strongest," Mr. Ortega replied sympathetically. He was a sharp-eyed man in a checked sports coat. "A brother is a brother."

"With all his faults—and he had plenty—Ludy was a nice guy."

"Everyone here thought the world of him. Such a cheerful personality. But what can you do?"

"Nothing now, I guess," said Harold. He rose to his feet and began buttoning his camel's hair coat. "Can I drive my car up to the door?"

"Certainly. The snow isn't deep," Mr. Ortega said. "You won't forget to return the key, will you?"

"Nah. Drop it off on my way back," said Harold, opening the lobby door to let in a frigid blast of New England air.

Even pacing himself, the job proved to be hard work, but at last he had piled all his brother's junk on the rear seat of the blue Cadillac. Only the footlocker under the bed remained, and that presented a problem. The thing was as heavy as an iron safe, and none of Ludy's keys fitted the padlock.

"What the hell's he got in there?" the lawyer muttered. "I try to lift that and I'll give myself another hernia."

Glancing out the cabin door he saw a tall woman striding up the snowy slope. A cloth coat was thrown over her broad shoulders, and beneath it she wore a wrinkled maid's uniform. As their eyes met, she called, "You are Ludwig's relative?"

"His brother—yeah," he answered.

"There is a family resemblance—the same hair. But it

is too terrible what happened. Poor Ludy. We all liked him very much, you know?"

"That's really gratifying to hear."

"I'm Nathalie," the maid said, entering the room.

"Pleased to met you," said Gilman, favoring her with a toothy synthetic smile. "Hey, could you give me a hand with this locker? Recently I had an operation, and it's more than I can lift."

"Of course. It's no trouble. I am very strong," she replied in her Gallic accent.

And strong she was, for she managed her share of the weight far better than Gilman did his. Into the car's trunk they shoved it.

"You are taking all his furniture?"

"Nah... not the furniture," Harold wheezed, unaccustomed to so much exertion. "I sold it all to the owner... the Spanish guy."

"Oh," she said, apparently disappointed.

"Want to buy any of what's left? The TV? Twelve inch, and it works great... nice, sharp picture... beautiful color. Cost you a hundred-and-a-half in a store at least."

"No, no. I don't need such a thing," she said, slightly contemptuous. "I must get back to work now. Good-bye."

"Yeah, so long. Thanks for the help."

Leaning wearily on the cold roof of the Cadillac, Harold watched the maid trudge down the hill. "Screw you," he said under his breath. "Another broad looking for freebies ...something for nothing. A ham sandwich she wants. The pig's ass I'll give her."

When he was well rested he locked the cabin, returned the key to the office, got back out on Route 3A and drove south. By the time he reached Arlington it was four-thirty. He stopped there at a seedy little pawnshop on Broadway, and with the aid of the proprietor—a man he had once defended against a charge of receiving stolen goods—unloaded the automobile.

Inside Ludy's trunk—they hacksawed the padlock— Harold found a couple of cameras, a Nikon and a Pentax. There were several additional lenses, too, including one that was a telephoto zoom, according to the print on the case.

But what had made the footlocker so heavy was a quantity of thick brown envelopes which were packed at the bottom. Opening a few, he found them full of photographs and negatives—tricky shots of churches, monuments, and curious old buildings.

The pawnbroker paid him a flat $300 for everything. It wasn't as much as Gilman had been hoping for, but he didn't haggle. It was found money. He never expected Ludy to leave him so much as a dime. His former client took the footlocker, too, though he showed no interest in the photographs. These were tossed back in the Cadillac.

Harold drove to a restaurant in Somerville and ate swordfish steak and Delmonico potatoes for his dinner. Afterwards in the parking lot he threw the envelopes containing Ludy's photographs in an iron garbage bin. Then, feeling satisfied with his day's work, he went off to a house in Wellesley and promptly lost the whole of his brother's estate playing deuces-wild draw poker with three other members of the Massachusetts bar. Bad luck dogged him. Even when he drew a fourth six, somebody beat him with a royal.

By midnight Gilman was home in Brookline. As he got out of his car in the basement garage he noticed that one of the thick brown envelopes was still on the backseat, somehow overlooked earlier. Not knowing what to do with the bundle, he brought it upstairs with him.

The building—it was called The Allerton Arms—belonged to his wife Magda, whose apartment was separated from his by a double door that she had been keeping locked for the past couple of years. Entering the living room he could hear her laughter coming from the other side of this door, and he assumed she was with her boyfriend, the Boston detective. But that didn't bother Harold. He and his wife were still on pretty good terms, though their lives were no longer intimately linked. She did her thing, he did his. It was an amicable arrangement.

He washed up, donned his pajamas, poured himself a small glass of crème de cacao, turned on the television and sat down. Memories of the night's poker game distracted him, however, and he soon switched the set off.

The envelope on the chest of drawers caught his restless eye. He rose, walked to the dresser, and emptied the fat packet on its polished surface. To his surprise he found that most of the pictures in this batch were pornographic—vivid scenes of abandoned sexual activity between men and women, men and men, and women and women. Harold, whose passions rarely expressed themselves carnally, was mildly revolted by this unexpected panorama of flesh and perversion.

"That ding-a-ling," he murmured. "He never changed."

Ludwig had been horny since birth, a natural sex fiend. As a kid this often got him in trouble. More than a few times Harold had gone hunting for the little schmuck, and caught him flagrante delicto up in the attic or in the garage, playing hide-the-baloney with one of his contemporaries. And they weren't always female contemporaries, either. Ludy wasn't finicky. He couldn't afford to be—not with the kind of itch he had to satisfy.

Engaged in these recollections of his childhood, Gilman began to notice a certain strangeness in the glossy 8×10 prints spread out before him. They seemed amateurish for someone of Ludy's camera skills. All were taken from above, shot straight down onto the rumpled bed. The lighting was terrible, too. And the setting never varied. The same furnishings appeared in every sequence—and it didn't look like the stuff in his late brother's cabin.

Something about the cast of characters bothered him. A lot of the participants were old and ugly or fat and homely—much more comic than sexy. None of them acted as if they were putting on a show. Nor had Ludy taken any posed close-ups—really explicit shots from interesting anatomical angles. But how the hell could he, if the camera was on the ceiling?

Sipping his crème de cacao, Gilman considered the problem, then suddenly chuckled. "They're candid photos," he murmured. "All those eager lovers—they're not posing. Ludwig snapped them on the sly in one of the motel units."

Sure, that was the explanation. Hadn't the crazy nut done exactly the same thing to Cousin Edna and her new husband when they came to live in the Gilmans' house for a couple of weeks years ago? Sure. Ludy had punched a hole high up on the wall, and through it photographed the sweethearts every night. He'd even stuck 200-watt bulbs in all the lamps to provide adequate illumination. By the end of their stay he had quite a stack of pictures, some amazingly distinct. Of course, he never showed them to

Edna—she'd have died of shame—but Harold had gotten to see the complete set, and he could still recall most of their more vivid details.

Voyeurism. Yeah, that was one of his brother's vices, too. Several times Ludy got caught peeping into bedroom windows, and once he fractured both wrists falling out of a tree suspiciously close to a dormitory on the campus of a girl's junior college in Newton.

Realizing now that the photographs had been taken without the consent or knowledge of the subjects, Harold Gilman viewed the whole matter much less critically. It became a practical joke to him, a fitting punishment for such raunchy behavior.

Get a load of these two freaks, he said to himself, studying one of the better prints. This old geezer must be sixty at least, but he's hung like a water buffalo. What a schwanz! And look at the bend in it. Unbelievable. When he's not shtuping floozies with that thing, maybe he rents it out to a hockey team.

Leisurely flipping the photos over, he began to hope that a familiar face might show up among the unsuspecting performers—a straitlaced judge, perhaps, or the snooty wife of a colleague. The lawyer was nonetheless astonished, however, when he actually did come across someone he knew—a shapely blond woman who wore her hair in long corkscrew strands.

"Well, well, well," he murmured, delighted. "Everybody's into mortal turpitude, these days. Imagine that."

The picture was fuzzy, so he couldn't distinguish much of her partner, but further on he discovered more shots of the pair and his eyes widened in wonder.

"Fantastic!" Harold whispered. "Both of them—and going at it like a couple of alley cats. The dirty bastards. Well, what do you know. Hey, these could be worth something—could be the key to a lot of doors. That dump up there must've been their private love nest."

With mounting excitement, he found other photographs of the two voluptuaries, though they were not always together. Each of them craved variety, evidently. Gilman didn't recognize any of their alternate companions. Not that it mattered. He had what he wanted.

Smiling at himself in the mirror above the chest of

drawers, his teeth shining with a phosphorescent gleam, he whispered, "Dynamite."

Then he carefully sifted through the pile again, hunting for the corresponding negatives.

3

Philip Delaunay's brick-and-brownstone Mount Vernon Street residence occupied the center slot in a seven-house row. Built shortly after the War of 1812, it had a two-step stoop and a white-painted paneled front door surmounted by an elliptical fanlight. A wan saffron radiance shone from this little window, gilding the crown of Detective Kevin Reedy's narrow-brimmed fedora.

Reedy gripped the cold brass knocker and rapped four times, and in that venerable neighborhood this sequence of percussions sounded as harsh as gunfire. Turning his back to the stiff breeze, he spied Delaunay's chauffeur, John Ruffing, huddled behind the wheel of a Dodge across the street. They exchanged nods of recognition, just as the door opened.

"Hi, Kev. How're you doing?" Phil greeted him affably. "Come in, come in. That air must be blowing straight down from Baffin Bay."

"Yeah, fierce. Wind's like a whip," Reedy answered, entering the warm vestibule and taking off his hat.

"Thank God it's not snowing. Storms are what devour the revenue and deplete the public coffers," said Delaunay, as he shut and bolted the door. "That damned nor'easter in December cost a fortune, and all the lads at the Hall are beside themselves. You'd think the money came out of their own pockets. But maybe it does...maybe it does."

He chuckled and paused for a moment beneath the old-fashioned chandelier with its scalloped glass shade, the soft light exaggerating the red tints in his hair and giving an added flush of health to his fair complexion, so that he looked ten years younger than he really was. Even his worst enemies had to acknowledge State Senator Delaunay's handsome features, yet there was something strangely artificial about them, something a bit theatrical. The square-jawed face was too perfectly proportioned, too symmetric, too free of natural flaw.

Kevin Reedy hung his hat and coat on the hall tree and trailed his friend into the parlor. To his surprise, they were alone—no city councillors, no precinct captains or ward bosses, no commissioners, no cronies, no loudmouthed wire-pullers.

"What you need is a drop of Old Bushmills, to get your blood circulating again," his host announced, stepping into the corner alcove where a marble-topped liquor cabinet rested under a huge colored lithograph of Faneuil Hall.

"Fine," the detective said, though in truth he would rather have had a glass of warm milk or a cup of tea. "Jeez, Phil—never seen this room so empty before. Where are all the favor seekers?"

"I threw them to hell out. Hughie Watson and Sal Calabrese left just before you arrived. They were pumping me—doing their damnedest to get inside information about the new tunnel proposal. *Free* inside information, mind you. Christ, what people! Jerome Foley used to say a contractor would follow you through the gates of Hell to find out if his bid was too high—and he was right. Remember Jerome?"

"Yeah, the old hump from Chelsea. Always wore a homburg and overcoats with velvet collars."

"That was Jerome. I once saw him in spats."

"His brother Tom had a Buick-Olds dealership over there—near Bellingham Square. I bought a Ninety-eight from him fifteen years ago. Jerome became attorney general, didn't he?"

"No—lieutenant governor. And that was as high as he ever got. He made the mistake of giving my father a hard time about a simpleminded nephew of his who needed a cushy job. So when Jerry Foley wanted the nomination for a seat in the House in D.C., Dad treated him like a pariah."

"Your father was a tough dude, Phil."

"I'll say." Delaunay came out of the alcove holding two squat glasses half filled with whiskey, handed one to his guest and raised the other aloft. "Here's to you, Kevin. Happy birthday. Hope you have fifty more, at least."

"I don't know if I could stand that many. But thanks, Phil."

They drank, then sat down. Delaunay said, "I was going to ask a few of the St. Columbkille's gang to drop by. None of them are around, though. Clarkie's in New York. Tim McPhee is out west somewhere, and so on. Don't want a real wild party, now that we're growing old and decrepit. Forty-one, eh, Kev? Getting a bit thick about the waist, aren't you?"

"Yeah. I ought to start jogging," said Reedy. "Where's Agnes?"

"My good wife is at a concert—Symphony Hall. Went with a couple of thoroughbred bluebloods from Louisburg Square. Are you hungry? Missy is upstairs watching some trash on television, but if you feel like a hunk of sirloin she'll come down and burn it for you."

"Nah, I'm okay. Had a boiled dinner an hour ago, and I couldn't even finish that. My stomach is still on the bum."

"Really? What's the matter? You used to have cast-iron guts, buddy. I'd get heartburn just watching you swallow those oysters drenched in Tabasco."

"Jeez, don't even talk about that stuff, Phil. Ever since the accident my belly's been acting up. Maybe I got an ulcer. But it's not only my stomach. I get a lot of headaches, too, and I feel lousy in general."

"Psychosomatic," Delaunay said confidently. "You've got to stop brooding."

"Sure, but it's not an easy thing to do," Reedy replied, staring into the small brick fireplace where sawtoothed flames consumed a pile of charred logs. "I keep seeing and hearing that woman. It's fucking uncanny . . . like a video cassette playing inside my skull. There ain't no way I can erase the tape, no way I can wipe those memories off my brain. Tell you the God's honest truth, Rita's more alive to me now than she ever was. It's like being haunted, Phil. She's with me all the time. I ain't had a decent night's sleep since it happened." Turning to face his friend, he asked, "You haven't heard anything, have you? About why she was up there on Route 495?"

"Like what, Kevin? Rumors? Gossip? No, I haven't—and I don't expect to. I've told you before that you're making a mountain out of a molehill."

"Maybe, but I don't see how. She was going to visit her mother, and her mother lives in Patchogue, Long Island. What was she doing in Chelmsford? That's the opposite direction, Phil."

"Didn't the mother collect antiques? Rita might've been looking for a gift up there—a teapot or some pewter spoons. For chrissake, give her the benefit of the doubt."

"How the hell can I? She left on Friday and she died on Saturday. Where did she sleep that night? In a flea market?"

A brief spasm of annoyance distorted Delaunay's symmetric countenance. "People often behave erratically. If Rita were alive, I'm sure she'd explain everything. Why are you so suspicious, Kev? She was alone in the automobile."

Reedy tipped more Irish whiskey into his mouth, and felt it tear down his throat like molten lead. "She was alone at the time, yeah—but that don't mean she was alone during the night," he argued, and wiped his lips with the back of a hand. "Listen, that girl had been acting strange for months. There was something on her mind. She got kind of dreamy, didn't pay attention when I talked to her. Started going to the beauty parlor a lot, too. Started dressing up more. Starting dieting...and buying fancy clothes."

"Kevin, you're letting your imagination run away with you. Rita always dressed well, always watched what she ate, always had her hair done."

"She must've been screwing around."

"I don't believe it."

"Plenty of other funny little things I remember, too," said Reedy, tapping the fingers of one hand on his knee. "Like she stopped asking me to marry her. Hadn't raised the subject for almost a year. Not a word, Phil. Even stopped making wisecracks about it."

"Interesting that you should mention that," Delaunay remarked, smiling slightly.

"Why?"

"Because maybe the marriage question is a big part of your problem. Isn't it just possible that you're trying to compensate for your own feelings of guilt by accusing Rita of infidelity? I don't want to sound like a shrink, but you lived with the woman six years and always laughed at her pleas to make the union legal."

"Hey, what arc you saying?" Reedy's crabbed fingers drummed rapidly. "That was the arrangement we had. I spelled it all out for her when she moved in with me, made it clear I didn't want a wife and kids, didn't ever want to get married. Phil, I was a hundred percent open and honest about that right from the start. I didn't bullshit her. Rita accepted those conditions—agreed to the deal—which is why I got sore later when she used to nag me."

In two quick swigs he drained his glass. Then he set it carefully on a cork coaster on a corner of the coffee table.

"But you know as well as I do how she was thinking," Delaunay said. "When a man tells a woman he's not going to marry her, it goes in one ear and out the other. They never believe it. They can't, buddy. If they did, the human race would become extinct. So far as the female of the species is concerned, remarks like that are only idle conversation—small talk, chitchat."

The detective slowly sucked air into his lungs, and just as slowly let it out. "We discussed it dead serious, Phil. No wedding bells, no kids. I explained it and explained it—told her about my old man and old lady, about the booze and the beatings, and screaming and yelling, the dirt, the humiliation, the fucking obscene misery. I never held nothing back. And Rita—she understood."

"Then why did she nag you, Kev?"

"Who the hell knows? Christ, that's why I used to get mad," said Reedy in a brittle voice, while his scrabbling fingers accelerated their tempo. "She appreciated that I wanted a decent life. She'd kid me about it. I was always kind of scared we'd go broke or something—wind up in a rat's nest on welfare. And I thought maybe I'd get to be like my father—a mean, drunken son of a bitch who belted his wife and kids around just because he . . . he . . . because he hated himself, probably. Okay, that was a kink in my head—a hang-up. Everybody's got a few of those, don't they?"

"But even if she understood the reasons behind your attitude," said Delaunay, "that doesn't necessarily mean she accepted the situation. I always had the impression that whenever Rita was at a big social function, surrounded by a crowd of legitimate wives, she tended to grow moody—to withdraw or become irritable. She probably had to listen to catty remarks, too. Regardless of her hip modern views, down deep Rita was an old-fashioned girl, in my opinion. And six years is a long time to be—"

"Jeez, Phil, give it a rest, will you?" Reedy broke in irately.

Elevating his trim eyebrows in surprise, Delaunay said mildly, "Whoa. Take it easy. We're all friends here. Merciful Mother of God, simmer down. I'm not blaming you, Kevin."

"Sure as hell sounds like you are."

"No, no. I'm only trying to help you solve the problem, shake you out of your fit of melancholia. The point is she's gone. You've got to forget her—at least enough so your health doesn't deteriorate. You need to come to terms with it." Vexed, the handsome politician clamped his mouth shut. The fire's crisp rustle filled the silence, until at last Delaunay stood up and laughed apologetically. "Hell, I'm jabbering too much—blethering away like a thick-headed hack in the legislature. Well, it's just that I can't bear to see my closest pal suffer." He finished his whiskey, pulled a wry face and exclaimed, "Jesus, Mary, and Joseph—what a birthday party!"

Reedy, suddenly ashamed of his outburst, said, "Listen, Phil, I didn't mean to get sore. I . . . I really ain't been myself lately."

"Come on, Kevin—forget it."

"You can say what you want to me—anything, anytime, anywhere."

"And you to me, buddy. Let's have a mite more of the Old Bushmills." As Delaunay took his friend's glass the phone rang. "Never a moment's rest," he said. "But my sister will answer it upstairs. She'll tell them I'm at St. Anthony's, making a mission. I'm getting so I hate phones. With all those sophisticated electronic devices they have now, you can't trust the damned things anymore."

"You still think your wires are being tapped?" asked Reedy, the tension gone from his voice.

"Sure. I've got some mortal enemies in politics. You didn't notice any suspicious characters hanging around when you came in just now, did you?"

"Only John Ruffing, playing the faithful watchdog in

his Dodge across the street. You're getting paranoid in your old age, Phil."

"Bullshit," said the politician, grinning cannily.

Three drinks later they moved out to the kitchen, where over plates of ham, cole slaw, and potato salad they reminisced about the carefree days of their youth—about other birthday parties, high school basketball games, wild weekends on the Vineyard, and hilarious hunting trips to Maine. After a while Kevin Reedy grew a bit maudlin.

"But the day that's real vivid in my mind, Phil, is the morning I went crashing through the ice there on the Charles. I can remember every single little detail about that, honest to Christ—the way Harvard Stadium looked, the boathouse with its ramp, that gray-black sky, the red wool hat you were wearing with the pompom thing on the top."

"Sweet suffering Jesus! Are we going to hear *that* heart-searing sob story again?" Delaunay grumbled, shoving his empty plate away.

"I remember falling, the scrunching sound—and all of a sudden the freezing water rushed over me. Went right up my nose, in my eyes, in my mouth. I could see the bottomside of the ice—a weird, sick green it was—and that fucking cold turned me numb instantaneous. Talk about being scared. Jeez! Then I felt your hand yank my jacket, and a second later my head popped out into the air again and I could breathe—like returning from the grave after being buried alive. I saw the trees, the sky, the bridge, the stadium—and you wearing that stupid hat. How long did you hold me up, Phil? Fifteen minutes?"

"Oh, shit! More like five, you silly clod."

"Never understood why your fingers didn't get frost-bite. Was it ever cold! And I must've been heavy as a sack of spuds."

"'He ain't heavy, Father Flanagan. He's me brother,'" Delaunay crooned in a boyish falsetto.

"Nothing to joke about," Reedy protested. "You were the first person who ever cared about me. You saved my life."

"A big mistake. Did it without thinking. Just never realized I was going to have to relive the whole damned dismal incident every time the two of us had a taste of hooch together down through the years. Stow it in the memory box, will you? A crying jag is what you'll be having next."

At that juncture Missy Delaunay pranced into the kitchen carrying presents and a small chocolate layer cake graced with a single pink candle. She was a pretty, blue-eyed girl, and her smiling face was framed by coiled strands of blond hair that the wavering candlelight transformed into spirals of brass.

Phil, who was fifteen years older than his sister, leaped up at once. Then the two of them joined their lilting voices in a fine rendition of "Happy Birthday to You," while the detective, taken by surprise, blushed and rose slowly to his feet. At the song's conclusion Reedy blew the candle out, though he forgot to make the traditional silent wish.

Two festively wrapped gifts were bestowed on him—a pair of fleece-lined bedroom slippers and a snuff-brown Donegal wool scarf. A lump developed in his throat and his eyes grew moist.

Missy cut and served the cake, and after the portions were appreciatively consumed the three friends trooped down to the rumpus room in the basement, where Phil settled himself on the piano stool and proceeded to play a medley of old favorites in his best barrelhouse style on the chipped-keyed, liquor-stained upright Baldwin. To these happy strains and amidst much laughter, Melissa and Kevin did some spirited dancing.

Delaunay's wife Agnes returned towards midnight, and not long after that the party broke up. Slightly befuddled by drink but very content, Reedy ambled into the vestibule and donned his hat and coat. There he was caught alone by Missy, who gaily said, "For God's sake, Kevin—give us a birthday kiss."

Though embarrassed by her sudden embrace, especially when she slid her tongue in his mouth like a warm and wet salamander, the detective didn't push her away until he saw Delaunay approaching.

Good nights were exchanged. Then, with the gifts under his arm, he stepped through the open door and descended the stoop to Mount Vernon Street. Johnny Ruffing and his Dodge were gone from the other side of the road and all was silent, dark and freezing cold.

4

As Reedy drove home to Jamaica Plain that night his euphoria slowly evaporated. Remembering the awkward conversation earlier in the evening, he came to the sad conclusion that Phil would never really understand the way things had been between him and Rita.

It's my own fault, the detective thought. I ain't got the gift of expressing what I feel. But, jeez, he must know how much I loved that woman, how I went for her the first night we met there at the Hyatt Regency, at Paddy Nugent's wedding, even though I figured I didn't stand a Chinaman's chance—not with a gorgeous dish like that.

The shapely, well-spoken girl had certainly seemed too sophisticated for a Boston cop. With her bright Irish face and quick sense of humor, Rita was the sort of ideal charmer a lonely man might imagine in a wistful daydream. Yet to Reedy's surprise and delight, she actually liked him. The two of them hit it off together beautifully. So in the weeks that followed, he saw her almost every night, and after a couple of feverish months of that she came to live with him in his eight-room house—the terrific Victorian place he had picked up for peanuts, for some unpaid taxes, through a political henchman of Phil's the previous summer.

It worked out great, too—at least for a year and a half. They settled into an easy, natural union that differed hardly from legal wedlock. But then she started complaining, Rita did—said she was only a surrogate wife—and nothing was quite the same again afterwards.

Reedy tried patiently to explain to her the strange dark fears he had of matrimony, tried to make it clear that he just couldn't handle the responsibilities of a family and children, but not being very articulate, he never managed to convince the woman. She didn't understand. She couldn't grasp that these crazy anxieties he had sprang from his childhood experiences, that their causes were buried deep in his heart and brain, and that he didn't think he'd ever be able to get rid of them.

The detective had grown up in the Allston section of Boston, in a poor, oddly isolated little neighborhood known locally as Hanoville. Until he reached the age of eleven, when his beloved Aunt Molly enrolled him at St. Columbkille's, the cramped streets of this area constituted his entire world. The Reedys lived on the top floor of a tumbledown triple decker. Their windows overlooked a rubbish-strewn empty lot, a desolate stretch of Boston & Albany railroad track, and a welter of other shabby wooden dwellings.

Kevin's father, a bruiser of a man named Gerald, was a bartender. In that trade there is an established rule of professional conduct that some now-forgotten wit long ago reduced to an easily remembered rhyme that runs as follows:

> You can drink it, steal it or give it free,
> But they'll bounce your ass if you do all three.

Gerry Reedy brazenly flouted this prudent axiom, however—he was a hardened kleptomaniacal dipsomaniac—and as a consequence rarely held a job for more than a few weeks.

Nonetheless there always seemed to be an innocent saloon owner somewhere in town who was willing to give him yet another chance. Gerry would then come home in a slightly disoriented state, his broad countenance rubicund and all the pockets of his clothes bulging with corked six-ounce 7-Up bottles full of 90-proof whiskey, and the family would know at once that Pa had found gainful employment again. They would know also that a roaring domestic brawl would occur before the evening was much older.

To make matters worse for Kevin Reedy, his mother Ethel behaved just as shamefully as her dissolute spouse. A slovenly overweight woman, her specialty was boosting merchandise from the First National supermarket or the Woolworth's on Harvard Avenue—so her clothing often bulged as well. This loot she later peddled to the denizens of the Limerick Lounge, across from the old Allston depot. But since Ethel would pass her ill-gotten profits over the mahogany bar of that taproom within moments of receiving them, she seldom had any cash in her voluminous pocketbook.

Kevin's sister, the oldest of the brood, ran away from home when she was fifteen. Her name was Ellen, and she'd had reddish-blond hair. Except for sending a snotty picture postcard from La Jolla, California, she never got in touch with them again.

Next in order of age was a pug-nosed brother called Junior. He'd been introduced to the beguiling charms of airplane glue at the grammar school, and by thirteen was sniffing the stuff regularly and moping around in a perpetual mental fog. One snowy January morning the police from Station 14 discovered Junior huddled in the backseat of an abandoned car next to the railroad track, and because he was shivering and incoherent, rushed him over to St. Elizabeth's Hospital. He died there three days later of aspiration pneumonia.

Suddenly Kevin found himself an only child, the last remaining target for his parents' harsh criticism and abuse. It was a rare day that he didn't get a few clouts from one of them. Withdrawing into himself, he soon began having strange and violent fantasies—wild reveries of poisoning his tormentors, or attacking them with knives, hatchets, or jars of flaming gasoline. If his sainted Aunt Molly hadn't arrived to take him off to live with her, a real catastrophe might well have happened in that house on Hano Street.

But it definitely had been a rough childhood. He had nightmares about his father that frightened him awake. Sometimes he dreamed he *was* his father, and that terrified him even more. Yet he couldn't be too different from his parents, could he? Their blood flowed in his veins. Their genes governed his thought and behavior.

Like them, Reedy had a hot temper and he wasn't slow to use his fists. He felt little sympathy for other people. Right from the start as a patrolman, he got into departmental hassles over battering wise guys on the street or evasive prisoners at the station house. He was labeled a head-buster, and that didn't do him any good when similar troubles arose after he was promoted to detective. While in Homicide he once broke a bookmaker's larynx—nearly strangled him to death because the man got snotty. Fortunately for Reedy, his partner, old Dinny Gates, supported his phony self-defense story a hundred percent, and when Phil put pressure on the bookie's boss, the charges were quietly dropped.

Of course, he had told Rita most of these things, but somehow she couldn't see the connection. Why had she made such a fuss about marriage? he wondered for the thousandth time. He'd given her everything else—plenty of spending money, the automobiles, the fur coat from that Russian on Newbury Street, a lot of expensive jewelry.

Then, as if it were fresh news, he suddenly realized the woman was dead. He flinched and trembled, his mind struggling to grasp this awful revelation. Rita was gone—gone forever. Rita had died months ago. She no longer existed.

"So it don't matter anymore, that marriage thing," he muttered weakly. "Nothing matters . . . nothing at all."

As he reached home and pulled into the driveway, his stomach started hurting again.

5

Nude except for a double strand of graduated pearls that circled her sleek neck—their existence forgotten during the concupiscent frolic earlier—Magda Gilman leaned back against the chair's brocade and closed her eyes. "My first husband? He was as different from Harold as night is from day. He was an intellectual, Gabriel—and good-looking, too. Dark, serious, deep deep eyes, lovely sensitive mouth. He came from right here in Brookline. Went to the high school, where he played on the chess team and belonged to the Chamber Music Society. My cousin Marcia took me to the school auditorium one night to hear a recital and there he was, my dream boy, fiddling away in a string quartet. Talk about love at first sight. One look, and I almost swooned."

"Was he Jewish?" Frankie Gates asked.

"Of course, but what's that got to do with it? You think only Irish Catholics from South Boston can be heavenly creatures?"

"Yeah, that's always been my impression," he admitted.

"You're an ignorant mick," she said severely, her eyes still shut. "Not only that, you threw too much wood on the fire and now I'm getting heat prostration."

"Really? I'm very comfortable, myself. Maybe you're hot for other reasons."

"If I still am, Frankie darling, it doesn't say much for you, does it?"

Gates, naked and sitting with both his legs up on the sofa, grinned and answered, "Must be the fire, then."

Magda ignored this rejoinder, though her eyelashes flickered. "My first husband was a prodigy—graduated at seventeen with the second best marks in his class. Harvard gave him a scholarship. He was brilliant there, too, but I couldn't wait for him to finish, so we were married at the end of his junior year. God, were we in love! A couple of innocent kids. Every night I used to think, 'Eat your hearts out, Romeo and Juliet.' We rented this cozy little apartment on Chauncy Street over there in Cambridge, full of books, paintings, sculpture reproductions, classical records. On the dining room table we had a big atlas I bought him, and in the living room there was a huge copper mobile hanging from the ceiling. I was happy every single day that first year. My angel Gabriel! He'd come home at lunchtime and play me a Schumann song on his violin. Then we'd go to bed and fool around for a while, nice and easy and tender—no rough stuff. And afterward we'd lay there and eat oranges—Gabe was crazy about oranges. Sometimes he'd read to me in his beautiful voice from *David Copperfield* or *War and Peace* or maybe *Lost Illusions,* which is by Balzac. We were babes in the woods, Frankie. And when he went back to the school I'd feel so incredibly lonely. It was an idyll, that year."

Lazily she pushed a lock of russet-brown hair up from her damp brow, and when her hand descended again to the cushioned arm of the chair, it was like a bird alighting on a perch.

Gates, his eyes flinty gray, watched the woman execute this simple movement and took great pleasure from it. Glimmering beams from the fire spangled her body with flecks of gold—her elegant throat, her shapely shoulders, her ample bosom and hips, the rounded stomach with its winking navel, her lush thighs and dimple-kneed legs.

Some men don't appreciate that zoftig kind of build, he ruminated, but far as I'm concerned it's state of the art. All those skinny broads in the movies—bunch of Olive Oyls. They're hardly even female—but you don't have to stare twice at this torso to know what sex it is.

Magda Gilman opened her eyes—they were a cocoa-brown shade—and said, "Gabriel got his B.A. that second year and went on to grad school—then the whole thing started to come apart at the seams. What happened was I had this crazy girlfriend—a kid I knew from the Webster-Parkman Academy. You ever hear of Webster-Parkman, lover?"

"Sure, Mag. It's that exclusive private school on Marlborough Street. Place is full of spoiled, snot-nosed brats," Frankie Gates said apodictically.

"Right—and my girlfriend Melissa was as spoiled and snotty nosed as a brat can get. Did whatever popped into her head, no matter how lunatic it might be. The family had her going to some high-priced analyst on Beacon Hill about ten hours a week, but it was a waste of time and money. For one thing, Melissa was always out of this world, always soaring on green dragons. So why did I become best pals with the girl? Who knows? I was an adolescent, and adolescents are all cuckoo. Once the two of us threw an armchair through a window of the faculty lounge. Shattered the glass and fell three stories into a snowbank, but it didn't even break. On another happy occasion we stopped up the sinks in the lavatory and turned the faucets on full blast. That was a sketch from the Marx Brothers, Frankie. Everybody up to her tookus in water, shrieking like schizos. A few weeks later we went to the other extreme and set fire to a lot of wastepaper baskets, which probably would've burnt the whole school down if Miss Salamanca, the bursar, hadn't happened along at the right moment and snuffed them out with a fire extinguisher. We were more fun than a barrel of monkeys. Most of the teachers guessed that Missy and me were the phantom vandals, but they just couldn't pin it on us."

Magda pushed the wayward lock of brown hair from her forehead. In the distance a telephone rang twice. Then a man's voice, faint and ghostly, could be heard uttering incomprehensible words.

"Your husband's home," Gates said.

"So what?"

"Kind of early for him, isn't it?"

"I suppose. Must be broke." She caught his eye and gave him an appealing glance. "Could you do me a favor, darling?"

"I just got comfortable, Magda," he said defensively.

"You're comfortable? That's nice—but I'm burning up from dehydration because of that stifling bonfire you made. Dash to the kitchen like a good boy and fetch me a cold Perrier."

Groaning, Gates lowered his bare feet to the thick Chinese rug and stood up. He was a tall, well-proportioned man of about thirty, with broad shoulders, a narrow waist, and long muscular limbs. His face, however, had a crude look to it, as though the features had been roughly hacked from a cobblestone by an inept sculptor; yet the overall effect wasn't unattractive. Indeed, Frankie's craggy aspect gave him a certain masculine charm.

"Liberated women," he mumbled darkly as he padded off to the kitchen.

When he was gone, Magda got up and went to a console table in a corner of the spacious room. There, from a center drawer, she took a handful of tissues which she used to wipe the perspiration from her brow and throat. The locked door that led to Harold's adjoining apartment stood close by, and through it she heard him say:

"Make it easy on yourself . . . strictly a business deal . . . maybe, but it would be impossible to prove in court . . . sure . . . you try to be cute, my friend, and you won't get a second chance."

A couple of inaudible sentences followed, then he continued more clearly, *"Nothing to be afraid of, if you play ball . . . you're just lucky . . . you're lucky I'm a civilized individual, and not . . . let me finish, will you? . . . and not a media guy hot for a sensational story . . . or suppose one of your enemies got ahold of this material? The scandal would bury you forever . . . certainly . . . you understand the instructions? . . . yeah, alone . . . okay, so long."*

The telephone clunked into its bracket. Under his breath Harold Gilman said to himself, softly but distinctly, "Why should I make concessions? A pool table he wants? Balls I'll give him."

Retreating footsteps punctuated these remarks, and

after that no further sound came through the double door.

Patting the area between her plump breasts with the tissues, Magda wondered what sort of sharp practice her husband was involved in. "Meshuga," she murmured, and walked languidly back to the brocade-covered chair.

Gates soon returned with two tumblers of effervescent water. "Who's that lady across the way?" he asked casually.

"Lady? Mrs. Petz, the rabbi's widow?" Her eyes widened. "I hope you didn't stand in front of that window."

"Should've warned me," he said, handing her a glass.

"Oy vey! The poor woman's probably having a conniption fit. Are you trying to show off, you klutz?" Magda clicked her tongue in dismay. "And you're not even circumcised. There goes my reputation again. The tenants would have me evicted, I'm sure, if I didn't own the building."

Gates leaned down and bestowed a lewd and lingering kiss on her soft neck just above the pearls. In his nostrils her perfume tingled sweetly, even as it tasted bitter on his tongue.

"Go back to the sofa, you exhibitionist," she said sternly. "Sit back down, so I can relate the rest of my memoirs—the confessions of a teenaged Jewish princess."

He did as he was told, stretched himself out on the cushions once more, and said, "Okay, sister—let's hear your story."

"Well, what happened was my girlfriend got expelled from the Academy," Magda declared, ignoring his attempt at humor. "They caught her performing an unnatural act with our chemistry teacher, Mr. Bates, a real cutie pie who looked like James Caan. We all loved him to distraction. Whenever he gave an exam, he would always call us his 'little testees.' Behind his back we referred to him as Master Bates. But the poor dear got bounced, too, after the headmistress discovered Melissa and him noshing among the board erasers in the supply closet. What an uproar that created! My goofy pal was given the heave-ho, and as a result I didn't see her again until several years later."

Magda stopped and slowly drank from her sweating tumbler, while the flames from the fireplace bathed her bare flesh in a sinuous coral glow. "One morning my young husband dropped me off in the Square," she went on somberly. "It was a drizzly October day, and as I walked away from the car I saw Melissa in front of the Harvard Trust Company, looking rather forlorn. But when our eyes met, she gave me a big smile. We went into Bailey's and sat there for hours drinking coffee and gabbing. From what I gathered, her recent life had been a real disaster—aimless trips around the country, sordid love affairs, drugs, liquor, family problems, shrinks—the worst of everything. She still had plenty of her old pizzazz, though, and the two of us laughed and laughed like we were kids again. I invited her to the apartment for dinner that night, and in the weeks after, we saw each other fairly regularly. Gabriel didn't care for her very much—"

"Not at first," Gates interjected.

"Clever you."

"Comes of being a Boston detective."

"Comes of having a nasty, cynical mind, darling," she corrected. "Actually Gabe didn't pay much attention to her during that period. He considered her boring, neurotic, and a complete dumbhead. When she visited he'd hang around for ten minutes to be polite, then sneak off to the Widener Library or go see his mother in Brookline. As for Melissa, she hardly exchanged any words with him at all. Hello and good-bye, that was it. If ever two people had absolutely nothing in common..." Magda Gilman shrugged her naked shoulders. "Well, several months passed and this weekend came up when we had to go to Westport, Gabriel and me, because my cousin, Frieda, was getting married to a corporate lawyer down there. When Melissa heard about it, she asked me if she could use the apartment while we were gone, and I said okay. She was living at home then, and I figured she had a boyfriend she wanted to sleep with. So I gave her a set of keys, and we took off. But after the wedding my sister Miriam talked me into going to New York with her—it was just before the holidays—and Gabe had to drive back to Cambridge Sunday night alone."

Frankie Gates shook his head knowingly, though he made no verbal comment.

"Wait—it wasn't like that," she said impatiently. "Listen, and don't jump to conclusions. He rang the bell when he arrived, not wanting to embarrass anybody, but there was no response. So he unlocked the door and went in. The rooms, as far as he could see, were empty, and there wasn't a sound. He threw his coat on a chair, peeled an orange and ate it. When he was finished he wanted to wash his sticky hands. He walked into the bathroom, and there was my girlfriend hanging from the shower pipe."

Magda paused to emphasize her revelation, and the man on the sofa said, "Nice houseguest."

"Gabe nearly passed out. He was always so sensitive, Frankie. Of course, the poor kid assumed she was dead—but then he heard a moan and her eyes opened, which must've made it even more shocking for him. Imagine staring up into the eyes of a person who's just hanged herself. Gruesome. Later on, when I finally dragged the whole story out of him, he said his knees were actually knocking. Somehow, though, Gabriel managed to slide the cord—it was really a tieback for the shower curtain—off the pipe and lower Missy into the tub. She was barely breathing, unable to talk, but with the noose off her neck she started to revive. He carried her into the bedroom, and there she had a fit of hysterics. Naturally he wanted to phone a doctor, but she begged him not to."

"How long had she been hanging?"

"I don't know. Couldn't have been too long, could it?"

"A few minutes is enough to kill you. Could she have staged it?"

"No, no. It just happened that way. You're so suspicious."

"I'm just wondering why she didn't die, Mag."

"She didn't die because she didn't do it right, obviously. Who knows from hanging? People screw up their suicides all the time. Look at Sylvia Plath. She had to keep on trying and trying before she finally succeeded."

"Sylvia who?"

"Oh, never mind." Magda raised her eyes to the heavens in exasperation, then pressed the cold tumbler to her right temple. "But let me finish, Frankie. The rest of the story isn't too easy to explain. Melissa was nude, you see. She'd been taking a shower and suddenly decided to end it all, I guess. However, there was more to it than that. To understand Gabriel's behavior, you would have had to know the man himself. He was a very *feeling* person—

incredibly humane. He happened to have this almost frightening supersensitivity. Everything affected him too intensely—joy, music, stained-glass windows, love, clouds, suffering, poems, movies. We'd go to the Museum of Fine Arts and he'd look at a Van Gogh and start acting manic. A pretty sunset could put him in a daze, or a German sonata alter his whole mood. He had this abnormal sympathy for things...and for people. So that day her crying was like a knife in his heart, he said. He had to console her, comfort her. He rubbed her wrists, stroked her neck where the tieback had bruised her skin, kissed her on the cheek and hugged her. And eventually she stopped bawling. Then he made love to her...the son of a bitch."

Magda's mouth closed in a taut crease, and she began to finger the double loop of graduated pearls as if performing some intricate computation on an abacus.

Watching her, Gates suddenly recalled a gruff pronouncement his Uncle Dinny had once delivered when he'd heard of an unmarried girl's pregnancy. "They *will* fuck," the old donkey had muttered sagely. Sensing that this was the wrong occasion for telling such an anecdote, the reclining detective kept silent.

After a minute or so Magda Gilman released the pearls and in measured swallows finished the rest of her bubbly mineral water. "So they became sweethearts," she declared, her voice subdued, "which certainly proves something about romance, doesn't it? It can sprout up under any circumstances anywhere, like ragweed. Unbeknownst to me, the two of them carried on all that winter—and I was too young and naive to suspect a thing. Gabe and Melissa? Ridiculous! Or so I believed until an acquaintance of mine dished me a few pointed hints one day while I was having my hair done at André Leduc's. Well, that night I charged Gabriel with his infidelity and he confessed. When I heard the whole squalid tale, I went insane, Frankie. The bottom just dropped out of my life. And he was shattered, too. We were totally demented, both of us. At one point I got a knife from the kitchen, and Gabriel—all he did was stand there with his arms open, waiting for me to stab him. Made no effort to get away or defend himself. I threw it at the wall, the knife, and it stuck in a landscape oil painting I bought him on Newbury Street as a first anniversary present.

"But even though I was only a nineteen-year-old kid, I wasn't about to let my beautiful bridegroom keep a mistress. No way. I laid down the law, told him he'd have to forget her. The louse was given an ultimatum he had to accept, because I was supporting him. Gabe didn't have a scholarship for his graduate work. I paid his tuition and the house rent, and for the car and everything. He didn't have a dime. His shirts I bought, and his underwear. I made it crystal clear to him that his little extracurricular activities were over and done with, and forced him to swear a solemn oath never to see Melissa again. As his wife, didn't I have a right to do that? And he kept his promise, too." Magda picked up a tissue from the table and pressed it to the side of her moist face. "You know what happened then?"

Frowning slightly, Frankie Gates replied, "I can guess. The girl, Melissa, killed herself."

"A detective you may be, darling, but a psychologist you're not," the fire-spangled woman in the brocaded chair said. "She didn't commit suicide—Gabriel did. He jumped in front of a subway train at Central Square station...one morning that spring. The young idiot! What kind of solution was that? At the mortuary they told me his death was instantaneous, but they lied. Nobody as mangled as Gabriel was could've possibly died in an instant. The wheels had cut him up...every part...his two hands...everything except his face. That, for some inexplicable reason, looked as calm and beautiful as it had on the day we...the day we were married."

A tear like a drop of molten silver trickled down her cheek. She wiped it away quickly with the tissue and tried to smile. Failing in the attempt, she bit her lower lip.

"A bad time for you," said Gates gently.

"Yes," she conceded. "I really cherished that boy."

"But it wasn't your fault, Magda."

"No? I hope not."

"What happened to the girlfriend? Ever see her again?"

"Only once, Frankie—couple of years later," she answered, hardness entering her voice. "At a fund-raiser for one of the Kennedys. She came over to my table—half pissed, she was—and offered me some stupid sort of apology. It was more than I could take. I stood up and slapped her right across the mouth. Almost caused a riot. Her brother is a big-shot politician—Phil Delaunay."

Frankie Gates's rugged countenance displayed surprise. "This Melissa was *Phil* Delaunay's sister? No kidding? She must've been Sunny Ned Delaunay's daughter, then. That family's had a lock on local politics for thirty-five years. My dad worked for Sunny Ned in Southie. Went to his funeral at the State House, when the old fox finally died. You ever meet him, Mag?"

"Yes. I spent a couple of weekends at their house in Brighton—when the two of us were going to Webster-Parkman. The father doted on her—spoiled the kid rotten. Anything Missy wanted, Missy could have—which is why she became so farmisht, I suppose." Her eyes still unnaturally bright, Magda stared into the dwindling fire. "So that's the story of my first husband," she said wearily, and used the crumpled tissue to wipe her lips.

The phone rang in the apartment next door, but no one picked it up and it jangled for a long while. Harold Gilman had apparently gone out.

6

That Friday evening Stanley Gloag emerged from an alley onto Exeter Street and turned left towards Commonwealth Avenue. Before he had gone very far, however, a grimy Boston Police cruiser pulled up alongside him at the curb, and the driver, a man with a bulbous nose, stuck his capped head out of the window. "Hey, you!" he yelled, sending wisps of vapor into the clear cold air.

His eyes sleepy, Gloag looked around. "Yes?"

"What were you doing in that alley there?"

"Taking a leak," Gloag lied, the barest trace of impudence in his tone.

A hand brake rasped and doors swung open. Both occupants of the dirty cruiser came into view, like genies popping from a bottle. "On the wall," ordered the driver, pointing his nightstick at the brick enclosure of some Back Bay citizen's garden.

"What do you mean?" Stanley asked.

The question was promptly answered with a forceful shove. "Get over there, you . . . spread those feet and slap your hands high on the wall . . . more, more . . . and move your ass back . . . quick, quick, quick. That-a-boy. Ain't you ever seen this on TV?"

"Guy's playing dumb," the other policeman remarked. He had a round, youthful countenance that was adorned with a sparse moustache. Having unsnapped his holster, he now stood a short distance away, lightly gripping the black butt of his undrawn revolver. "Nobody could be such a total boob."

"I never had this kind of experience before," said Gloag, still lying. His pale face almost touched the rusty red bricks. "Didn't do nothing wrong. Just relieved myself . . . shed a tear for Ireland. If you want, officer, I'll show you where I did it—up against a garbage can."

"Gee, thanks, but I think I'll skip an on-the-spot inspection," the large-nosed driver said, tucking his stick under his arm and running his fingers over Stanley's chest, side and back. "I seen pissed-on garbage cans before, and to tell you the truth, they ain't much to look at. Where do you live, slim?"

"North Cambridge, with my eighty-year-old grandmother."

"That's nice," said the cop benevolently, as he explored his suspect's waist, thighs, and pants pockets. "So how come you're loitering in this neighborhood?"

"I'm not loitering. I was visiting a friend on Beacon Street."

"Yeah? Your face is kind of familiar. What's your name?"

"Stanley Glowak," Gloag replied.

"Glowak . . . Glowak. Don't mean nothing to me. How about you, Aram?" the driver inquired of his partner, while he tapped Stanley's calves and ankles with his nightstick. Having just eaten a heavy dinner, he was reluctant to bend over. "Know any Glowaks?"

"Nah. Must be a Polack," the young policeman sneered, snapping his holster closed.

"Still think he's playing dumb?"

"Polacks never play dumb, Lou. Don't have to. Reminds me of a story. This guy goes in and holds up a bank—okay? And the teller says, 'Hey, you must be Polish.' So the guy says, 'Yeah. How did you know?' And the teller says, 'Because you sawed off the wrong end of the shotgun.'"

"Not bad, Aram—not bad."

"What about this one," said the boyish-faced cop, encouraged. "Lady goes into a store and orders a pound of Atalanta ham, a hunk of kielbasa, and a jar of Krakus pickles. So the guy behind the counter says, 'You must be Polish.' And the lady says, 'I am, but how did you know?' And the guy says, 'Because this is a hardware store.'"

The driver laughed loudly, his bulbous nose luminous in the glow of the streetlamp. "Where do you get them all?" he said appreciatively. Then he poked the suspect in the small of the back. "Okay, slim. You can lower your hands now and turn around."

Gloag did as advised and declared, "That's racial prejudice."

"What? Them little jokes?" Aram retorted. "They ain't nothing of the kind."

"Of course not," his partner said. "It's ethnic humor. Besides, Stanley—who the fuck are you to talk? How about shedding a tear for Ireland? What do you call that?"

"Racial prejudice. You're right. I shouldn't have said it," Gloag answered. "I apologize."

"Don't bother. You didn't insult us. I'm Italian, and Aram here is a Armenian. We wouldn't neither of us give a good crap if all the Irishmen in Boston dropped dead tomorrow morning while they was drinking their breakfast. That happens, we might get a chance at a promo—trade in these grungy blue bags for plainclothes." Lou, the driver, sniggered. "But enough bullshit. In the future if you want to shake the dew off your kidneys, Stanley, use a barroom toilet."

"Yeah. In this country we don't do wee-wee on the street," said Aram truculently. "It's against the sanitary code."

Gloag nodded, clasping his mittened hands behind him so he wouldn't be tempted to try anything foolhardy.

At that point a series of urgent croaking sounds came over the car radio, and the two lawmen looked at each other before hurrying back to the blue-and-white vehicle. The doors slammed, the engine snarled, the tires screamed—and off they sped.

"Real chumps," the man in the peaked cap said to himself as he watched the cruiser veer around the corner. "Who buttons their uniforms for them, I wonder."

Then, from out of the surrounding gloom, an eerie lilting voice called, "Been a naughty boy again, Stanley?"

Turning, he saw a yellow Mustang double-parked on the opposite side of the street, and seated in it a pretty blond girl wearing a voluminous polo coat and a maroon beret.

"What are *you* doing here?"

"Did you forget I live right down the block?" she said, a pout on her painted lips.

"Guess I did," Gloag admitted, stepping over a small snowbank to reach the street. "If I'd remembered, Missy, I would've dropped by and rung your bell."

"Yeah, Stan—you're good at bell-ringing. First class, and don't I know it," the girl said in a teasing voice.

Around the front of the Mustang he walked, opened the off door and slid in beside her. "How long you been watching? Those cops saw me leaving the alley, so they patted me down. Figured I was perpetrating a crime, I suppose. Cops always think the worst of people."

"And were you perpetrating something?"

"No, no. I just came from a cocktail party on Fairfield Street. An old pal of mine from Cambridge gave it. He got out of Billerica this morning after doing twenty-eight months for stealing whiskey. The cocktails were made from that same hooch, and it's great stuff—but whether it was worth all those days and weeks is something else."

"And you cut through the alley to save a few steps?"

"I cut through the alley because I like dark places."

Missy Delaunay met his gaze directly, and in a tone of wonder said, "Stanley Gloag, you're a genuine weirdo."

"Nothing wrong with alleys," he answered, peeling off a mitten and letting it fall in his lap. "They're interesting, nice and quiet, shadowy, soothing, lonely, spooky." He laid his hand on the girl's knee. "If you want, Missy, I'll show you what I mean, give you a tour of that alley right now. What do you say? It's got some beautiful dark doorways, and a lot of mysterious little courtyards and corners. We can explore them together, just me and you. Be like an old black-and-white movie, where the heroine is stalked by a homicidal sex fiend. Be very strange and thrilling. How about it?"

She shivered under his hand, then laughed nervously. Nevertheless, her wide open blue eyes glittered like stars. "You're kidding me, aren't you? It's freezing cold out there, you hopeless loony."

"So you'll have chills to go with your thrills," he retorted, sliding his hand beneath the polo coat and her skirt and up onto her bare thigh. "Anyhow, you won't be cold long, Missy."

"No, I can't. You're too much. But I really can't, because I have to meet somebody tonight," she told him, a bit breathlessly. "Stan, you're a mental case—honestly. Sane people don't prowl back streets in the dark in the dead of winter. There are rats in those alleys, and muggers. Aren't you afraid of being hit on the head, you silly goop?"

"I meet any muggers, it's the muggers who are going to be scared," he said, his fingers gently kneading her soft warm flesh. "Come to think of it, I did get jumped by a kid recently in an alley—a black kid, over by Field's Corner. Came at me with a linoleum knife. But I happened to be wearing my Knapp heavy-duty work shoes, with the steel safety caps in the toes, so I kicked him in the leg. Should've seen the expression on his face. Lucky for that dinge his knife went flying under the automobile. Otherwise I would've made him eat it."

"God! You're a ferocious beast of the jungle."

"No, I'm not. I'm a businessman with a lot of principles."

"Oh, go on. You told me once that you murdered people. Stanley Gloag, you're a professional assassin. You admitted it."

"But, girlie, that doesn't make me a beast of the jungle. I'm a bill collector. I square accounts, get chiselers to pay their bad debts. Of course, there are all kinds of ways of doing this."

To keep from laughing, Missy Delaunay seized her nether lip between her teeth. Her foot jiggled the Mustang's accelerator pedal, provoking intermittent purrs from the idling engine. "No wonder the police stopped you," she said, peeking out at him from behind the curtain of her blond hair. "I'm surprised they didn't run you in."

"Funny thing is, I know that cop with the big nose," Gloag replied, still caressing her leg. "Years ago a fellow named Peanuts Klein operated a creeper—a floating craps game—in Allston, and I used to straighten out deadbeats for him. But one night a Black Maria pulled up while I was pounding this guy in Union Square, and the next thing I knew there were blue uniforms all over me. The cop with the schnozz I knocked flat on his duff—caught him with a sucker punch—but after that I got slugged myself a few times, and they flung me headfirst into the wagon." Gloag smiled at the memory, and stared through the windshield at the cars on Commonwealth Avenue. "It was an exciting ride. See, when you're alone in the back of a Maria with your hands cuffed behind you, you're helpless. There's a narrow little bench there, but the slightest little bump will knock you off it. Naturally, the cops know this—so that night they whipped around corners on two wheels, jumped curbs, and went zigzagging down the worst potholed streets they could find. For me in the back, it was like tumbling over Niagara Falls in a barrel. By the time we reached Division 14 station house I had a dislocated shoulder, a couple of cracked ribs, and knobs all over my skull. Next morning, after the bondsman sprung me, I took my clothes off at the doctor's and my body was bruised every color of the rainbow. I looked like one of those parrots in the zoo."

"I wish I could've seen you," said the girl, prodding the accelerator.

"So running into that cop again annoyed me," he said. "I wanted to haul off and whack him—put a dent in his big snout."

"There were two of them, Stan. And they had guns."

"Takes time to draw a gun. If you're quick enough, you can stop it from happening—and nobody's quicker than me." He smiled at her, moving his restless hand higher on her leg. "I'm so fast I can turn off the light and jump into bed before the room gets dark. You don't know me, Missy. I move like a shadow. I got eyes in the back of my head, and I can see around corners. Not only that, I'm the kind of scrapper who never gives in, never gives out, and never gives up."

Her shrill laughter filled the small car. "You're a raving maniac, Stanley Gloag. Some night you'll have to show me that trick—switching the light off and hopping into bed with me before the place gets dark. But right now I have to go. I'm running late, and my brother will kill me if I don't talk to this Gilman guy tonight."

His heavy-lidded eyes aglow with curiosity, Stanley asked, "Your brother, the big-shot politician? What's happening? Who's this fellow you're going to see?"

"It's all hush-hush, and I can't tell you any details. The guy's trying to blackmail us, though. Phil's worried sick because he wants the nomination for the U.S. Senate this summer. So I have to find out what the son of a bitch wants—have to talk to him."

"Blackmail?"

"Yeah—isn't that a riot?"

Gloag chuckled, and pinched her thigh. "What have you been up to, girlie? What's the shaker got on you? I can't believe a hip lady like you would get caught in a badger game."

"Never mind. It's no joke," she said, yanking his hand out from under her skirt.

"Want me to come along for protection?"

"You can't, dummy. If the guy sees me with somebody, he won't show. I don't need protection, anyhow. I've got my gun—the one I tried to shoot you with that time, remember?"

"I remember all right. Never could figure out why you did that."

"I did it because I was scared, you loony."

"But you could've blown me away with that thing. Small guns can be more deadly than big ones. Those little slugs ricochet off bones like they're in a pinball machine. Cut you up good. But I made a mistake that night. I never should've untied your hands. Doesn't pay to be too nice a guy." Gloag slipped his mitten back on. "Well, it's interesting—this blackmailing business. Better handle it right, or you'll be opening a can of worms. If things get complicated, Missy, give me a call. I'd be glad to help."

"Gee, aren't you chivalrous? You mean you'd work for me for nothing?"

"Can't do that—but I'll give you a sizable discount because you're my pal," he said, opening the car door. "Thirty percent off list price. You want me to break a leg? Only cost four hundred dollars."

"That's all?" said Missy Delaunay, giggling. "Maybe I'll get you to do one of mine, since they're such a bargain. Stanley—we'll be seeing each other, won't we?"

"Sure. And soon, I hope," Gloag said.

He kissed her on the mouth and got out of the Mustang.

7

Shortly before twelve that same night the last customer, a demented old man in a red-checked hat with elephantine earflaps, left the Suds for Duds Laundromat carrying his well-worn clothing, still hot from the dryer, in a wrinkled plastic garbage bag.

"Every day we get more and more of those deinstitutionalized characters in this dump," Ossie Peña soliloquized, watching him shamble down the street.

Then the attendant locked and bolted the front door, rolled all the hampers beneath the long Formica tables, switched off the lights, and went back through the shadows to the cubbyhole that served as an office. From around his scrawny neck he took the earphones of his Walkman WM-7 and adjusted them to his head, after which he splashed another generous dose of Bardolino into the chipped teacup, recapped the half-gallon jug, and lit up a *porra*.

Ossie, a swarthy youth with curly black hair, stood only five feet tall and was built proportionately. Once upon a time he aspired to being a flyweight boxer, but in his second amateur bout an overhand right caught him on the bridge of the nose and knocked him unconscious for several minutes. The next morning, as he examined his two black eyes in the bathroom mirror, he decided to retire from the ring and become a jockey.

However, that grandiose scheme didn't work out, either. For a year he had haunted Suffolk Downs, offering to do practically anything for practically nothing, but no one would hire him because a clocker he knew had spread a story around that Ossie Peña was a sneak thief. The cops all believed this lie, and used to chase him out of the paddock. It was a dirty rotten trick to pull, in Ossie's opinion, especially since he had never stolen a thing from the clocker—only a pack of cigarettes, maybe.

Sitting on a corner of the desk, he filled his lungs with marijuana smoke and gazed blankly at the unpainted concrete-block wall. Friday night and what am I doing? he thought despondently. *Nada.* Other people are out there having a ball—dancing, laughing, eating good food in fancy restaurants, making time with pretty girls—and where am I? No place. On my *fundillos* in a rat hole. How come it always happens to me this way? But at least it's better sitting here than in that miserable furnished room on Symphony Road. At least it's warm.

Gradually he began to feel more cheerful. The pot, the wine, and the exuberant improvisations of John Coltrane flowing from the earphones mingled together in his mind, creating a dreamy sense of well-being.

Out of the office he wandered, and up to the building's back door, where, lingering in front of the barred window, he fell to contemplating the almost empty parking lot and the sporadic traffic off to his right on Tremont Street. Ossie enjoyed spying on the world from dark and secret places. It was like being invisible. You were there, but you weren't, like directing a movie or something.

An automobile entered his field of vision, rolled slowly to the distant end of the desolate lot, executed a sweeping turn, and came to a halt less than twenty feet from the door behind which he was lurking.

"A brand-new Audi. *Coño,*" the youth whispered. "They going to leave it there?"

Everyone knew that Audis came equipped with expensive stereos. Jake Mints, the humpbacked guy who operated a secondhand store on Chandler Street, had only recently mentioned to Ossie that he'd go as high as a hundred dollars for a real good Alpine or Blaupunkt. So the sight of this car immediately triggered larcenous thoughts in the Laundromat attendant's slightly anesthetized brain.

Engine idling, the Audi discharged ghostly clouds of vapor into the frigid air. After a moment the interior light came on, and Peña got a glimpse of the occupants. Two people sat in the front seat. Of the pair, he could distinguish the man most clearly—a well-dressed dude with a suntan and a lot of wavy hair. The lady beside him wore a dark beret and a loose-fitting beige coat that had its collar raised. Not much of her face could be seen.

Can't be lovers, Ossie thought. A classy guy like that ain't going to bring his chick to a parking lot. Why don't they get out and go where they're going?

He took another gulp of red wine from the teacup and another profound drag on the reefer, and forgot about the car for a minute or two while Coltrane's tenor sax flooded his head with mellow variations of "But Not for Me." Only when the track came to an end did his mind grudgingly return to reality. Standing on his toes to obtain a better look, he peered out at the shiny automobile. In it, the wavy-haired man was gabbing away like some street hustler trying to peddle a fake Rolex, while the woman was busy shuffling through a pile of papers.

"Why don't they go home or wherever?" Ossie muttered fretfully. "Why don't they leave so I can slap a little masking tape on the window, give it a crack with the boss's hammer, and glom that stereo?"

The woman, he now saw, was upset about something. She was making a lot of gestures, and moving her head jerkily the way people do when they're arguing. Yet the man just sat there grinning, his mouth full of brilliant, nicely matched teeth.

Hoping to eavesdrop, Peña put his teacup on the lid of a Maytag and slid the earphones down onto his thin neck, but though he could faintly hear the woman's high-pitched voice, the drone of the idling motor completely scrambled the things she said. The papers in her hand rose and fell angrily, and for a moment it actually looked as if she might strike her companion with them. Finally, however, she folded the sheaf in half and, with manifest violence, jammed it into a large leather handbag. Then, like a magician performing a bit of hocus-pocus, she brought forth a small gun, pointed it at the man's chest, and shot him. Two infinitesimal tongues of flame licked the weapon's muzzle, while the double recoil sent a tremor up her extended arm.

"Holy shit! *Qué está pasando*?" Peña said in a hushed voice, unwilling to accept the testimony of his own eyes. "Did she really zing him? It ain't possible."

There were plausible reasons for his doubts. The gun, for instance, just didn't seem big enough to be a deadly instrument. It might well have been a toy, a joke-shop gadget—one of those cigarette lighters in the shape of a miniature automatic. And the shots sounded so feeble—hardly more than the hollow pops you heard when you snapped the caps on a couple of cans of Budweiser. Not only that, the gunfire hadn't produced any noticeable effect on its target. The wavy-haired dude hadn't even blinked. There he sat, still grinning, still flashing his glittery white teeth.

But while Ossie grappled with these conflicting impressions, the self-satisfied smirk abruptly faded from the man's mouth. Back against the car door he fell, with his nose pointing up in the air.

Is he dead? the watcher in the shadows wondered, heart thumping. He pressed his face to the cool iron bars of the window. This is crazy. Am I dreaming?

Evidently the woman herself was also astonished by the swift and vicious deed, for she remained perfectly motionless for the next minute. When she recovered her composure, however, she wasted no time. The Audi's headlamps and interior light were suddenly extinguished, and its rumbling engine switched off.

An eerie quiet descended on the murky scene, but it was soon terminated by the stealthy opening and closing of the car's door. Beyond the hood a spectral figure materialized. Then, to the accompaniment of heels clicking rhythmically on the black pavement, the woman in the beret and polo coat hurried towards Tremont Street.

"*Sarito!* How do you like that? She smoked the guy—

drilled him *quemar ropa*—and now she's going home to bed," Ossie said incredulously. "How am I supposed to handle this? Cold-blooded murder, and I'm an eyewitness." He took a quick puff of the reefer and let the hot fumes warm his lungs. "But I don't want to talk to no cops, so what am I hanging around for? Better split, like the lady."

Despite his words, he didn't stray from the barred window. Faint saxophone music seeped from the earphones looped on his neck—a ululant chorus of "Everytime We Say Good-bye"—sounding like a shortwave broadcast from Europe.

Now that the woman had vanished, not a single pedestrian strolled the shabby gray streets. The automobile traffic had diminished to a trickle, and the usual city noise sunk to a discontinuous murmur. Down towards Shawmut Avenue a pair of windows glowed on the topmost floor of the Mass Pike Towers, like beacons shining from a distant promontory.

Peña made an effort to regain his calm and think clearly. But why should that chick go to the cops? They're the last people she'd want to see. So there's no sense in me rushing off. If she don't call them, they won't show up till tomorrow morning. Why should I chuck away a hundred *bolos*? She didn't even lock the door.

The undersized youth finished his cup of wine, and loped back to the office for a refill. Feeling drained by the excitement, he plopped into the swivel chair and took a final drag on the *porra* before dinching it in a tinfoil ashtray. For the next quarter hour he sat at the desk half asleep, but growing suddenly aware of the passage of time and fearing he might doze off and not wake until daylight, Ossie got up and again went to the window.

Nothing had changed. The Audi, a dark mass almost concealed by the angular shadow of the one-story building, looked exactly as it had before. There was the wavy-haired man slumped in the front seat in the same tragic pose, his white teeth vaguely glinting in his partially open mouth.

"They ain't coming tonight," the Laundromat attendant said decisively, and went back to the office to get some tools.

Two minutes later he slipped through the rear door and scampered like a rat across the parking lot. A pungent whiff of old cigar smoke, sweet perfume, and burnt gunpowder greeted his nose when he hopped into the still warm automobile. Ignoring the grim figure behind the wheel, he left the door ajar to keep the light on, ducked his head under the dashboard, and began extracting screws and disconnecting cables. Though the cotton work gloves he was wearing slowed him down some, he still managed to slide the compact radio free in short order. It was a Blaupunkt digital—AM-FM, Dolby. Peña placed it on the leather-covered seat, straightened up and glanced at the Audi's other occupant.

Seen from that distance, the man appeared older. There were flecks of gray in his crinkly hair, and he had flabby jowls. Beneath the suntan, his complexion was sallow. Three ropy filaments of blood depended from a corner of his slack mouth. Where they had dribbled on the notched lapel of his camel's hair overcoat, they coiled into a bright scarlet galloon. A crooked arm lay athwart his pudgy stomach. Just above it, two dime-sized red blots disrupted the pattern of his pin-striped shirt.

Genuinely affected by this dismal spectacle, Ossie Peña crossed himself. But business was business, and when he noticed a heavy gold watch ticking away on the dude's wrist, he decided to appropriate that, too.

He lifted the limp arm timidly and sought to undo the small strap buckle with his gloved fingers—a frustrating task. And while he was engaged in it, the dead man's hand came to life and fiercely seized his own.

For the space of a dozen rapid heartbeats Ossie remained as still as a graveyard monument. Panic numbed his brain. By dint of an enormous effort, however, he regained control of his petrified limbs at last, and with a jerk liberated his hand from the macabre grip. Through the open door he backed, but to his horror something grabbed him by the nape of the neck and prevented his retreat. He let out a yelp and wriggled like a belly dancer, and this energetic activity soon revealed the cause of his problem. The Walkman wire had tangled itself around the car's shift, and it was the metal band of his headphones that had clutched him by the throat.

"Mierda!" he swore.

Then, as he struggled to free the treacherous cord, the revenant behind the wheel suddenly groaned, and in a peculiar gurgling voice said, "Hey . . . hey, get me a doctor . . . please, a doctor . . . I'm dying."

Later Peña remembered slamming the car door, but could recall nothing whatever of his headlong flight back to the Suds for Duds. The power of coherent thought did not return to him until he was safely inside the building again with the door firmly bolted.

"Aagh! The guy's still alive," he wailed, his hundred-pound body shaking convulsively. "*Por Dios!* He ain't dead. Holy shit! Did he see my face? *Hombre,* I got to get the hell out of here."

He was trembling so badly that he nearly dropped the Blaupunkt before he set it safely down on the handiest washer. A wave of nausea came over him, and he gasped for air as if he had run a great distance instead of only a few yards. Talking to himself, he hastened to the cubby-hole office to replace the tools in the chest and retrieve his jacket. But a noise out in the parking area quickly brought him back to the barred window. He arrived there just in time to see a large American automobile—an Olds, he thought—its headlights flaring, come to a smooth stop at the extreme end of the gloomy lot.

When a robust man in a narrow-brimmed fedora alighted from the vehicle, Ossie Peña commenced to quiver again. He lingered at the window only long enough to observe the husky newcomer stride purposefully towards the solitary, dark green Audi and yank open its door.

"Coño," whispered the attendant, donning his jacket.

With the stolen radio crudely wrapped in a plastic laundry bag and tightly tucked under his arm, Ossie headed for the front of the store.

Minutes later, seated on the thick cushions of his beat-up Ford Granada, he was on his way home to Symphony Road.

8

Less than a half hour before Peña fled from the Suds for Duds Laundromat, Detective Kevin Reedy hit the Jamaicaway and turned his siren on, obliging what traffic there was at that hour to squeeze off to the right and give him an open road. The steering wheel was cold as ice, and there were icy sensations in the pit of his stomach as well.

That girl must be mentally sick, he thought.

For a change Reedy had gone to bed early that Friday night, taken a couple of Nembutal and buried his head beneath the pillow, but only a short while later the jangling phone had dredged him back up from the depths of sleep. He was so disoriented he couldn't even answer the thing at first, and it rang on and on like a shrieking banshee. Finally, the fog lifting from his drugged mind, he managed to pick it up.

"Hello," he growled.

"That you, Kev?"

"Yeah . . . yeah."

"I'm in a pay phone. Don't want to run any unnecessary risks. Kevin, we've got a real problem here. I'm going to need your help. A crook was hassling her—got smart. And she lost her head and shot him."

"Who is this?" the detective mumbled woozily. The illuminated dial of the electric clock showed 12:10. "Who is this talking?"

"It's me. Who do you think?" the answer came, swift and tart. "Listen closely, will you? She got the son of a bitch downtown. Got hysterical. He had these photographs—wanted to blackmail her."

"This you, Phil?"

"Good Christ! Yes, it's me. Aren't you awake yet?" Delaunay said irately. Then he lowered his voice to a whisper. "I absolutely can't afford to let a story like this hit the front pages, Kevin. My enemies—Everett Wheeler and his crowd—are just waiting for such an opening. They'll crucify me. That damned idiot, Missy. You were right. I never should have bought her the derringer."

Reedy rubbed his eyes. "And she shot a guy—a blackmailer," he said, doing his best to assimilate the information.

"Right, right. Got upset. You know how she is."

"Has she been taken into custody, Phil?"

"No, no, no. The police haven't been notified—and they're not going to be. Mum's the word on this one. It only happened minutes ago, in a car on Tremont Street. You'll have to get rid of him, Kev."

"What do you mean? Get rid of who?"

From the other end of the line came the impatient rasp of stertorous breathing. Then Delaunay said, "The dead man, the blackmailer—who else? I can't handle it myself. It isn't humanly possible. He has to disappear—vanish completely and forever."

Pushing himself to a sitting position and knocking his king-sized pillow off the bed, Reedy exclaimed, "You're asking me to dispose of a corpse, Phil?"

"You're the only person I can turn to."

"Jeez! That ain't something you want to screw around with. Homicide is a serious business. Even a man with your clout—"

"Damn it, Kevin, I know what I'm doing. I'm a lawyer. You don't need to explain the statutes to me. But I'm at a crossroads. Either I get rid of this bastard tonight or I resign from public life tomorrow. My Dad and I—forty years we've been running the show. We've created a dynasty here—and I'm not about to give it up just because that flaky sister of mine threw a tantrum and plugged some sleazeball down in the South End."

"Hey, Phil—wait a minute. Let me get it straight. If Missy did it, why the hell should they put the heat on you? You're not responsible for her actions. Anyhow, if the guy's a blackmailer, we can fix it. She should turn herself in."

"No, no, that's exactly what I don't want. Goddammit, you can't appreciate what's at stake, Kevin. Listen to me—Clarkson is stepping down. His wife's dying, and he's not in such good shape himself. If I can nail the nomination this summer, I'm sure to win in November—and a chance to become a U.S. senator doesn't come along too often, buddy." Delaunay paused to take two deep breaths. "But those hicks out in the western part of the state are giving me a hard time. They'd rather have Evie Wheeler, that sanctimonious old hypocrite, as the candidate—and the race is going to be close because of all the half-assed liberals in the suburbs. Even a hint of scandal could tip the scales. You don't understand the subtleties of politics, Kev. Everybody wants to back a winner. If I start losing ground, the ward bosses will drop me like I had AIDS."

Reedy, surprised to hear that his friend had so little control over his supporters, listened as he rambled on about Watergate and Chappaquiddick and James Michael Curley. None of it made much sense to the detective, but he didn't interrupt.

Finally the monologue came to an end, and he said, "Covering up a homicide is dangerous as hell, Phil. You sure there weren't any witnesses? And if she was the last person to see the guy?"

"Nobody saw anything. I'm not stupid, Kevin." A slight tremolo was now audible in Delaunay's voice. "If the man vanishes, the mess will vanish with him. Remember that high-tech executive out in Athol? The respectable husband and father who murdered the teenaged hooker? They found her bloody automobile in the woods, along with her bloody clothes and *his* bloody hatchet, and the D.A. could prove he'd seen her the day she disappeared—but that exec is still free as a bird in a tree, because he buried the remains in some impossible to find back-country ravine. No corpus delecti, no indictment."

Reedy switched on the beside lamp, then averted his fleshy face from its harsh light. "That was a whole different situation. Hiding the corpse didn't place the guy in any extra jeopardy. But in this case it's like an admission of guilt. See what I mean? You're taking something that ain't so bad, Phil, and turning it into a potential disaster—"

"You're not scared, are you? Christ Almighty!" Delaunay's voice soared into a higher register. "If you're going to show a yellow streak, you picked a hell of a time to do it. No, no, I didn't mean that, Kevin. You wouldn't let me down—not in a matter as vital as this . . . a matter of survival. Without Kevin Reedy's help, Philip Delaunay's dreams will die aborning. I'll be washed up. And why should that happen? Just because some psychopath snapped a few pictures of my sister balling a couple of guys in a motel?"

"Take it easy, Phil," Reedy said softly. "I ain't refusing to help. All I'm trying to do is explain what you're getting yourself into."

"I don't need your explanations. I'm fully aware of the dangers. You've got to have faith in my judgment. Just get rid of this dead rat, and I'll handle the rest. Aren't you remodeling that brownstone I gave you in the Fenway? Maybe you could stick him under a layer of concrete in the cellar. But Mother of God, get a move on. Missy's waiting for you in her automobile on the corner of Tremont and Shawmut, and she's a nervous wreck."

"Tremont and Shawmut," the detective echoed.

"Yes, so hurry. Take care of it, but don't call me back tonight. I'll be in touch tomorrow. Good luck, Kevin."

"Yeah," said Reedy resignedly as the phone clicked.

He crawled from beneath the blankets, sat on the side of the bed and passed a hand across his mouth. The lamplit room, its shape distorted by shadows, looked unfamiliar to him. Yet there, hanging from a hook on the closet door a short distance away, was Rita's blue cotton nightgown with its frilly collar, the one he had bought her only last April for her thirtieth birthday. For a minute he stared at it longingly, wanting to get up and touch it with his hands. But he didn't. Instead he reached for his pants on a nearby chair.

Huntington Avenue was virtually free of traffic, so Reedy, feeling cold despite the car's heater and the heavy down jacket he wore, flipped the siren off. The dispatcher on the police band of his radio mentioned a Hyde Park gas station holdup and a burglary on Ruggles Street, but there was no report of a South End shooting.

Melissa Delaunay. She'd been a headache from the age of twelve, he reflected morosely. Gave the family nothing but trouble. The nuns claimed she was sexually precocious, and nobody could argue with them about that. She went straight from an innocent child playing with dolls to a nympho playing with dicks, practically overnight. The kid couldn't set eyes on a guy in tight jeans without making a grab for his zipper—like a cat going after a mouse.

Her father, Sunny Ned Delaunay, sent her to a lot of psychiatrists, but it didn't do any good. Young Missy just kept on rubbing her ass or her pointy little tits on any healthy looking male who happened to visit the house. That, of course, usually led to other, more serious activities. Phil always claimed the problem was glandular, whatever the hell that meant.

Memories of those days stirred in Reedy's mind like maggots. Once he had slept over at the Delaunays' after a particularly wild stag party for an old school friend from St. Columbkille's, and around five A.M. Melissa, naked as a snake, had entered his attic room and crawled into bed with him. Still half smashed, it took him a while to realize what was going on, and then he'd been frightened and revolted. Hell, this was his best pal's kid sister—thirteen years old, with braces still on her teeth. But luckily he hadn't gone beyond the point of no return. When he came to his senses he pushed her from the bed, escorted her out to the hall, and locked the door.

The next morning Kevin Reedy couldn't believe the incident had actually occurred, until he saw Missy at lunch and she gave him a whorish, knowing grin that sent a chill down his spine. Jeez, thirteen years old. Naturally, he never mentioned the matter to Phil—yet he'd never forgotten it, either.

At the time Reedy was twenty-seven, a five-year veteran of the police department. Even now it made him sweat to think of how they might have been caught in the sack together that night. Ned Delaunay probably would have had him arrested for statutory rape. The old guy had always been crazy about his dippy daughter.

Afterwards Reedy avoided the girl, though this proved increasingly difficult as she grew older. The Delaunays threw so many parties, and there were plenty of inauguration balls, campaign kickoffs, and fund-raisers, too, at which they met each other. Missy would hang around his neck like a scapula, drag him out on the dance floor, and right there in public ram her pelvis up against him and slip her wet tongue in his ear. It was some tongue, too. Even at that little birthday get-together at Phil's house a few days ago, she had danced with him in the same brazen way. Dry humping, that's all it really was.

Rita used to say the kid was a pervert. They didn't much like one another. A lot of snotty remarks passed back and forth whenever the two women were in the same room. But Rita must've been right because lately he'd been hearing funny stories about Missy Delaunay—how she was running with street bums and petty hoods, and how she even hung out in nigger nightclubs and messed with cocaine and other shit. That's why Phil had bought her the .25 caliber derringer, a little two-shot, over-and-under thing. Reedy had warned him not to do it, because years back the girl had been suicidal, for chrissake. And now she had killed a guy with that gun.

Copley Square loomed up in front of him, supernaturally bright in the clear cold atmosphere. Behind the Plaza the glazed Hancock Tower rose to the dark sky like an iridescent column of ice.

He swung right and drove into Bay Village, where the deserted brick pavements were awash in eerie yellow lamplight and the old attached houses seemed to huddle together to keep warm.

Reaching the Tremont-Shawmut intersection, he had no difficulty spotting Missy's car, a sleek Mustang with louvers on its sloping rear window. Engine puffing exhaust, it sat in front of the Don Bosco Technical High School—and there was a tall, well-built black man in a bulky long-haired fur coat standing next to it on the driver's side.

Reedy made a tight U-turn, double-parked slightly behind the small car, switched his ignition off, climbed out and paused for a moment to take in the whole scene. The black man treated him to an insolent leer, while Melissa gazed back at him with anxious eyes. She'd always had such a pretty face, Reedy thought, but her feelings were so ugly that it affected her looks. Now, as she watched him approach, her blue eyes squinted beneath a worried brow and her lower lip sagged like an idiot's.

"This guy a friend of yours?" he asked her.

"No way, Kevin," she answered, her voice nervous and eager. "I told him to take a hike, but he only laughed at me."

Fixing the fur-clad intruder with a hard stare, Reedy

said in a grim voice, "Move it, jigaboo, or I'll roust you for vagrancy."

"Hey, who you talking to, Mr. Jones?" the man inquired contemptuously, straightening to his full height of well over six feet. "You ain't no cop, so don't jive me—less you want me to wax your ass for you."

"Jeez, will you listen to that?" the detective remarked, as if thinking aloud. Shaking his head in disgust, he parted the flaps of his down jacket to display the ebony handled .38 clipped on his belt. "Even the nigger nellie-fags give you guff nowadays. Get going, Aunt Jemima, or I'll have to flatten your nostrils for you. Do it so bad you won't be able to snort stardust for a year."

Eyes focused on the revolver, the object of this threat suddenly grinned. "Hey, how about that. Guess you the genuine police after all," he declared flippantly. "But don't get your shit hot, man. I only being cordial to this woman. Thought she might want to party—chug a cocktail, do a little shuffling. Ain't against no law to be friendly, is it?"

Not deigning to reply, Reedy glared at him until the fur-coated dandy, still smiling, pivoted forty-five degrees and sauntered off towards the corner. In the nocturnal gloom he resembled a carefree grizzly bear walking on his hind legs.

They watched him vanish onto Tremont Street, then Missy moaned plaintively. "It was an accident, Kevin—I swear. Oh, God! I never meant to shoot the guy."

"Not so loud," he cautioned her.

"I went crazy when I saw the pictures. He wanted to blackmail me, this damned Jewish wimp. Kevin, what am I going to do? He's back there in his car . . . dead."

"For chrissake! Keep it down, will you? Want the whole neighborhood to hear about it?" Reedy snapped. "Unlock the door, Missy."

He got in beside her, and immediately the distraught girl began to weep on his shoulder. Patting her back, he waited. Eventually the tears ceased. She pushed the snakelocks of blond hair off her wet cheeks, and blew her nose in a handkerchief fragrant of musk.

"Honest, I couldn't help myself. It was like an accident," she said weakly.

The detective nodded impatiently, raised her chin so

he could see her face, and commenced asking questions. Who was the blackmailer? A guy named Gilman, she told him. How did he get hold of the pictures? She didn't know. When did he contact her? That afternoon, by phone. Who else knew about the meeting? Just Phil—nobody else. Was she seen anywhere with Gilman that night? No, she didn't think so. Where did she meet him? On that corner, right across the street. He was waiting, and she got in his car—a green Audi. And what happened after that?

Sniffling and trembling, Missy Delaunay said, "We drove down a couple of blocks... past the project, to where the stores are. He swung off into this empty lot and parked. Made a few wise cracks... showed me the photographs. I flipped and started yelling at him. Then I shoved the pictures in my handbag. The gun was there... so, like a dope, I pulled it out and shot him... twice, in the chest. And I... I ran away from the car... found a phone booth and called Phil." Her mouth puckered. "Jesus, Kevin, was I ever terrified."

"Give me the gun," said Reedy, unable to generate much sympathy for her.

"What?" she mumbled, pushing the hair from her face.

"I want the gun—the derringer. Don't tell me you left it there, for chrissake."

"No, Kevin. I've got it." She wiped her eyes with the musky handkerchief and started digging in the leather bag, tilting it forward to catch the street light. Out fell a folded package of glossy colored pictures that hit the floor and scattered. "Shit!" the flustered woman exclaimed.

Dark as it was, Reedy could perceive that the photos were of nude people playing around, though he couldn't distinguish the details. When he picked one up for a closer examination, Missy snatched it away from him.

"What the hell are you doing, Kevin Reedy? Looking for cheap thrills?" She bent hastily to gather up the pictures and stuff them back in the handbag. "Believe it or not, I still have some pride left."

After a moment's groping she found the derringer and gave it to him. The detective tipped the barrel of the small gun, saw that both chambers were empty, closed it again and dropped the weapon in his jacket pocket.

"Gilman, you say his name is?"

For a minute she gazed at him silently, her expression one of fear and misery. "I really *hate* these situations," she said at last. "They're so *heavy*... so depressing... such a drag... so fucking *dismal*."

"Come on, will you? You're depressed, Missy? What about the dead guy?"

"Don't yell at me, okay? Right now I just can't take it," she said in a brittle voice. "If you want to turn me in, Kevin Reedy, go ahead. I don't care. Do your duty. But stop yelling at me."

"Missy, cut the dramatic bullshit, huh?" he said, exasperated. "Time's flying. Any minute a car thief might check out that Audi, see the stiff in there, and phone some cop with the news so he can score a few points for a rainy day. How do you know this Gilman?"

"I don't. He's not a friend of mine. He said he was a lawyer... and that he was looking for a political job. Seemed to think Phil could get him one."

"Are you talking about Harold Gilman? That schmuck with the wavy hair who's always hanging around the State House sucking up to people?"

"Yeah, him. You know him better than I do."

"I'll be damned," said Reedy. "But didn't I hear that he married that real estate woman with all the millions? The one whose father was involved in them big developments—the Pru, Park Square, the Waterfront? The girl you went to school with, Missy. Don't you remember? What was her name? Marcia?"

"Magda Margolis? Are you saying this Gilman was married to Magda Margolis?"

"Yeah, yeah. Jeez, that's a funny coincidence, ain't it?"

"Fantastic, Kevin. Magda Margolis."

"But if a guy's married to a millionairess, why the hell would he want to blackmail anybody?"

"Didn't I just tell you? He wasn't after money. He wanted an appointment to an executive position. He wanted Phil to make him the Property Commissioner or the Assessor or some stupid thing. The guy was a real dink. He said he needed a springboard for his political career. Must've been a little soft. But how did he ever get to be Magda's husband? That's kind of fishy." A crafty gleam suddenly illuminated Missy Delaunay's blue eyes. "Maybe she put him up to it, Kev. She hates my guts, that girl."

Reedy opened the car door. "We ain't got the time to talk about it now. You drive straight home—understand? Anybody comes to ask you questions, say you went to bed at eleven o'clock and slept like a baby."

"Jesus, you think they might do that? I couldn't bear to be grilled," she said, sounding slightly hysterical again. "Listen, Kevin—you come to my apartment afterwards, okay? If you're there, I won't be scared—won't feel so wired. Anyway, I want to know how you managed."

"I'll call you, Melissa."

"Shit! That's not the same. I'd be afraid to answer the damned phone. Come and stay with me—please!"

Eager to be off, the detective nodded. Then he climbed out, slammed the door behind him, and hurried to his Oldsmobile.

9

Awakened from a stuporous sleep by the heat of the room, Whitey Frainer grumbled aggrievedly and sat up on the bare hard floor. His gaunt bearded face was slick with sweat, and he could feel his pearl-buttoned cowboy shirt clinging to his back.

Samantha shoved that thermostat too high, he thought groggily. Must be a hundred degrees in here.

Earlier that Friday night Whitey had got his crutch from the car and, braving the arctic wind, had mooched eleven dollars in a couple of hours on Boylston Street. Then he'd given the Haitian shoplifter, Claude, eight of the eleven for a fifth of Cossack, a pint of blackberry brandy, a pint of peppermint schnapps, and a bag of assorted nips—the peewee bottles Samantha liked so much. So after they crawled into the vacant house through the cellar window and turned up the thermostat to get warm, the two of them were able to have a real nice party.

But why did she shove it so high? he asked himself, looking at the plump Samantha, now sprawled against the baseboard of the unfurnished room, bundled in her mangy imitation fur jacket and snoring peacefully.

As the lanky vagabond listened to her measured breathing, he gradually became aware of another and stranger noise, a crisp snapping and crackling that seemed to come from out in the hall. Glassy-eyed, he lumbered to the door on hands and knees and peered into the corridor. Everything looked perfectly normal. To his right some planks were stacked beneath the boarded-up windows, while a sheet of plywood leaned against one wall. To his left he saw only the gaping hole in the middle of the landing, where the renovators had ripped out the staircase to the ground floor.

Nevertheless, he still heard the peculiar sound, and now he began to smell the distinctive odor of burning wood. Whitey, not much of a deductive thinker, grappled with these two curious phenomena and soon came to the conclusion that the building was on fire.

Concerned but not alarmed, he crawled down the hall past the chasm in the landing, negotiated a corner and observed a bright glow issuing from a doorway a little farther on. He scrambled towards it and poked his shaggy head across the threshold. The room within had no floorboards. They had been stripped from the rough-hewn joists—and Whitey, to his befuddled astonishment, found himself staring down into the chamber below. There, a massive tiled fireplace containing a roaring blaze provided a simple explanation for the heat, noise, smoky smell, and rosy flickering light.

At first momentarily dazzled by the flames, Whitey didn't notice the sturdy man in the narrow-brimmed fedora crouching motionless on the hearthstone, but when he did, he quickly withdrew his head. Then, more cautiously, he took another peek.

The man—he was dressed in a white sweater and dark trousers—had an iron poker in his hand. His face was florid and beefy, and he appeared to be muttering to himself.

In Whitey Frainer's life fantasy and reality often became confused. Seeing this odd scene below him, he wondered if he was dreaming.

Around the squatting figure the spacious room looked

ready to disintegrate. Most of the wainscotting had collapsed, and the frames were gone from doors and windows. On all sides tattered strips of faded paper hung limply from decaying walls like parasitic growths in a dungeon. The floor was warped in some areas, pocked by dry rot in others, and here and there piled with crumbled plaster and splintered laths.

Who is this bozo? Whitey wondered. And what's he building a fire for? Place was warm already, on account of Samantha setting the thermostat. Does he belong here or did he sneak in the window, too?

But then the bewildered wino caught sight of the fat wallet on the marble mantelpiece above the raging fire, and became so preoccupied with the question of how to steal it that he forgot all his other speculations. Expensive looking, this billfold was. And it lay there all by itself, as if waiting for somebody to come along and pick it clean.

The problem was solved almost immediately, however, since the man in the white sweater straightened up, left the poker on the hearthstone, and hurried out of the moldering room. His footsteps could be heard in the hallway, and subsequently on the wooden stairs that led to the basement.

Whitey blinked his bleary eyes, scratched his shaggy head, and stroked his sandy beard. Slowly he got to his stockinged feet and cautiously stepped across the threshold onto the closest of the thick and ancient joists. It supported him with scarcely a murmur, so he nimbly hopped to the next beam over. Six more strides brought him to a spot near the front of the house where some workman had providentially erected an aluminum stepladder between the two plywood-sealed bay windows.

He paused to listen. Only the fire's peevish cackle disturbed the stillness. Down the ladder like a bearded gibbon Whitey went, and across the littered floor he raced. Fingers trembling from anxiety and alcohol, he snatched up the wallet and feverishly searched its inner compartments. But as luck would have it, they yielded no cash at all. He found quantities of business cards, several credit cards, a dry cleaner's ticket, an automobile registration and license, and three blank checks. That was it. Not so much as a dollar bill in ready money.

"Darn it!" he whispered, disappointed, and after slipping one of the credit cards in his trouser pocket, replaced the wallet on the chimney piece.

He turned and surveyed the rest of the forlorn room. Spying a bulging plastic shopping bag sitting atop a pile of old newspapers on the hearth's edge, Frainer hastened to it and pulled the handle flaps apart. What he saw when he looked inside—or, at least, imagined that he saw—was an elaborate Halloween mask, a rubbery horror complete with livid complexion, gore-stained lips and teeth, and jagged glistening neck wound. But his initial impression faded swiftly when a sudden flaring of the fire showed him the details much more clearly. With a great shock he realized that the sunken brown eyes regarding him so sadly from the depths of the bag were not just synthetic globs, nor was the grim countenance itself merely painted polymer. The thing was made of flesh, blood, and bone. It was real. It had been alive once—and not so long ago, either.

In the course of a rough and vagrant existence, Whitey Frainer had seen more than his share of disagreeable sights—some while sober, some while drunk, and some while in the cruel throes of delirium tremens—yet never before had he been face to face with a severed human head.

"Cripes!" he said softly, his lanky body commencing to quake.

But though he was frightened, he was entranced as well, and continued to gaze into the dead eyes long after his brain had advised him to flee. All this vibration soon had an effect on the object he held, for the detached head, as if wishing to avoid his concentrated scrutiny, at last tumbled over on its sallow cheek. When that occurred, two amputated hands appeared beneath it in a carmine pool of blood. And at almost the same moment Whitey thought he heard a noise out in the corridor.

Startled, he released the bag's limp handles and swung around—but no one was coming through the hall door. The only sign of animation was a restless fret of light and shadow cast high upon the ruined walls by the fluctuant play of the fire.

He exhaled silently, and just as silently hurried back to the aluminum ladder.

* * *

Minutes later the man returned carrying a snow shovel and a galvanized iron tub, and these he deposited on the floor. Out of breath, he gasped for air, exhibiting his uneven, widely spaced front teeth.

The wino had long since reoccupied his point of vantage on the landing above. After his recent experience he was more interested than ever in this curious denizen of the lower floor. With the intensity of a hawk he watched the man pick up the shopping bag, together with a few newspapers from the stack to prevent blood from dipping on the hearthstone, and effortlessly fling the whole grisly, gruesome bundle into the frenzied flames.

Sparks flew. The thin plastic caught fire at once, melted and curled away. An incandescent gold ring circled the head, which lay facedown on the burning paper. From the wavy hair tendrils of gray smoke seeped, and slowly meandered up the chimney. One of the severed hands, having fallen on a length of charred timber, now clung there like a small animal on the withered branch of a tree.

Whitey watched it all, still not entirely convinced that he wasn't having a new kind of nightmare. The odor of roasting flesh reached his nose and made him queasy. He wondered drowsily if he should go back to Samantha, wondered if the two of them shouldn't skedaddle the heck out of there. But maybe that would be risky. The husky bozo might hear them when they tried to sneak down to the cellar.

Time passed, yet it didn't seem like real time. Then suddenly, amidst a meteor shower of embers, the mound of burning wood collapsed, sending the well-done hand skittering into the darker depths of the inferno. At the same instant the head fell. Down and over it rolled, not coming to a rest until it crashed against the sooty bricks of the fireplace wall.

Frainer winced. Where the pale jowly face had been, there was now only a coarse mat of carbonized tissue and bone—a reeking black wound, devoid of human characteristics. Nothing remained but the teeth, and these were larger than they had been in life because the lips and gums were gone. From the smoldering skull they shone with surprising brilliance, shone in a death smile full of mockery.

The man, who had been wandering aimlessly about the

big room in a somewhat distracted manner, rushed back and retrieved the iron poker and with it deftly maneuvered the charred head into the center of the fire again, much as a suburbanite might rearrange a broiler on an outdoor barbecue grill.

That accomplished, he added a few more dusty slats of wainscotting to the blaze, retreated a step or two and crouched down on the granite hearthstone. For the next half hour he stayed in this position, scarcely moving while the harsh glare transformed his fleshy face to bronze and his eyes to luminescent jewels. In a more exotic setting he could have been a heathen idol before a holocaust.

Meanwhile, stupefied by heat and fatigue, the vagabond on the second floor kept to his vigil. With his bearded chin on the doorsill and his bloodshot eyes fixed in a hypnotic stare, he drifted in a limbo midway between wakefulness and slumber.

By the half hour's end the head was reduced to a riven contour of blackened bone barely distinguishable from the cinders on which it nestled. But the capering flames were now appreciably shorter. Furtive shadows advanced from the four corners of the room like famished gray wolves closing in on a dying campfire.

The man below arose, grabbed the galvanized tub and trudged off towards the rear of the house. When he was gone, Whitey Frainer rolled onto his back, stretched his arms and legs, and mopped his sweaty face with the sleeve of his cowboy shirt.

If me and Samantha go, where can we go to? he asked himself. Ain't no place open this time of night, not even the bus station. And it's freezing cold. Maybe we could get a motel room with the credit card. But I better wait and see. They might not let us in, a motel, and this time of night there ain't no places open. Cripes, I sure could use a snort of that Cossack.

Somewhere in the old house water began to run. The sound persisted for several minutes, and shortly after it stopped the man returned, struggling under the weight of the now full tub. Beneath his arm he had a lit flashlight that cleared a path through the deepening darkness for him. Going directly to the fire, he set about dousing it with the water. The embers hissed furiously, and an opaque column of smoke billowed pell-mell up the flue. Sooty water flowed out of the fireplace, crossed the slab of granite, and formed an inky pool in a hollow of the warped floor.

With the snow shovel the man quickly removed the damp debris, and soon the full fireplace was empty and the empty washtub full. He then tucked the flashlight under his arm again, picked up the loaded basin, and left the room.

Whitey Frainer, lying in the total darkness, listened to him descend to the cellar. After a while some doors slammed and an automobile engine roared behind the house, and though it alternately raced and stalled, eventually it warmed to a steady rumble and the car drove off.

"Darnedest thing I ever saw," the lanky wino said, and he got to his stockinged feet and yawned.

10

Missy's blue eye, lackluster with sleep, appeared in the small round lens of the judas. The lock clicked and the door opened.

"What happened? I must've dozed," she said, blinking at the glare in the hall. "You look strange. What happened, Kevin?"

Reedy walked past her into the living room. "Get me a drink, will you?"

"It went wrong, didn't it?" the blonde said, snapping the door bolt in place. "I knew it would. I just knew. My luck has always been rotten."

"Nothing went wrong. I took care of everything. The guy's gone—gone forever. You don't have to worry." He started to shiver, but swiftly regained control of his barrel-chested body. "What I need now is a shot of something—a double, and no ice. I'm half froze."

She hesitated for a few seconds, a slim figure tightly swathed in yellow satin, then nodded and went off to the kitchen.

After he struggled out of the worn oilskin slicker and

draped it on a chair, Reedy caught a glimpse of himself in the mirror and frowned. The shadows under his eyes were like welts, while his hair and stubble of beard, dusted with sea salt, were as gray as an old man's.

I looked like my father after a binge, he thought.

Somewhere a small motor was droning. The sound annoyed him. He wondered if it were a blender. Suddenly his tired mind conjured up a lurid image—the saw, the blood, the open eyes—and his whole burly frame jactitated violently.

When Missy Delaunay returned, she found him huddled in a corner of the couch. "God, you look awful, Kevin," she said bluntly, giving him a glass. "You smell funny, too. And why are you wearing those grotty clothes?"

Reedy downed the whiskey in two gulps. For an instant he thought it was going to come back up again, but then, hot as fire, it gradually settled in the pit of his stomach. He coughed, wiped his lips with an index finger, and said, "I fell overboard."

"You what?"

"Almost drowned, for chrissake. You wouldn't believe how cold that water was. Just like the time I went through the ice on the Charles. Feels as if your heart's going to seize up and stop, like your blood ain't circulating any more. It was only dumb luck that I happened to come back up close to the dinghy. A couple feet farther away and—sayonara."

"Gee, must've been terrible," she said sympathetically, sitting down beside him.

"I never figured I'd make it to shore, Missy—honest to Jesus. Thought I'd pass out in the boat and die of shock and exposure." The detective gave her a gap-toothed smile. "But I'm a tough cop. I got back somehow, tied up the dinghy and staggered to the car. Unlocking that door with my frozen fingers was a real bitch. Kept dropping the goddamn keys. Wasn't till the warm air started coming out of the heater that I figured I might not croak after all."

"God, Kev—I'm sorry I caused you—"

"Its okay... forget it. Had to change into these old clothes. They ain't too warm, but at least they were dry."

"I shouldn't have asked you to do such a risky thing,"

Missy said contritely, her face half hidden by her long hair.

"Why not? The Delaunays have been helping me for years. I'm just glad I could do one of you a favor for a change," said Reedy. "That's loyalty—and if a friend ain't loyal, he ain't nothing."

She touched his stubbly cheek with a warm hand, chucked him under the chin, and said, "Well, I won't *ever* forget it. From now on, Kevin Reedy, you're my knight in shining armor. But why is your face so cold? Want another bourbon?"

"Yeah, that'd be great."

When she stood the yellow satin kimono flared, and he caught a brief glimpse of creamy flesh. His eyes continued to follow the shapely woman as she ambled towards the kitchen in her backless, high-heeled bedroom slippers.

Once again Reedy became conscious of the droning electric motor sound he'd heard earlier. Could it be a ringing in his ears? Prompted by the thought of electricity, he remembered the loose wires in the Audi and experienced a fresh pang of fear.

Melissa returned, filled his glass with Jim Beam, and put the bottle on the table.

"That guy's automobile—Gilman's," he said. "Did it have a radio?"

"A radio? I guess so. Why?"

"Because it didn't have a radio when I got there. The wires were hanging loose from an empty hole in the dash."

"I would've noticed an empty hole. You mean somebody swiped it?"

"Yeah."

"Then he must've seen the dead guy. Shit!"

"Yeah. That ain't too good," said Reedy, shaking his head. "Maybe he seen other things, also."

"What do you mean?" she asked, sitting next to him again.

"Ordinarily a thief won't go into an occupied car. Gilman just looked like he was sleeping there. See what I'm getting at? The only way the thief would know he was harmless was if he happened to eyewitness the shooting."

"Oh, Christ!" Missy stamped her high heel on the carpet. "That's all I need."

"Could be he was still hanging around when I showed up later, too. Might've took my license number."

"Kevin, I didn't see a soul there. The streets were deserted." She picked up a pack of Benson & Hedges cigarettes, shook one out, and wedged it between her lips. "So where does that leave us now?"

"There were three or four other vehicles parked in the lot. I was going to check them out, but there didn't seem no point in doing it. Even if I flushed the hump, I couldn't have taken him in, could I? Besides, I had enough on my plate already, and I didn't want to waste any more time. For all I knew, the radio might've been hooked a couple of days ago." The detective drank some whiskey and blinked his red-rimmed eyes. Then he glanced at her bare leg and cleared his throat. "But I can absolutely guarantee nobody followed me when I drove that Audi out of there. Which means if there was some maggot watching, he ain't going to know what happened to the corpse. And if he can't produce a corpse, who the hell's going to believe his story?"

Two lines creased Missy's forehead between the serpentine strands of her yellow hair. "You used Gilman's car?"

"Had to. Guy was bleeding," he said, shrugging his wide shoulders. "Maybe we're worrying about nothing. Whoever clipped the radio—what can he do? Probably just some nigger junkie trying to support his habit. Can a guy like that run to the station house and tell the desk sergeant he found a dead man in a car while he was perpetrating a little petty larceny? And why would he bother? Those jigs never help the police. It's against their religion."

"I sure hope you're right," the woman said, and lit her cigarette with a disposable lighter.

"Nothing we can do about it now," said Reedy. He coughed, and had another taste of the bourbon. "Jeez, I hope I'm not coming down with the flu or something. My throat's scratchy—and I'm still cold."

"You ought to take a hot shower, Kevin."

"I'll do it when I get home."

"Don't be a dope. Do it now. By the time you drive home you could catch double pneumonia. Half the people I know have been sick this winter."

"Yeah, might be a good idea. Probably take the chill off me." He finished the whiskey, flexed his legs, and stood up. "Hey, what's that buzzing sound I keep hearing, Missy?"

"My white noise machine. Blocks out the traffic from Storrow Drive," she responded, releasing a cloud of smoke from her narrowly parted lips. "I'd lie awake all night long if I didn't have that thing." She pushed herself from the couch and added, "I'll get you a towel. Wash the salt off and comb your hair. You look like something left on the beach after the tide's gone out."

Reedy laughed hollowly, set his glass on the table and trailed her as she left the room.

Once the door was closed behind him, he drew his .38 revolver and examined it for rust. The gun had gone into Cape Cod Bay with him, and he'd have to clean it thoroughly in the morning. He set it on the toilet tank and got out of his sea-scented clothing.

The shower felt wonderful, but its steamy warmth intensified the effect of the bourbon he'd drunk. By the time he finished, he was a bit giddy.

Arriving back in the living room, he found Missy sitting in a chair. The couch-bed was unfolded and made up with blue sheets and gray blankets.

"What's this? I can't stay over."

"Why not?" Missy asked negligently. She pointed a thumb at the banjo clock on the wall. "It's five in the morning, almost. Be daylight in another hour, and you have to go all the way to Jamaica Plain."

"But I don't want to put you to any trouble. J.P. ain't that long a drive."

"It's no trouble. I already fixed the bed, didn't I?"

"Mightn't look right, Melissa—me staying here," he argued, although he knew he was exhausted and a little drunk.

"Are you serious, Kevin?" she asked, giving him a scornful, sidelong glance from behind a loose fall of her curly hair. "Quit talking like an old lady. I'll bet you can hardly keep your eyes open. Stay. Don't be a loony."

Too weary to engage in a debate, Reedy capitulated. "Okay, okay. Don't let me sleep too late, though, will you? Phil's supposed to phone me tomorrow."

"I'll wake you around ten for breakfast," she said, getting up from the chair. "You can tell me the rest of the gory details about what you did with that wimp Gilman."

"Nah, I've told you all I'm going to tell you. The less you know, the better. Good night, Missy."

"Good night, Kev."

Off to her bedroom she went. The detective noticed with relief that the droning white noise ceased as soon as she closed her door.

He removed his shoes, discarded his shabby clothing, put out the two lamps, and crawled between the cool sheets. Under the weight of his fatigue he sank almost immediately into a profound slumber. And he dreamt of Rita.

They were together in a vast park, a place of emerald-green lawns and little round hills and shady groves of trees. Everywhere flowers were growing, and in the golden sunshine these many-colored blossoms dazzled the eye like bursts of flame. There were butterflies, too, and flocks of songbirds who warbled their harmonious melodies even as they dived and darted in the crystalline air.

Yet none of the park's marvels was half so beautiful as Rita herself. She lay on the grass beside him, her pretty face surrounded by soft brown hair. Through the flimsy white gown she wore, he could clearly see her slender body. Tender expressions of love and longing gleamed in her eyes, and when he heard her provocative laughter he grew delirious with joy. But just as he was about to caress the alluring woman, something hot and moist wriggled into his ear.

Like a magnificent stained-glass window shattering in slow motion, the dream disintegrated. The hills, trees, flowers, birds, sunshine broke into pieces that blew away like autumn leaves. Only a trace of sweet fragrance remained behind. Even the thing in his ear withdrew, but now he could feel balmy breathing on his face and warm flesh urgently pressing against his body.

"Caught you at last, Kevin Reedy," a tantalizing voice whispered.

The perfume smelled wonderful. He ran his hand down a naked back to the curve of a buttock, nuzzled a mass of scented hair, kissed a smooth shoulder. Then it dawned on him that the seductive voice hadn't been Rita's.

"Hey," he said woozily, and opened his eyes to the gray darkness of the room.

"Hey, yourself," Missy retorted, fondling him.

"Jeez... don't. Quit it, will you?" he muttered, as he attempted to push her away. "Cut it out, for chrissake. Nah... it ain't right."

"Feels right to me," she said breathlessly, climbing on top of him like a playful child.

He put up a weak resistance, but not for long.

Afterwards she lay there panting, her sweaty forehead and damp blond hair on his heaving chest. Reedy wanted to get out from under her so he could breathe, but his strength seemed to have evaporated.

"Never should have done that, Missy," he said finally.

"Why not?" she asked innocently, rubbing her nose on his nipple.

"A person's got to have some scruples. Certain things just ain't right."

"Oh, bullshit! What's the matter, Kevin Reedy? Afraid you've committed a mortal sin? Don't be a feeb. The priest in the confessional will understand—and, even if he doesn't, wasn't it worth a few extra Hail Marys?"

Giggling, the woman slithered off his body. The springs squeaked as she left the bed.

"Nighty-night," he heard her say, but when he turned and looked for her in the darkness, she was no longer there.

Down the hall the toilet flushed. Tap water rushed noisily into the sink, followed by faint splashing. Finally the drain gurgled, the light switch clicked, and Missy's high-heeled footfalls receded into her bedroom.

The detective shut his eyes and did his best not to think, hoping sleep would quickly overtake him again. But too many shocking things had happened to him in the preceding five hours, and his brain refused to rest.

To make matters worse, his hostess hadn't closed her bedroom door and he could hear the white-noise machine humming away like a swarm of bumblebees. He ducked beneath the blankets, only to discover that it was unbearably hot there and that he couldn't breathe. A fit of coughing came over him. By the end of it his throat felt sore—especially when he swallowed. From time to time he did manage to doze off, but the nagging drone always awakened him, and once, half in a dream, he thought it was the sound of the jigsaw, thought he was back again in the basement of the Fenway brownstone with Gilman's hulking body stretched out on the dusty workbench.

When the banjo clock's single chime indicated that it was six-thirty, Kevin Reedy muttered, "Goddammit," and dragged himself from under the tangled bedclothes. Within minutes he was dressed, out of the Beacon Street apartment, and on his way home through the bleak light of a winter dawn.

He felt a little better in his own house. Getting two Nembutals to pass down his constricted throat proved something of a problem, but after he succeeded in doing so he fell asleep at once, a sleep rife with physical discomforts and bad dreams.

Saturday morning, when the alarm clock went off, he was too sick to get up. His black part-time housekeeper, Mrs. Williams, telephoned the doctor for him, and when the physician arrived at eleven-thirty he promptly diagnosed a strep throat and gave his patient a shot of penicillin.

By nightfall Reedy was feverish to the point of delirium. Mrs. Williams, afraid he might become even worse, remained with him till the next morning.

11

The trip from the police laboratory on Commonwealth Avenue to Magda's Brookline apartment house, the Allerton Arms, took Frankie Gates less than fifteen minutes. He swung onto the driveway between the neatly trimmed hedges, stuck his cardkey in the slotted post to raise the overhead door, entered the basement garage, checked for oncoming vehicles in the convex mirror that depended from the ceiling, made a sharp right and parked the Gilman Audi next to the

Gilman Cadillac Seville. Then he got out, nodded to the attendant who was washing the whitewalls of a Lotus, and rode the elevator to the fifteenth floor.

She was in the corner room she used for her business office, dressed in a frilly white blouse and seated behind her mahogany kidney-shaped desk.

As he sat down across from her, Magda studied his irregular face and said, "It was blood, wasn't it?"

"Yeah," Gates admitted, "but not enough to get excited about. A few smeared drops. Might not even be Harold's. There are plenty of other possibilities. Some drunken kids might have snatched the car from the lot out at Logan, taken it for a joyride. Maybe they had a fight about who was going to drive, and one of them got a rap in the mouth. Then they dumped it in the South End and went on home."

"Very plausible, Frankie," she said, rocking gently in her chrome executive swivel chair. "So you're still convinced he flew to Florida?"

"The man likes to travel, doesn't he? In the seven months since I met you he's been to Vegas, L.A., Atlantic City, Tampa, the Bahamas."

"The caretaker at the condominium hasn't seen him. This morning I phoned Tampa."

"So maybe he went straight to Lauderdale—caught a charter flight to Nassau. Gambling's his thing, isn't it, Magda?"

The woman pondered this reply, transferring a small stack of papers from the center of the desk to one of the rounded ends. "Well, for starters, Harold never leaves his car at the airport. He takes a cab. Furthermore, whenever he goes on a trip like that, he usually tells me in advance. Thirdly, I checked his apartment yesterday and his suitcases, his electric shaver, his toothbrush and hairbrush, his summer clothing—everything is still there. And last but by no means least, my husband didn't have the money for such a junket. On that very Friday morning, Sherlock, he put the bite on me for two hundred dollars to pay some of his office bills."

"But he could have had a streak of luck, couldn't he? Gamblers can be broke one night, and flush the next. And when they're hot, they like to play in big games—like to take on the casinos."

She fixed him with a hard and steady scrutiny. "Are you being honest with me, Frankie? Or aren't you as smart as I thought you were? When a person is missing three days and his car is found abandoned in a slummy area with bloodstains on the front seat, Albert Einstein you don't have to be to conclude that something nasty has happened to him. Are you trying to protect me from harsh realities or what?" Magda folded her hands on the leather-framed blotter that covered the middle of the desk, and released a barely audible sigh. "Perhaps you're not taking the matter seriously. Is that how it is?"

"If you're asking me if I'm worried about Harold—if I care whether or not he shows up again—I'd have to say, not particularly," Gates conceded. "And it isn't just a question of my personal feelings, Mag. He's a grown man. Missing adults almost always turn up."

"This missing adult happens to be my husband—a member of my immediate family. Maybe I don't sleep with him anymore, maybe I don't like him very much, and maybe I wish I could dissolve our miserable marriage—but I still want to know where the idiot is. Stop handing me a spiel, Frankie darling. You're supposed to be a police detective. Give me the benefit of your vast experience. What did your forensic friend at the lab say?"

As a form of retaliation, Gates would have liked to put his size-twelve shoes up on her gleaming desk—yet he didn't dare. "How come whenever you're in your office, Magda, you start acting like a high-powered business tycoon?" he said instead. "I'm not complaining. I'm just wondering."

"That's easy. I act like a tycoon because I am a tycoon. Now let's dispense with the chitchat. Tell me everything you heard from your pal Harvey what's-his-name, so we shouldn't have an argument. Okay? For instance, did he check for fingerprints?"

"Yeah, and there were more than a hundred of them. All the local grifters ran their hands lovingly over that Audi. None of them drove it off, though, which is hard to figure. Ordinarily your average South End kid would steal a space shuttle, if you left it parked there overnight—but the radio is the only thing they snitched." The detective shrugged, mystified. "As evidence, any of those fingerprints are worthless, Magda. Harvey Gunther didn't even bother to photograph them. He vacuumed the car, though. Got sample bags of dirt and dust filed away for further reference—in case it comes to that. There was clean sand in the tire treads, so he thinks they were driven on a beach or through a sandpit maybe. What else? Let's see. The blood on the upholstery—he estimated the quantity at less than half an ounce. And it's type O. Would that be Harold's blood group?"

"I haven't the vaguest. Don't even know my own," she said, puckering her brow. "I'll phone his doctor. Why in heaven's name would he go to a beach in January?"

"Probably he wouldn't—but joyriding kids might."

"I still don't buy it, lover. Doesn't he have any theories about what happened to my husband?"

Gates smiled tolerantly. "Come on," he said. "Be reasonable. Harvey's a first-class scientist, but he can't perform miracles."

"Harvey's a first-class schlub, it seems to me. If Philip Marlowe went over that automobile, he would've found all kinds of clues."

"Who?"

"Oh, never mind," said Magda Gilman disgustedly.

The telephone rang and she grabbed it. "Speaking... Oh, yes, Mr. Selwyn. How's it going?... Did they? Well, they're lying to you," she said austerely. "Pettigrew has no interest whatever in that property. Those people are trying to bid us up—turn the thing into an auction... absolutely... Listen... listen, Mr. Selwyn, for a building that size on a measly eighteen acres of land it's a very generous offer. Route 128 isn't Louisburg Square, tell them. Okay?... No, I'm busy with something else right now. Get back to me in an hour. 'Bye."

She hung up, pushed the phone away from her and, just as if they hadn't been interrupted, said, "Frankie, I'm disappointed. I always thought the Boston Police Department was chock-full of clever Irishmen—shrewd, hard-nosed professionals. But I must've been mistaken. Harold's disappearance can hardly be a unique case in the annals of American crime. Has it occurred to anybody—you, Harvey, headquarters—that perhaps, because his wife is wealthy, the poor man might've been kidnapped? That he's being held for ransom?"

"You receive a phone call from someone, Magda?" Gates asked, sitting up in his chair. "Or a note demanding money?"

"Not yet—but that doesn't mean I won't."

"Yes, it does," he flatly contradicted her, shaking his head. "Kidnappers don't wait seventy-two hours before making contact. Delays only increase the risks for them. They want to do the deal quick. Even a schlub like me knows that."

"Okay, okay. What about other possibilities? Harold lost a fair number of cases, and some of those clients were absolutely furious. They threatened to kill him as soon as they—"

"Magda, felons always threaten their lawyers when they're sent down—they never carry out those threats. Know why? Because if they did and they got caught, no lawyer would want to defend them." Frankie Gates grinned at her for a moment, then his rugged face grew serious and he leaned forward. "Look, Mag—the key to a missing person case is usually something in that person's private life. You're a better source of clues than Harvey Gunther. So let's work on your memory. When did you first notice he wasn't sleeping next door? How did he act the last time you saw him? Does he have any big problems? Financial? Professional? Marital? Health? Tell me what *you* know, and maybe I can give you a couple of deductions and theories."

"That reference to marital problems—is that supposed to be a wisecrack?" She favored him with a frosty glare.

"Nah—I'm just trying to be a shrewd, hard-nosed Irishman. Like you said, he is your husband—right?" he replied, sitting back again and folding his large hands over his lean stomach. "Even when two people are separated, marriage relationships are complicated."

"All right, Frankie. I'm just asking," the woman said in a conciliatory tone. She paused and collected her thoughts before going on. "Sunday afternoon I noticed it was quiet in his apartment, and it occurred to me that it had been quiet the day before as well. I went in and looked around. When I saw that the bed was made I knew he hadn't slept there, because the girl doesn't come on Sunday and he'd never make it himself. But I wasn't worried about one night. On Monday I had to go into town, and the minute I arrived back home they called to say they had found the car." She fell silent, gently rocked, and absently contemplated the stack of papers at the end of the desk. "As for Harold's problems," she continued, "I can't tell you much about them. He's always short of money. His legal practice is not quite mediocre; he's overweight and has high cholesterol. He had a hernia operation six months ago. You already know the man's a degenerate gambler. What can I add?"

"Has he been acting strange lately?"

"No stranger than usual. When I gave him the two hundred dollars Friday morning, the last time I saw him, he did a lot of extravagant talking—lot of nonsense. Said he was going to surprise me. Said he was going to land an important political appointment, and that his picture would be on the front pages of all the newspapers. But that's always been one of Harold's big fantasies."

"What else did he have to say?"

"Nothing. He just rambled. Started reminiscing about his brother Ludwig, who died recently up in New Hampshire. Ludy, they called him—a horny little bastard who always wanted to play Doctor with me when we were kids. May he rest in peace. I was surprised to hear Harold wax so sentimental over him." Magda slowly revolved forty-five degrees in her chair and gazed out the picture window at the distant Boston skyline, a silvery-gray range of blunted peaks. "I never should have married that man, Frankie," she said wistfully.

"I couldn't agree with you more. Why the hell did you?"

"Because after Gabriel killed himself, I was meshuga—crazy in the head. I'd get so lonely, so down. Believe me, my heart was broken. And Harold was around. His father and my father started Primrose Realty together fifty years ago—but Sol Gilman was another born loser, and Dad had to buy him out before they both went under. My father never liked Harold. Thought he was a yentzer—a person you can't trust—and warned me not to marry him. Only it was too late. I'd already agreed. A couple of nights earlier he had proposed to me at the Casa Valparaiso, and I must have been shikker on those potent pisco sours because I said yes."

"Funny your father thought he was dishonest."

"Not really. Harold worked at Primrose for a while and did a few shady deals under-the-counter. When Dad found out, he fired him."

"Was the guy dishonest with you, Magda?"

"No worse than most husbands, I suppose. But he never had access to my money. We didn't share and share alike, darling. Right from the start I put him on an allowance." Suddenly the woman's eyes gleamed with suspicion. "Hey, why did you say '*Was* he dishonest?' Is Harold dead, Frankie? Do you know more than you're telling me?"

"Stop imagining things. I said 'was' because we're talking about the past," Gates answered reproachfully. Then he gave her a calculating look. "Beforc you mentioned that maybe you should've dissolved the marriage. How come you didn't, Mag?"

Fingering the lace on the neck of her blouse, she weighed the question. "The truth of the matter is, I didn't dare divorce him," she said finally. "Harold's a fox in some ways. He has a lot of proof of my . . . my escapades. The settlement could cost me a couple of million. Maybe even more. And a sensational trial wouldn't do my business reputation any good, either."

Gates nodded, a joyless smile on his craggy face. All she worries about is money, he thought with regret. So what if she paid the bastard a million or two? Still be plenty left, and she'd be free. But the woman doesn't understand how much I like her—doesn't take me serious. I might as well be a rented escort as far as she's concerned.

"It's late," he said abruptly, standing. "Got to get back to work."

"Good idea." Her eyes were inscrutable. "Find my louse of a husband for me, why don't you?"

"I'll try, but my heart won't be in it. Besides, I'm a burglary specialist, not a Missing Persons cop. See you tonight, Mag?"

"Come around eight, Sherlock—and bring encouraging news."

The telephone rang again as he passed through the door.

12

The investigator, Frederick—Fritz, to his close friends—Pomerantz, conducted his modest business from a room above a sandwich shop in a flat-roofed, three-story brick structure that, according to an engraved stone tablet on its blackened facade, had been erected in 1904. The place smelled of stale tobacco smoke, scorched dust from the ornate cast-iron radiators, and salami, oregano, and provolone, courtesy of the restaurant below.

Pomerantz was of medium height and build, but he had a noticeable paunch that caused him shame. On formal occasions he wore a corset to hide this deformity. The best feature of his homely face was a full walrus moustache that he kept black and lustrous by the skillful application of the same Clairol dye he used on his hair and eyebrows.

He smiled, uncovering a set of large yellowish teeth, and said, "Where exactly did they find it, Mrs. Gilman?" in his gravelly voice.

"Right here on Tremont—downstairs, no more than a block away," Magda replied, opening her cashmere polo coat because the office was overheated. "That's why I dropped by. I thought Harold might've come to see you on Friday. But you say he didn't."

"Hasn't been around in more than a month. His last visit was about a kid charged with mugging a Jap businessman in South Station. I interviewed the victim through an interpreter, and checked the defendant's alibi. Case comes up the tenth of February, I believe. But Harold disappearing like this—that's unprecedented." Pomerantz tugged at the vest of his three-piece gray worsted suit, and adopted a look of paternal concern. "Would you want me to find him for you, Mrs. Gilman?"

"What makes you think you could, Frederick?"

The investigator laughed. "Got to have confidence in this profession," he said affably. "Don't get me wrong. The police are very adequate, generally speaking, but they can't expend a lot of their precious time on a single individual. Now a free-lancer like me—he can devote his whole undivided attention to the problem. Makes all the difference in the world. Besides, I know the subject personally."

Patently unimpressed, Magda let her eyes rove the room. On one wall above two oaken file cabinets a cheap reproduction of Gilbert Stuart's *George Washington* hung, while near the dingy window there stood a Morgan Memorial bookcase that had a few odd volumes of *The Annotated Laws of Massachusetts* on its dusty shelves.

"What do you charge?"

"The professional rate for you. Forty-five an hour, plus expenditures. Same as I charge your husband."

"Well, you're ideally located to find out about the car being left here, aren't you? Okay, you're hired. Just keep in mind that I expect results for my money, Frederick—and don't go hog wild on those expenditures, either. Do you want a retainer?"

"From you, Mrs. Gilman?" Pomerantz looked flabbergasted. "Nah, I'll bill you later." He opened the center drawer of the desk and pulled out a pad of lined paper. "Right now what I need is information—his customary schedule, what you know about his plans for the day he vanished, a description of the clothes he was wearing, etcetera."

Nodding once, she concisely told him everything she knew, and he scribbled it all down with a blue Flair pen, interrupting occasionally to request more details. The lawyer's gambling habits seemed to be of special interest to him. But Magda could provide few particulars. She wasn't acquainted with any of her husband's fellow cardplayers. Harold's secretary at his downtown office would probably know some of them, she suggested.

When the woman finished, Pomerantz continued to stare at his pad for a minute or two, as though memorizing each and every word. But the truth was that his mind had wandered.

This Jew broad is solid gold. Owns condos, shopping centers, hotels, he thought greedily. Her father was Abe Margolis. Margolis had so much money he couldn't count it, they used to say. Had to weigh it in canvas bags. If I handle this right, I ought to be able to take a couple of grand off her, maybe more. God knows, I could use it.

Finally, he tapped the tip of his shiny moustache with the end of the pen, and said, "Not much to go on, is there? You mentioned that the blood in the Audi was his. How did you arrive at that?"

"I didn't say it was definitely his, Frederick. I said it was the same type," she corrected him. "It's been analyzed as type O—and Harold's blood is type O, according to his physician."

"Yeah, that's what I meant," he answered glibly, striking a businesslike pose in his leather-upholstered chair. "I wouldn't rush to an unwarranted conclusion, though, Mrs. Gilman. Two out of three people in this world have type O. Your husband, seeing as he likes to gamble, might've gotten himself engaged in a marathon poker game someplace and left his automobile vulnerable in the street. A couple of kids could've swiped it on him, and he wouldn't even know about it yet. You follow me?"

"Yes, Frederick, very easily," the woman said with unconcealed irony.

"Right. Okay. Well, what I'm going to have to do is interrogate the people in this immediate vicinity—see if I can pick up a thread. A lot of the characters around here spend all their leisure loitering on corners or gawking out windows, so one or more of them might've seen how the vehicle got parked there. Means plenty of legwork, but it's standard procedure."

"That was more or less what I had in mind."

"But I'll require a photo of Harold. If you could arrange—"

"I have three right here," Magda said, cutting him short. She drew a white envelope from her bag and passed it across the desk to him. "I gave the police several this morning."

"Terrific," said Pomerantz, inspecting the pictures. "I'm all set then. I'll get on it this afternoon—start asking around."

"One more thing. I have a boyfriend. His name is Frank Gates, and he's a detective at the District D station house," she declared matter-of-factly. "Friday night he went to a hockey game at the Garden with two other detectives, one of whom is named Dolan. I can't remember the second man's name. I don't suspect my friend of any hanky-panky, but I'd like you to verify all this. Can you do that?"

At the mention of the word boyfriend, Pomerantz's dyed eyebrows wriggled involuntarily. He lowered them fast, resumed his worldly manner, and recorded this additional information on his lined pad. "Shouldn't be a problem. I have confidential connections in the department."

"Fine. Confidential is what I want. Be discreet, Frederick—okay?" she said, getting up to leave.

Gallantly he insisted on accompanying her down the stairs to the front door.

The traffic light was red. She bade him a quick good-bye and dashed across Tremont Street to where her Seville was parked a yard from the Suds for Duds Laundromat.

13

Pomerantz watched the well-proportioned woman till she got in her expensive automobile, then he walked a few steps and entered the submarine sandwich shop, intending to buy a container of coffee he could take back upstairs with him. Just inside the door a wiry man in a corduroy jacket and a peaked cap tried to brush past him—but the investigator, recognizing this departing customer, deliberately blocked his way.

"For crying out loud! Hey, Stanley—don't you know me any more?" he exclaimed indignantly.

"Fritzie! How've you been?"

"Great. And you?"

"Not bad, not bad—but I'm in a little hurry right now. Got to meet a pal. You don't mind if I—"

"What are you saying, Stan? Ain't I your pal, too?" Pomerantz declared, making as if to grab the other's arm, though not actually touching him. "I haven't seen you in more than a year. Let's sit and have a cup of jamoke. Won't take five minutes."

Stanley Gloag, his heavy-lidded eyes fastened on the decal-decorated glass pane of the shop's front door as if he were captivated by the sight of the Tremont Street traffic, held his ground for a while—but in the end he smiled meagerly and said, "Sure, why not?" and allowed his friend to steer him to a corner booth.

"Two regulars," Pomerantz called to the counterman. To Gloag he said in an undertone, "Somebody told me you took a bad fall down in Connecticut, Stan—that you got sent to Enfield."

"Not Enfield—Somers. Fifteen to twenty the judge dropped on me. He couldn't make it stick, though, and I left the joint after seven months," said Gloag, not without pride. "Didn't have time to take my shoes off."

"You're not . . . ? I mean, did you get out legally or what?"

"Of course, legally. You think I dug a tunnel or scaled the wall? I'm a civilized person, Fritz—you know that. We filed an appeal and won. I had a very persuasive lawyer— and one of the witnesses revised his story." Stanley pushed the bill of his cap up, and the change gave his pale face a youthful look. "Business must be pretty good for you, Frederick. You've put on weight."

"Can't complain. Lately I've been catching a lot of lucrative personal injury cases," said Pomerantz in the casual manner of a flourishing executive. "And before that I was snowed under with resumé checks and curriculum vitaes, which are these references people have to submit when they apply for top-flight positions in commerce and industry. I verify the true facts and search for derogatories.

It's disgusting the way all the job seekers tell lies nowadays, Stanley. Like a guy'll say he's got a degree from Harvard, and you find out he never even finished high school. Or maybe he'll allege he pulled down fifty K last year as a mining engineer in Idaho, and a few discreet inquiries reveal the bum's been living on welfare in Roxbury for as long as his relatives can remember. This country's full of phonies. Doing verifications on resumés and curriculas has ruined my whole faith in human nature—but the pay is good because you can pad the expenses."

Gloag cocked an eyebrow at him, and said, "It's a wicked world." Then he winked broadly and asked, "Was that one of your undercover agents you were talking to a minute ago, Fritzie—out there on the sidewalk?"

"You saw her, huh?" The investigator smiled, showing his blunt yellow teeth. "Nah, she's a client. Her husband disappeared on her. Just a simple locate, but the woman is financially secure—got money up the kazoo. So maybe it will develop into a windfall for me. Classy broad, ain't she? You ought to see her with her coat off. Got a pair that would beat a full house. He must be soft as a one-minute egg, the husband, if he's cheating on that Kewpie doll."

"Why don't you cheat on the husband?"

"Wish I could, Stan."

The coffee arrived, steaming hot. Each man scooped sugar into his stoneware cup. Pomerantz blew on his and began drinking it in small, cautious sips, glancing at Gloag from time to time.

It wasn't exactly true that he and Stanley were friends. They had grown up together—gone to the same schools in North Cambridge, hung out with the same gang of roughnecks on the street, even worked together as busboys one summer at the Hotel Commander—but they'd never really been tight. Gloag was too weird to be anybody's friend. You always had to handle the guy with care, like a jar of nitroglycerin.

Remembering the fight Stanley had with Lenny Klinger years ago on Russell Field, Pomerantz repressed a shudder. Neither of them was more than eight or nine, but it was one of the worst battles he'd ever witnessed. Gloag almost tore the other kid's ear off. Then he bit him on the throat so bad the blood started spouting like a fountain. If a neighbor hadn't rushed poor Lenny to Mount Auburn in a cab, he probably would've cashed in his marbles and baseball cards. Going for the jugular wasn't just a figure of speech with Stanley Gloag. The guy was a vicious animal. The rules went out the window when he fought. He'd use his feet, knees, elbows, thumbs, head, hit you with everything in his arsenal. And he could be crafty, too. You wouldn't even know Stanley was sore about something until he snuck up behind you and gave your kidneys a crippling thump with his fist or the thick end of a pool cue. After he came out of the Lyman State School, he was worse than ever. No wonder the Mob hired him to collect their debts.

"Hey, Stan—you're not working for Alfie Jay, are you?" he asked, suddenly uneasy.

"Not at the moment," Gloag replied, shifting his hooded eyes from the restaurant's fogged windows to Pomerantz's face. "I hear you owe him a pile of money, Fritz. That a fact?"

"Yeah. Word sure travels fast in this town," the investigator acknowledged. "But I got no cause to worry about Alfie. I pay that vig every week, right on time. He should be ecstatic with happiness. Trouble is, he's a very moody individual."

"You don't gamble, don't have vices. How'd you manage to get into a tight bind like that?"

Pomerantz straightened his cup on its saucer. "A person I trusted roped me into a deal involving a truckload of video cassettes—the best stuff. They had *Raiders of the Lost Ark, Rambo, Return of the Jedi, Back to the Future*—everything. I laid out twelve thousand bucks—most of it borrowed from Alfie. I figured I could turn those cassettes over quick and be able to pay him off in four or five days. But it didn't work that way. The load was stored in a little warehouse in Charlestown near the Navy Yard. I sold forty of the boxes for about two grand, but before I could move the rest, the fucking warehouse burnt down. Did I get stiffed? I don't know. What do you think, Stan?"

A skeptical smile contorted Gloag's narrow lips. "Could've been an accident if it was anyplace else," he answered.

"But nothing bad ever happens by accident in Charlestown—judging from my past experiences over there."

"Yeah, know what you mean. Anyhow, that's the story of my financial obligation to Alfie Jay and why I got to bust my ass to meet those payments so I don't have an accident myself."

"With this rich client now, maybe you'll be able to wipe out the debt completely. Who is she, Fritz? How'd she make all her money?"

"A Jewish girl, Stanley. Comes from Brookline. Owns a lot of property," Pomerantz said confidentially.

"And her husband's run out on her?"

"Or something. He's a compulsive gambler. He's probably down Atlantic City. You want anything to eat, Stan? Sandwich? A salad?"

Recognizing that Pomerantz was changing the subject to avoid discussing his business affairs, Gloag replied, "No, thanks. I've got to get going." He finished his coffee, adjusted the peak of his cap, and slid out of the booth. "Nice seeing you again, Fritzie."

"Leaving so soon? Hey, where are you staying these days?"

"With my grandmother—in the old house there on Rindge Ave. Phone number's in the book, if you ever want me. Take it easy, pal."

"You, too," said Frederick Pomerantz as Gloag walked off towards the front door.

14

Clenching the phone between her ear and her shoulder, Melissa Delaunay lit a Benson & Hedges 100 and drew on it vehemently. She slipped the lighter in her shirt pocket and expelled a rack of smoke that slowly diffused against the windowpane.

"Where on Tremont?" she asked.

"At the end of Clarendon. She went there after she left the police headquarters," Stanley explained. Some flaw in the electronic transmission gave his speech a sepulchral intonation. "His office is in a brick building across the street from some stores—a spa, a Laundromat."

"And there's a parking lot, too—right?"

"On the corner, yes. Pomerantz." He spelled it for her. "You could get his address from the Yellow Pages."

"That's a coincidence—him having his office across from that parking lot."

"Why?" Gloag asked.

"Can't tell you, Stanley. It's a secret," Missy said provokingly. "But you lost Magda Gilman?"

"Couldn't help it, girlie. She jumped in that Caddie and sped away like a bank robber. Actually it worked out pretty good, though, because it gave me a chance to question Fritz."

"What did he tell you?"

"That she hired him to look for her husband, a gambler, who's gone missing. He also said she's a rich woman from Brookline," Gloag answered reverberantly. "What's all this about, anyway? You never mentioned the lady was rich."

"Did you think she got that Cadillac with Ronzoni coupons, dummy? What else did you learn?"

"That's all. I tried to squeeze Pomerantz for more details, but he got cozy and buttoned up on me."

She clicked her tongue in annoyance. "You're not giving me too much for my money, Stanley Gloag."

"Don't complain. At least you know I'm trustworthy. I won't be spilling any beans, Missy—like about you going to see a blackmailer the other night, and how you were carrying an automatic for protection, and now all of a sudden some habitual gambler isn't around anymore and you're hiring me to shadow his wife. Some people might think it peculiar that you didn't employ a regular private detective, the way this Magda did."

"You're too damned smart, Stanley. But I don't want to discuss that part of it. Will you pick her up again tomorrow?"

"Sure. Not that I'm crazy about this sort of work. It's boring—and I'm a man of action. Thought I'd throw a fit waiting for her outside the police station, although I did see a couple of fellows I know... handcuffed to each other."

"It's good discipline for you," Missy said, smiling mischievously as she gazed through the picture window at the

Charles River and MIT beyond it. "So what are you going to do now?"

"Maybe I'll come over and see you, since you're home alone. We can examine this question of discipline, if you feel up to it."

She took the phone from her shoulder, sat on the couch and flicked a spray of ashes into a heart-shaped ashtray. "On my time? You've got a lot of nerve."

"Well, you just complained about not getting much for your money, didn't you?"

"What kind of remark is that, you savage?" she snapped with mock anger. "I hope you don't think I have to hire my lovers."

"Don't get sore. I'm only fooling. In twenty minutes I can be there. What do you say?"

A curl of blond hair had fallen before her face, and she swung it aside with a toss of her head. "I don't know," she retorted, sounding curiously innocent. "If I say yes, what will you do to me when you get here?"

"I'll do whatever I feel like doing. It's no fun if you have to restrain yourself, is it?" His laugh flowed eerily out of the telephone.

"God, you're a loony. I'm not sure I want to, Stanley Gloag. You go too far. The last time I thought I was going to need help. Almost went to a doctor. You don't know when to quit, you maniac."

"If I keep going, it's because I know you want me to," he said reasonably. "See you in twenty minutes, Missy. We'll talk about it then."

The line went dead. For a while, however, she continued to hold it to her ear. Then she placed it back in its cradle and got up from the couch in a single languid movement. She went into the bedroom and dabbed musk on her throat and between her breasts.

15

"Kevin, you're looking much improved," Phil Delaunay, neatly attired in a pencilstriped dark blue suit, declared cheerfully. "That first night—Saturday—I almost sent for the priest, buddy."

"Yeah? I can't hardly remember you being here. Ain't it funny how a fever turns everything into dreams?" Reedy said. His complexion was a mottled melange of pink and pallor. "Mrs. Williams—she told me I had the delirium all that day. But I didn't do any wild raving, Phil, because I couldn't talk. Felt like there was a fucking golf ball stuck in my throat. Yeah, I've been real sick. I ain't well yet, either."

Delaunay's eyebrows formed an inverted V of concern. "This doctor you have—is he competent? I know a throat specialist who's a wiz. All the lads use him at election time, so they don't develop laryngitis or pharyngitis out on the hustings. I'll send him over, Kev."

"Nah, don't bother. Doc Boyd's okay—even if he ain't expensive. Told me this morning that George Washington died of a strep throat. What do you think of that? They didn't have penicillin in those days. So it's a pretty classy disease, Phil," the detective said with a harsh dry laugh that quickly changed into a raucous cough. He wiped his mouth with the back of his hand and resumed speaking, but now the humor was gone from his voice. "I guess you're anxious to know what happened—how I handled that guy."

"Only if you feel up to it."

"Might as well get the thing over with," said Reedy, his fingers moving restlessly on the counterpane. "Well, I didn't have no trouble finding him—and the keys were in the ignition. Had to shove him over onto the other seat. Then I drove it out of the lot and went to my brownstone by the Fens—just like you suggested, Phil. Place is still a mess. Barry O'Keefe gave me a cheap price to renovate it, and for the cheap price he's giving me a cheap job. Son of a bitch only works there when he's got nothing better to do. Hasn't been there since before Christmas."

"Contractors are all the same, Kevin. Big ones, little ones—it doesn't matter." Delaunay dragged his chair closer to the bed, and in a low voice asked, "What did you do with it?"

"Brought it straight into the cellar. Jeez, the guy weighed a ton. But when I looked around for a good spot to hide him, Phil, there wasn't any. You can't just tuck a full-grown man under a loose floorboard." Kevin Reedy closed his eyes, breathed shallowly, and opened them again. "I hauled him up on this bench against the wall and took off his coat, his clothes, his shoes, his watch. Had to make the bastard anonymous, right? Erase his identity—otherwise none of us would ever be able to rest easy. The God's honest truth. Anyhow, there was an old electric jigsaw on the workbench, covered with dust. Belonged probably to the previous owner, the tax delinquent who put up all those faggy corner cupboards in the kitchen and bathrooms. Must've made them himself. The blade on it was rusty. When I pushed the plug in though, the motor started humming . . . started operating fine. So I used it."

"Used it? For what, Kev?"

"To . . . to cut the head and hands off, Phil. How else could I erase his identity?"

"Christ," Delaunay whispered. "Wait a minute." He hopped from his seat, dashed to the door and flung it wide. No one was there. "Thought I heard something." He shut the door quietly, drew an immaculate white handkerchief from his hip pocket and patted his forehead. Returning to the chair, he said nervously, "Better keep your voice down."

The detective watched these antics with listless eyes, while his hands kept wriggling on the counterpane. He coughed, cleared his throat, and continued his narrative. "O'Keefe left some plastic dropcloths in the cellar there. I spread a couple of them over the body and the saw to prevent the blood from spattering. The plastic was clear, so I could see what I was doing pretty much—but maybe it would've been a damned sight easier if I couldn't. Jeez, never thought I'd ever cut a man's head off, Phil—not in my worst nightmares. It ain't like slicing a Thanksgiving turkey, let me tell you. Came close to puking. Almost passed out." Reedy stirred beneath the mounds of blankets. His breath had a rasp to it, like background static on a defective radio. "Somehow I got the job done, though. Then I went upstairs and built a fire in the fireplace, and when it was roaring full blast I tossed the head in. The hands, too. That smell—it's been coming to me in my dreams. After an hour or so, only the teeth and a few bones were left. I was going to burn the clothes, too, but I just didn't have enough time. Well, to douse the fire I threw water on it—and the wet ashes I shoveled into a big washtub. What was left of the guy I wrapped up in a dropcloth, tied the bundle with a hunk of clothesline, and stuck in the Audi's trunk. Put the tub in there, too. The overcoat, the shoes, and the rest of his stuff I flung on the backseat. Then I cleaned the basement as best I could, hosed the bench and the jigsaw down, wiped everything with rags, locked the door and took off."

A fit of scratchy coughing interrupted the sick man, and Delaunay poured him a glass of water from a carafe on the night table. Reedy gulped it greedily.

"I still feel lousy, Phil," he gasped. "Too bad Rita ain't here. She'd have me on my feet in no time. Jeez, I really miss that girl. You don't appreciate people till they're gone."

"Keep your chin up, buddy," Delaunay said, sounding rather rattled himself. "You're going to be okay. All you need is a good rest to recharge the batteries."

As if deaf to these remarks, the detective abruptly plunged into the tale of his harrowing journey to the Cape that night—how he drove so carefully on Route 3 because he was scared to death of having an accident, how he discarded pieces of Gilman's clothing in the woods along the way, how he dumped the ashes in a brook that ran under the road, how he threw the tub in a ravine, and how he finally reached Barnstable and rolled through the country darkness to his beachfront cottage.

"Looks weird down there in the winter. No leaves on the trees. Lot of snow on the ground. All the houses closed up and shuttered," he said in a tone tinged with wonder. "And my place—it was cold as a fucking morgue."

He had dragged the ten-foot aluminum dinghy out of the garage on its trailer, manhandled it off into the water, and hooked the two-horsepower Johnson on its stern. Filling the outboard with gas syphoned from the Audi, he loaded the corpse into the boat, tied some cinderblocks and perforated bricks to the clothesline that bound it, and shoved off into the sea. There was an icy breeze, but it wasn't strong—and the water seemed calm for that time of year. Across Barnstable Harbor he chugged, past Sandy

Neck and out into Cape Cod Bay. No other craft were visible. Nevertheless he kept his lantern extinguished, navigating by the glow of a cloud-veiled sliver of moon and the fuzzy lights strung randomly along the shore.

"I didn't go too far. Only a few miles," Reedy explained in his croupy voice. "After I threw the guy overboard I swung around and started back, but the goddamned motor stalled on me. And it wouldn't restart, either, so I got pissed off, which was a mistake, because then I gave the fucking cord a good hard jerk and fell right out of the boat. That water—Christ! Must've been one degree above freezing, no shit. Thought my heart was going to quit on me, Phil—my nuts wrinkled up to my chin, I was so cold and scared. It was just like when I went into the Charles that time. Suddenly, no warning or nothing, you're staring death in the face." Spasmodically the sick detective clutched a loose fold of the counterpane in his left hand and grinned bleakly. "But I was lucky. The outboard motor didn't kick over. If it had, that dinghy would've gone put-putting off into the dark and I would've drowned."

Here he stopped and rested. Delaunay filled the interval with a monologue of his own, a gushy hymn of praise and commiseration to which the man in the bed paid scant attention.

When it was over, Reedy took up the thread of his grim story as if it had never been broken, vividly describing how he struggled back into the little boat, and how after many failures he managed to get the balky motor going once more. Nor did he spare his listener any details of the hellish return voyage—the slashing of the frigid wind on his wet flesh, his uncontrollable shivering and dread of frostbite, the bone-chilling sea spray, the formation of ice on his clothing and hair. He told of reaching his bungalow on the harbor, of hauling the boat up on the shingle, and of all the problems he had getting the car door open.

"Honest to Christ, Phil, I was shaking like a leaf. Thought I'd die of exposure before I'd be able to crawl inside and turn that fucking heater on."

Worn out by reliving his ordeal, Reedy gave only a sketchy description of its concluding chapters. About his visit to Missy, he said scarcely anything. A dullness crept into his eyes. He looked far more the fragile invalid now than he had earlier.

Patting his square-jawed face again with the handkerchief, Philip Delaunay said emotionally, "You've been nothing less than heroic, Kevin—made a superhuman effort for me and my sister. Believe you me, I won't forget it. Jesus, Mary, and Joseph, what a horrendous experience! But in spite of every difficulty you got the job done. Buddy, you've salvaged my career . . . pulled me back from the brink of a political debacle." He shook his head as if amazed and stuffed the handkerchief in his pocket. "And the automobile—you left it on the street in the South End?"

"Yeah, with the door unlocked and the keys in the ignition," said Reedy tiredly. "By this time some nigger has run it off to a chop shop to be dismantled."

"You didn't find any photographs in it, did you?"

"Nah. There was a briefcase on the backseat, but it was empty. I got rid of it with the clothes because I thought Missy might've touched it."

"And the little derringer that caused all the trouble?"

"I smashed that with a hammer in the cellar. Broke it to smithereens and scattered the pieces here and there alongside of Route 3."

"Beautiful, Kevin. You're the soul of efficiency," the handsome politician exclaimed. "Just one more thing now—this business of the radio being stolen out of the Audi. Will that be a complication?"

"I doubt it," Reedy answered. "Nothing's happened yet, Phil, so chances are nothing's going to happen. The thief probably didn't actually see either of us. And a hump like that—he ain't likely to go to the cops."

"Of course. I agree." Delaunay stood up and ran a hand over his reddish-brown hair. "Well, I've got to be on my way. I think I heard Ruffing beep the horn a minute ago. When you're feeling better, we'll talk some more." His too-perfect face radiated benevolence and gratitude. "Is there anything you need, Kev?"

The invalid appeared not to hear the question. His eyes had narrowed to slits, and the fingernails of his busy hands were audibly scratching the chenille counterpane.

"What's the matter?" his friend asked, frowning. "You okay?"

"Phil, listen. There's a part of the story I didn't mention to you. I . . . I wasn't going to, but I guess I better," Reedy whispered.

"Oh?"

"This Gilman . . . the lawyer—when I covered him with the plastic and shoved his head up against the blade of the saw, he . . . he all of a sudden . . . came back to life."

"What? Came back to life? What are you saying, Kevin?"

"I'm saying he wasn't dead. I'm saying the son of a bitch was still living."

"But . . . but if he was still living, why the hell didn't you stop?"

Reedy's eyes slid around between their narrowed lids and slowly focused on Delaunay's face. "How the fuck could I, Phil? Jigsaw was in his neck, for chrissake. Guy was bleeding like a butchered pig. Tell me—what do you think I *should've* done? Taken him back to the parking lot? Called a doctor? Brought him to the fucking Mass General? Dumped him in the Fens? What, Phil? I ain't no mastermind, and I had to decide quick. He was making these noises. . . . I didn't want to torture the poor slob, so . . . Besides, he probably would've croaked anyway—right? Ain't that right, Phil? Had two slugs in his chest. So . . . so I . . . I kept on sawing. He struggled . . . not much, though."

"Merciful Mother of God . . ."

"I wasn't going to say anything about it, figured it might be easier for you if you didn't know. But it's sort of . . . bugging me, and I just can't keep it to myself no more."

"Sure . . . sure. Of course. That's understandable, Kev. Christ!"

"The guy was a louse—a blackmailer."

"Right . . . absolutely."

"And there wasn't any other way of handling it, Phil."

"I agree. I understand. But that means . . ."

The unfinished sentence hung in the air like a malediction. To hide his confusion, the politician shook his head and scowled.

"Yeah," said Reedy, his voice so weak that the word

might have been a sigh. "It means your sister didn't murder Gilman. I did."

An awkward silence followed this flat statement, then in a rush Delaunay exclaimed, "Makes no difference whatsoever. You did it for us, Kevin. You saved us from a calamity. For chrissake, we're all in this together."

An automobile horn honked impatiently out in the street.

"People should be loyal," the detective said as he went back to scratching the bedspread. "A guy who ain't loyal to his friends ain't nothing—right? I only did what I had to do."

Delaunay bent down, patted him on the shoulder and murmured a few more comforting words. A moment later he was gone from the room.

Hearing the car drive away, Reedy groaned and turned heavily on his side. One of his black oxfords protruded from beneath the bed, and he fell to staring at its tip like a man in a hypnotic state. They were hand-crafted calfskin, expensive shoes, the kind he's always liked ever since that day his Aunt Molly had taken him in the taxi to Jordan's and bought him those new loafers so he would look decent when he started out at St. Columbkille's.

Decent was a word she often used, he remembered. What would the poor woman think of him now, if she were still alive? *Do the right thing, Kevin.* He'd heard that a lot from her, too. But sometimes the right thing changed while you were doing it—went from being right to being wrong. And sometimes no matter what you did, no matter how hard you tried, you wound up acting like a no-good bastard.

One day soon he'd have to go to confession and tell the story to a priest. "Jeez," Reedy whispered, rolling onto his back again.

Through half-shut eyes he spied Rita's blue nightgown hanging like a ghost of the girl herself on the closet door. If only she were here, he thought.

16

As he had been doing every morning, Frankie Gates phoned Magda at the Allerton Arms to tell her there were no new developments. Harold Gilman hadn't been found wandering the streets in a daze or lying comatose in a local hospital, and while seven additional dead bodies had arrived at the two city mortuaries during the previous twenty-four hours, none of them answered her missing husband's description. Reacting as usual with a little relief and a lot of irritability, she brought a smile to Frankie's rough countenance by referring to the Boston Police as a pack of Irish schlemiels.

The conversation ended on a cordial note, nonetheless, and he was in a happy frame of mind when he left Station D to begin his day's work.

A short drive took him to an automobile accessories wholesaler on Columbus Avenue, where he interviewed the owner and his warehouse manager about a $3000 shipment of spark plugs that had been left on a loading platform "for only a couple of minutes" and somehow mysteriously disappeared. It was a familiar story. Past experience convinced Gates that the manager or one of his men had deliberately turned his back on the merchandise so that a confederate could cart it off. Everybody gambled these days, but not all of them could pay their markers. When the bookie or the loan shark leaned on them, they soon agreed to steal their boss's property to square what they owed. Spark plugs were perfect for such a hustle, relatively expensive for their size and weight, and easy to sell.

Solving that kind of crime was almost impossible, though, unless you dropped everything else to work on it. Since the owner was only interested in collecting the insurance, there wasn't much sense in making an all-out effort. Yet Gates dutifully wrote up a report and solemnly promised to investigate the matter.

After a cup of coffee at Bailey's, he went to the ground-floor apartment of a tidy two-family house on Belvidere Street and listened to the maundering complaint of an elderly man, a Boston Edison retiree, whose television had been snatched from a table near a window the night before. The victim, despite his seventy-four years, had rushed out to the sidewalk and copied down the license number of a Ford Granada he saw fleeing the scene a moment after the theft.

Gates left the old man and called the Registry, where he learned that the car belonged to Osvaldo Peña. He was not surprised. He had picked Peña up for petty larceny twice before. On to Symphony Road he drove.

The rooming-house vestibule appeared cleaner than it had on his last visit, but it was still pretty grubby. He started climbing stairs. Through the dimpled windows of the landings a milky daylight filtered, quickly absorbed by the indigenous gloom.

Somewhere above him a door opened. Coming to a halt, Gates heard a few stealthy footsteps and peered up the shadow-filled stairwell. A childlike face surmounted by curly black hair protruded out over the topmost banister, but only for an instant. Then it was gone.

Saw me from a window, the detective thought, and continued his ascent.

Attaining the top floor at last, he rapped the door vigorously with his knuckles and, though short of breath, yelled in a voice of brass, "Open up, Ossie. I know you're in there."

Thirty seconds of silence ensued.

"Hey, stupid! You think I didn't see you?" Gates hollered, rattling the knob. "If you piss me off, *cholo,* I'll kick the fucking door in—*entiende?*"

Even as he spoke, however, he wondered if his quarry hadn't fled to the roof. The thought angered him. But then the lock clicked and slowly the door began to open. In the widening gap there stood an exceptionally small young man with a swart complexion and the large brown eyes of a faun. He wore a white terry-cloth bathrobe and pointy patent-leather bedroom slippers. Around his thin neck a radio headset was looped like a sloppily made bow tie. From it a wire trailed down into a pocket of the robe.

"What do you want with me now? I ain't done nothing."

Frankie Gates shouldered him aside and strode into the room beyond, which was as long and narrow as a bowling alley. It had probably once been somebody's hallway. A few sticks of secondhand furniture were aligned against one wall, while piles of magazines, phonograph records, cassette decks, and paperback books formed a ragged revetment against the other.

"Ought to open a window once in a while, Ossie." He grimaced. "Place stinks of *grifa*."

"It's cold outside, and they don't give you no heat here," the youth replied, closing the door. "Lady downstairs died of hypothermia."

"That's a shame. Hey, where did you get the fifteen-inch Sony?" Gates jerked his long thumb at a TV on a table next to the rumpled iron bed. "I'll bet you bought it at a yard sale."

"Yeah, I did. In Newton, out near B.C. You like it? Forty-five dollars I paid."

"Shit me easy, *panita*. That's a KV1515."

"So what?"

"So I've caught you dirty again," said the detective. "You glommed that set from a man named Thomas Lyons, from his house on Belvidere Street."

"*Hombre!* You crazy or something? Sony—they make millions of KV1515's," Peña squawked, his slight body rigid with indignation. "And who said you could come busting into my private room, anyhow? I didn't invite you. Ain't I got U.S. Constitution rights same as other people?"

"Sure, but the U.S. Constitution doesn't guarantee the right to commit burglary," Gates responded, plopping himself down in a heavily-painted wicker chair and stretching his legs out before him. "Get your clothes on, Ossie. We're going bye-bye. Better bring a toothbrush."

"*Coño!* You can't arrest me for *nothing*. Is this Nazi Germany? Is this Russia? I didn't commit no burglary."

"Osvaldo, I'm not arresting you for *nothing*. I'm arresting you for larceny. That Sony is highly probative evidence. Last night Mr. Lyons walked into his front room to get a pair of eyeglasses, and he happened to notice that his TV was floating out the window. Naturally, this aroused his curiosity—"

"A nut case, obviously. Must've been hallucinating."

"—so he ran to the street and saw his television being loaded into a Ford Granada, so he copied down the license number. And guess what? The Registry of Motor Vehicles tells me it's identical with yours."

"How could he see the license number if he wasn't wearing his glasses?" Peña asked, angrily jerking the cord of his bathrobe. "Besides, yesterday I was home all night—right here—and my car was parked on Mass Ave. Any of the neighborhood junkies could've popped the ignition and used it to go out stealing. Those *moyetos* . . ."

"Yeah, except that Mr. Lyons described the perpetrator—and how many ninety-five-pound sneak thieves with curly black hair can there be in this part of Boston?" Frankie Gates pulled a notebook from inside his jacket. "Do you spell Osvaldo with an *s* or a *z*?"

"I need a lawyer."

"To help you spell your name? Stop worrying. The Commonwealth will be happy to furnish you with legal aid. An *s* or a *z*?"

"An *s* . . . an *s*," Peña answered, suddenly looking miserable. He removed the radio from the pocket of his bathrobe, unhooked the earphones from his neck, and laid both on the foot of the cot. "You think I'll get sent down this time?"

"Probably. It's your third offense, isn't it? And you're still on probation for clouting that snowblower in Dorchester. After a while the law gets impatient."

"They stick me in the *penitenciaria* and I'll go loco. I'll die. I got to have sound in my ears. Without my music, ain't no way I can go on living. They take my Walkman and I'll hang myself."

"*No problema, chico.* These days everybody in the can has a radio. Place is like a country club. Bet you make a lot of new friends. Put your pants on, Ossie."

"In the newspapers I read where hanging yourself is easier than people think," Peña continued, his dark eyes now moist. "Happens real fast, they said. I believe it, too. You ever think of hanging yourself?"

"Not recently."

"I mean, how bad can it be? You dangle a couple of minutes, then you pass out. Ain't messy like cutting your throat or diving off a high-rise or plunking a bullet in your head. To tell you the truth, the idea of hanging doesn't even scare me hardly. But that's the worst part, because it's so *frightening* that it don't scare me. If I ain't afraid, I'll go and do it—right?"

"Seems logical," Gates agreed. "In the meantime, though, put your clothes on, will you? I'm getting high from the fumes in here. You'll have plenty of leisure for planning your future after the turnkey slams the gate."

The youth took a pair of blue jeans from a hook on the wall and began wriggling into them. He stopped abruptly, however, and his childish face brightened. "Holy shit! Why didn't I think of this before? Me and you, amigo—we can do a deal."

"A deal?" The detective laughed. "What the fuck have you got to deal *with,* Osvaldo?"

"Something big, that's what. Something *sensational.* I seen a murder."

"Yeah?"

"Don't laugh. It's true. I swear on the head of my mother. Happened in the parking lot, back of where I work... last Friday night."

Gates lifted an eyebrow. "What were you smoking?"

"Be serious. You could get a promotion. Listen, with my own two eyes I saw this chick shoot this older guy with a little mini-automatic. Bang, bang—twice in the chest." Peña zippered his fly loudly to emphasize the point. "Then she jumps out of the Audi and struts off down Tremont Street like nothing happened. *Hombre!* It was like a program on television."

"*What* kind of automobile?" Frankie Gates asked, no longer smiling.

"An Audi. They pulled in behind the Laundromat I work in—the Suds for Duds. Don't you remember? You collared me there the last time... about the snowblower." Having slipped out of his terry-cloth robe, Ossie stood naked to the waist. His skinny chest was matted with coils of glossy black hair. "Friday 'round midnight, right after I locked the front door."

"What color was it?"

"The Audi? Green—but dark green," Peña said, and went on to unfold the whole story of what he had witnessed from the time the car came to a stop in the parking area to the arrival of the husky man in the narrow-brimmed fedora, only deleting the circumstances surrounding the theft of the Blaupunkt radio.

"Why didn't you phone the police?"

"Me? Hey, come *on*! I don't have nothing to do with you guys voluntarily. Besides, if I told the cops *then,* I wouldn't have no secrets to trade *now*—would I?" the undersized youth replied plausibly.

"Okay, but where's the cadaver? A person gets killed, there's always a corpse. What happened to it?" Frankie Gates asked, thoughtfully studying him with gray eyes that were like chips of granite. "The only stiffs that turned up in the South End last weekend were a hooker with a needle in her arm, and some old skel who got himself brained with a wine bottle outside the Missionary Baptist Church on Dudley Street."

From the top of the turquoise painted chest of drawers, Peña grabbed a wrinkled velour shirt. "*No sé,* amigo. Like I told you—I didn't hang around to see what the husky guy did with the body. *Sarito!* I was too scared," he said, as he slipped the shirt on and began to button the buttons. "Must've been a friend of the lady's—got rid of the evidence for her. I ain't seen nothing in the papers about it yet, so I guess he done a good job. Maybe they're Colombian drug wholesalers...or mafiosos. Lots of real tough dudes in this section of town."

Pretending disbelief, the detective assailed him with a stream of questions. Was the woman tall? Was she fat or skinny? How old? What color hair? How was she dressed? Was she pretty? And what did the victim look like? What was his age? Was he heavy? What was he wearing? Could you tell if he was tall or short? These papers he gave her to read—were they letters or what? And the husky guy—what kind of car was he driving? Did you get the license number? How was he dressed? Did he wear glasses? Have a moustache? Were all these people white Caucasians?

By the end of this rapid-fire interrogation Gates had learned that the woman had been fairly tall and around twenty-five years of age. Peña couldn't tell him anything about her build, however, because she was wearing a loose coat. Nor could he give a description of her face and hair, as they were covered up by the brown beret and the raised coat collar. He knew more about the two men, and rattled off all these details—the wavy hair of the victim, his camel's hair coat and suntanned face, the husky man's down jacket, the big Oldsmobile—just as if he'd watched the whole drama only an hour earlier. But he hadn't noticed the license number—couldn't even say what state it was—nor did he remember anything of particular interest about the papers the woman stuffed in her handbag. None of the three people had been black, and none had been Hispanic, either, as far as Ossie could tell.

"Sounds like a crock of shit to me," said Gates. "And even if it was true, Osvaldo, it's not worth a thing because you can't produce a corpse."

"What do you mean? Of course it's worth something," Peña whined in alarm. "*Por Dios!* A human being gets zapped, and the cops ain't interested? The body's got to be someplace. The man's got to be missing. Put out a bulletin or whatever."

"Who else did you tell this story to?"

"Nobody—and maybe I shouldn't have told it to you. I thought we had a deal. Now you're acting like you're still going to bust me. What kind of business is this?"

"I never made you any promises, *cholo.*"

"*No me diga eso.* Didn't you ask me all those *questions*? And didn't I give you all those *answers*?" A tear rolled down the thief's brown cheek, but he swiftly wiped it away with the tail of his shirt. "You tricked me—and that ain't *fair.*"

Entirely unmoved by these demonstrations of despair, Gates feigned sympathy and said, "Hey, kid, don't go to pieces. Maybe you are on the level. I'll check around and if I find any solid substantiation of what you've given me, we'll talk about it again."

"You're not going to take me in?"

"Not right now—but I can't swear—"

"That's okay. You check and you'll find I told the truth." Peña beamed at him through glistening eyes. He kicked off his patent-leather slippers. "You're going to solve the case and get a big promotion. Wait and see."

"First I've got to bring the TV back to that old man and talk him into dropping the complaint."

"*Claro,* amigo. Take it. The set don't work too hot,

anyway. Got a double image. Don't know how the guy can stand to watch it. Of course, I ain't confessing I robbed it—but you can have the crummy thing."

"Thanks," Gates said dryly. "One other small detail, Ossie. I don't want you repeating this story to anybody. Keep your yap shut, *chico,* or you'll land deep in a world of shit. *Entiende?* I can't catch a promo to Second-Grade if some Homicide hotshot crowds me out."

"Don't you worry. I won't spill nothing to *nobody*—on the head of my mother," Peña swore devoutly as he wiggled his tiny foot into a wing-tipped loafer that had a two-inch stacked heel.

The detective had no doubt that Gilman was the wavy-haired, suntanned victim in the camel's hair overcoat. Green Audis weren't common, and didn't they later find the car parked on Tremont Street? Harold had got himself killed, all right, but Frankie couldn't really grieve for him. With the husband gone, the wife was finally free. That, to Gates, represented a definite improvement.

Who the hell shot the guy, though? Magda? Frankie, having gone off to a Bruins game, hadn't seen her that Friday night. The woman stayed home alone. She had no alibi. And since most homicides are committed by relatives, family members were always prime suspects in any murder investigation.

They're bound to hassle her, he thought uneasily.

Marrying Harold had been a great mistake, Magda acknowledged. She admitted, too, that divorcing him would cost her millions. Such damaging information could be dug up by a reasonably competent cop, as could the fact that the lady had a lover. Dynamite stuff. If the investigator also got hold of Ossie Peña, it would give him enough for a grand jury—and the grand jury would probably bring in an indictment.

It was strange how the pieces fit together so neatly. Magda even owned a polo coat exactly like the one Peña described on the murderess—beige, long, big patch pockets, high collar—and with this coat she often wore a brown beret. Only a coincidence? Too bad the kid hadn't gotten a good look at the woman's face. That might've solved the mystery, settled the thing once and for all.

If it actually had been Magda, though, why would the two of them meet in a South End parking lot when they lived right next door to each other? A smart prosecutor would say she lured him there, of course, and argue that she planned the crime in advance. Yet Peña believed the woman suddenly got sore—drew the gun and plugged Harold on impulse—which flatly contradicted any premeditation theory.

What were the papers she was looking at, and why did they make her angry? Did the lawyer try to work some kind of swindle on his wife? Or was he outlining the financial settlement he wanted in exchange for an uncontested quicky divorce? And who was the husky character who arrived later to dispose of the body? A friend? Employee? Lover? The questions were many, the answers few.

All the same, Frankie couldn't quite see Magda as a killer. She was too cool, too smart, too civilized. People like her used their brains, not their hands. Besides, unless he misread the lady completely, she was genuinely concerned about her lost husband. Hadn't she been nagging everybody to find the guy? A guilty party wouldn't do that.

Unfortunately, the Homicide Squad didn't know Magda as well as he did. All they'd consider were the circumstances, the general pattern of the case. Detectives might be shrewd, but they weren't infallible—and the truth of that could be vouched for by more than one innocent citizen in the joint.

Frankie Gates, having recently begun to suspect that he loved Magda Gilman, wasn't about to toss her to a pack of bloodhounds. Therefore he decided to keep what he knew to himself until the whole situation became a lot clearer.

"Been using the radio," Mr. Lyons said, "but it's not the same thing at all. Puts me to sleep in ten minutes."

He was so pleased to get his television back that he scarcely listened to the detective's mendacious explanation.

Gates set it down, then suddenly remembered the Audi's missing radio. That little *cholo* was the one who snitched it, he thought, surprised that this simple deduction hadn't occurred to him before.

After he hooked up the TV for the old man, Frankie

refused a can of beer and left. From Belvidere Street he drove directly to the parking lot behind the Laundromat to survey the scene of the crime.

17

Fluttering her eyelids, which were coated with silver glitter dust, Rubyjewel wound the long end of the purple feathered boa twice around her otherwise bare neck. The concavity of her navel and the corrugation of her ribs were both clearly visible through the thin fabric of the tight black frock she wore. She picked up the pony of anisette, dipped her tongue into it, took a few unhurried sips, and said, "Why should I remember automobiles, daddy? I ain't no meter maid, you know."

"The car belongs to a guy who disappeared," Frederick Pomerantz explained patiently in his gritty voice. "His wife has employed me to locate her husband's whereabouts."

"She did? What the hell for? He come dragging hisself home soon enough, when he wore out and hungry. And if he don't, so what? Ain't no shortage of men in the world. Why, you keep running into them everyplace you go—like cockroaches."

"This vehicle was abandoned on Tremont Street near the project, and since you spend a lot of time in that vicinity, Ruby, I surmised you might've noticed who parked it there. Allegedly he vanished on Friday night. Here's the guy's picture. Does he look familiar?"

The girl inspected Harold Gilman's photograph for three or four seconds, then shook her head and said, "Not to me he don't. I ain't outside too much now, anyway. It's freezing cold, daddy. I hang in the hotel, or around one of the clubs down the Zone. Scipio, he thinks I'm dogging it when I do that, but he don't understand. If I can't keep the thing warm, ain't nobody going to want to *buy* it. Tricks don't favor putting their frankfurters in a freezer. What they all hankering for is a microwave oven, dig?" She nudged him in the side with a pointy elbow and laughed lasciviously. "So that's why I probably never saw this here gentleman who's gone. And he must be *real* gone, if his woman is shelling out money to a private detective to get him home again."

"You're positive you don't know him?" Pomerantz said, not entirely convinced.

"Well, I can't swear I *never* met him. A girl like me has a real large acquaintance," Rubyjewel declared, twinkles of light reflecting off her painted eyelids. "If you was to calculate according to the law of averages, chances are I did something to the dude sometime or another, but I can't recollect his face right this moment. Maybe you better ask Scipio Africanus. Ain't much happening on the street that my honey man misses."

The investigator shook his head, disappointed. "Scipio Africanus," he repeated, and ran a forefinger over his dyed walrus moustache. "Where the hell did he ever get a name like that, Ruby?"

"You mean he never told you that story?" she said. "I must've heard it a hundred times, 'cause he's *real* proud of it. Seems like he got this cool name from his great-granddaddy who worked down Carolina chopping cotton in the scorching sun eighteen hours a day for a hunk of cornbread and a bowl of cow pea soup, whatever the hell *that* is. Back a hundred years ago, I'm talkin' about, back when you whiteys could ball us black chicks for nothing on account of you owned our asses. 'Course you can have the same thing now, baby, but you got to pay."

The girl twirled the end of her boa, and gave him another dig in the ribs.

"Where did his grandfather get the name, though?" Pomerantz asked, leaning an elbow on the bar. "Scipio Africanus sounds like something out of a prayer book."

"Near as I can remember, my honey found out about all that when he was down Lorton Prison," said Rubyjewel. "When they give him the five years for panhandling."

"How could he get five years for panhandling? It's only a misdemeanor."

"Well, yes and no. Depends on how you do it. Now my Scipio, he discovered one day that if he have a razor sticking out of his coat pocket, the people he asked for money was a lot more generous. Then he find that if he *hold* the razor, they start handing over dollar bills 'stead of dimes and quarters. And when he actually open the razor up, folks give him all the money they had on them, even offer to run home and get some more. Honey was scoring real good till he hit on a police decoy."

Pomerantz chortled, and reached for his beer.

"And it was while he was doing them five years," the lean black girl said, "that he meet this professor who tell him all about the first original Scipio Africanus, who was a big-shot general that lived long, long ago, way back before Jesus. He got hisself a famous reputation, the first Scipio, by whomping and stomping another boss general in a humongus army battle involving thousands and thousands of soldier boys wearing them old fashioned tin hats and cast-iron tank tops. So that there is where the name come from at the very beginning. My honey man—he a real *historical* character." Flickering her gaudy eyelids, Rubyjewel raised the pony of anisette and emptied it down her throat. Then, entwining the feathery scarf around a caramel-hued arm, she cooed, "Why don't we go upstairs to my place, baby, and I'll fix you something to eat."

At that instant she saw a tall black man in a brindle fur coat approaching them from the barroom's entrance, and changed her conversational chat to a shrill squeal of surprise.

"Woman, how come you ain't out there on the street?" the newcomer demanded of her in an irate baritone. "You taking a furlough?"

"No, sugar—I was just now going. What are you doing up so early for, honey? It's only two o'clock. You going to ruin your health if you don't—"

"You trying to jive me, Ruby? Don't hand me that shit. It's a quarter to three. How much you been drinking?"

"Drinking? Nothing. One little old thimble of anisette, Scipio—just to sweeten up my breath," she replied, batting her tinseled eyelids.

"Where's Lucinda at? She still in her room copping zees?" the tall man said irritably.

"Lucy ain't sleeping. She up there shaving her pits and frying her hair. You want her looking pretty, don't you, honey?"

"Yeah? Well you go and tell her to stop frying her hair, because if she ain't down Washington Street in five minutes, I'm going to fry her nigger ass with that iron. And that goes for you, too, 'cause I'm tired of this old shit."

"Okay, papa. I'll do anything you say. But how about a little sugar before I go?" Rubyjewel declared, lifting her dusky face to him and puckering her lips.

Scipio Africanus ignored this offering, however, though he almost smiled as he pushed her towards the door and said, "Get on out of here, woman."

Giggling, she grabbed her white vinyl coat from the back of a chair and strutted off, the purple boa trailing behind her like a semaphor flag from the stern of a warship.

18

"You got questions, Fritz, ask me, not her," Scipio said dourly.

He unbuttoned the fur coat and signaled the bartender with a wave of his knobby-knuckled hand. The thick gold herringbone chain bracelet on his wrist chinked and sparkled.

"It's just a run-of-the-mill marital case," said Pomerantz. "A lady from Brookline. Her husband went missing last Friday night, and the cops recovered his automobile down the street in front of the project. So I theorized Ruby might've remembered seeing him, but she didn't."

"'Course she didn't. That's six whole days ago, and Rubyjewel don't remember most things for more than a hour. That girl hates remembering. She mainly likes to forget. And if you done the kind of things Ruby does, you probably feel the same way." The pimp laughed sardonically. "What color automobile you talking about?"

"Jade green—a four-door Audi with mahogany brown leather upholstery, license number—"

"GK947 833," Scipio finished for him, as the bartender arrived bearing a bottle of Chivas Regal.

Pomerantz smoothed his moustache with a thumb. "You noticed it, huh? I should've figured you'd spot a luxury set of wheels like that. Here's the subject's picture, Scipio. Do you recognize him?"

"Never saw him in my life," the pimp said, glancing briefly at the photo. "He look rich. Must be, if he own a Audi and live there in Brookline. What's the cat's name?"

"Can't reveal his identity. It's confidential." Pomerantz tossed a ten-dollar bill on the bar to pay for the scotch. "How come you memorized the license number?"

"How come you expect me to answer your questions, pops, when you ain't even polite enough to answer mine?" came the tart reply.

"The nature of my business is I got to be discreet. I'm sorry, but that's how it is. If you got any solid information, I can probably pay you for it."

"How much? Twenty dollars? Shit, I won't even rap with you about the weather for that." Africanus leaned lightly on the cavetto edge of the bar with his furry coat sleeve barely an inch from a puddle of spilled beer. After a moment he added, "'Cording to my calculations the stuff I know ought to be worth some real heavy bread. Been thinking on it all week. Twenty thousand—that'd be a nice round figure to open up with."

"Twenty K? What are you talking about?" the investigator asked, astounded. "The missing person isn't Patty Hearst. He's just a lousy criminal lawyer with hardly no practice to speak of."

"Yeah? Must've bought the Audi with food stamps, huh? Fritz, maybe I got colored balls, but that don't mean I fell off no Christmas tree." Scipio picked up his scotch and drank it in a single gulp. Putting the glass down on the wet bar, he regarded himself with approval in the tarnished mirror that lined the wall behind the shelves of bottled liquor. "You ain't being too smart, 'cause I could cut you into this proposition. You could have yourself half of that twenty K, man."

Staring at the pimp's smug profile, Pomerantz said cautiously, "I ain't averse to acquiring ten thousand dollars, but it would have to be something that's not too hairy."

"Them's my feelings, too, pops. Believe it. Safety first. This ain't no trick bag. It's so undangerous, it's almost legit."

"I could lose my license, which would jeopardize my whole livelihood."

"Nothing like that going to happen here, Fritz. What we got is a dream scheme, a foolproof hustle that could make us dirty rich. Ten grand is only the beginning, man. With your confidential information and my confidential information, us two would have the entire play all to ourselfs—dig? And I need a partner—a white guy who can talk good, handle the negotiating, maybe write a educated letter." Africanus watched his companion's moustached face in the mirror. "So what's the missing dude's name?"

"He ain't been kidnapped, has he?"

"You answer my question, I'll answer yours."

Pomerantz weighed this rejoinder for the space of half a minute, then said, "Okay. His name is Harold Gilman."

"I don't know him—but that don't matter none."

"Has he been abducted?"

"Has he been what?"

"Kidnapped . . . snatched."

Turning away from his image in the mirror, Scipio bestowed a look of mild derision on the investigator. "No, he ain't been snatched, pops. Who want to do a thing like that to a man what ain't got no money?"

"Very funny—but let's dispense with the bullshit, huh? You going to volunteer some information or ain't you?"

"You going to be my partner, Fritz?"

"I already divulged my client's identity, didn't I?" said Pomerantz, his moustache quivering. "You want me to call my lawyer? Get him to draw up a contract?"

"I don't think so, baby. Nothing in writing." The pimp smiled at him condescendingly. "Okay, partner, let me explain you what happened Friday, now that we in business. 'Round midnight I leave the room, 'cause I'm supposed to meet a brother in Roxbury. It were real cold out. So I cut across the street heading for my Eldo, and I glim this nice shiny car parked on the corner with its tailpipe puff-puffing. And inside it is a young fox all by herself—blond, and not bad. Naturally, I stop and—"

"She was sitting in the Audi, Scipio?"

"Nah, nah. You going to have to be patient, man. This gasser were a Mustang—banana yellow. So I stop and say hello to the lady, only she point her pretty little honky nose in the air and ignore my conversation. She act like something bugging her, like she all tore up over something. And while I'm jiving the woman, a Oldsmobile suddenly pull in on us, and out hops this dude wearing one of those funky lumpy jackets full of chicken feathers. And right off he starts talking tough. Well, I ain't about to take no shit from him, so I tell him real polite to shag ass before he get his fat head busted on the curbstone. Trouble is I misread the guy. He just grins and unzips his tacky jacket, and that's when I notice a short .38 hanging off his hip, and snap to the fact that he's the Man, and not some lame from Newtonville."

"A plainclothesman?"

"Or a D.T. Normal folks don't walk around all holstered up like that, do they?"

"And they were white people?"

"White as you are, Fritz. Whiter, even. Three hundred and sixty degree white—a couple of bed sheets, fresh out of the laundry. Anyhow, ain't no profit in arguing over a frail eel on a cold night with some guy who's carrying a loudspeaker, so I tip my cap and do a fade. But soon as I'm round the corner, I hear the blonde start in yelping. 'I never meant to shoot this blackmailer. Now he's dead. What am I going to do, Kevin?' she say."

Pomerantz made a soft percussive noise with his tongue, but remained otherwise silent.

"Well, the cop—he get pissed off and tell her to hush up her big mouth, 'cause he realize I ain't far away. Then he climb on into the Mustang with her, so I can't hear their talk no more. Long about now my ass is cold as ice, and I'm doing a little boogie there on the bricks to keep my feet alive, but I don't quit and leave 'cause I real anxious to find out who got hisself bumped by this pretty creature. After what seem like a hundred years the door open up again and the cop come out, and a minute later they both gun their engines and go scooting off—him one way, her another. So I cut on down a few steps to where my Eldo at, jump in and follow the Olds, figuring the police is going straight to the scene of the crime—dig?"

"Yeah," said Pomerantz, now on the edge of his bar stool.

"Solid. Well, he only travel a couple of blocks on Tremont 'fore he swing into a parking lot—the one 'cross from the Grotto. I'm careful about keeping my distance, naturally, so I stop by the corner. And I watch the Olds pull up at the back of the lot, the headlights switch off, and the cop crawl out. And where did he go? You listening, partner? He walks lickety-split over to this dark green car—an Audi, I figured—and peeks in the window. Then his whole budgy body get kind of stiff like he seeing something evil, and he starts looking 'round over his shoulder to make sure ain't nobody spying on him. That's when I decided I better depart the hell out of there, 'fore he glim my automobile sitting cross the street."

"This is the Eldorado you're driving? The Kelly-green Eldorado with the white walls, the whip antennas, the chrome and everything?"

"It ain't Kelly green, pops. It chartreuse."

"A car like that isn't real conducive to surveillance work," Pomerantz pointed out.

"No shit? Never even considered that when I bought it, Fritzie. But suppose he do notice my flashy gasser? Ain't going to mean nothing to him."

"That parking lot, it's right across from my office."

"Yeah, it is, ain't it? Too bad you weren't up there that night with a pair of them high-powered binoculars," Africanus said in his deep baritone. "Then we'd know for sure what was inside that Audi. I'd be awful amazed if it weren't a dead lawyer name of Gilman, wouldn't you?" Raising his knobby hand, he beckoned the bartender again. "After I leave I drive on to Roxbury and meet my old chum from down the District, and we have a natural ball with a couple of chicks who go to the Berkeley School—real fine piano players, both of them—and when I 'rive back here 'round daylight, the first thing hits my eyes is that exact same Audi automobile parked out in front of the project."

The bartender glided in from the darkness, refilled the pimp's glass with Chivas Regal, glanced at Pomerantz's almost untouched stein of beer, collected two one-dollar bills from the change on the bar, rang them up on the register, and rolled off again into the ambient shadows.

"Nobody in it, dead or alive, and the window is wide

open," Scipio continued when they were alone once more. "I feel the hood. It's cold—been sitting there a while. And, believe it or not, the keys is dangling from the ignition, just like as if the person who left it there wanted to make it real easy for a thief to steal the thing. You dig it, partner?"

"Yeah—smart bastard," said Pomerantz.

"But not smart enough. If the police in the lumpy jacket want that car cut to little bits in a chop shop, I decide I'm going to stop it from happening that way. So I took them keys, shut the window, and locked the Audi up tight as a bank. Then I slip a few bucks to the kids who always hang in the hall of the 'partment house there—they the early-warning system for the private club that operates in that building—and tell them don't let nobody jump the wires on the nice green gasser and run it off, which is why it sat there for three days."

"Why'd you do that?"

Africanus looked sage. "'Cause I figured that after a while something might happen. And you know what, pops? Something did happen. You came 'round and pulled my coat. Now we in business."

He laughed resonantly, snapped his fingers, and did a series of quick dance steps that caused the skirt of his fur wrapper to jounce and whirl. Then he ceased his capering and drank his scotch.

Meanwhile Pomerantz gazed intently at his stein of flat beer as though it were a crystal ball. At last he said, "Maybe I ain't bright, Scipio, but I just can't decipher or perceive what your plan is. How do you anticipate a big score off a mystery like this? You haven't got any names except the dead guy's. You ain't even got a body. Where the hell's the twenty thousand coming from?"

"That cop's name is Kevin," Africanus said.

"Yeah, and maybe only two or three hundred other cops on the Boston Police Department have the same Irish handle. You can't be absolutely sure he is a cop, can you?"

"Anyhow, that don't really matter none. Listen close, partner. This bale of hay in the Mustang, this blondie, she appear kind of familiar to me when I first see her, only I couldn't exactly recollect why. That Saturday morning after I hop in bed, though—click, click—the whole remembrance suddenly mesh together in my mind. Couple of years back there used to be a after-hours glad-pad on Columbus Avenue run by a blind guy name of Ernie something, who everybody call the Mole—and the joint, they called that The Mole's Hole. Mainly black folks hung out there—hip gees, fly chicks—but whiteys came 'round, too, and this blonde I'm telling you about was one of them. At the time she the girlfriend of a prizefighter, a black boot from down Brooklyn who fought Marvelous Marvin once and nearly got hisself killed. The blonde give him almost as much trouble as Hagler did. Believe it. Girl love to snort, and when she have a noseful she get worse than a hound bitch in heat. So the fighter were kept pretty busy slapping her upside the head and dragging her ass off of people. Yeah, The Mole's Hole. A cool place, but the police shut it down early one Sunday morning—and the Mole say it happened on account of that blond fox. Missy, her name is—Missy Delaunay."

"Missy Delaunay," Pomerantz echoed meditatively. "For crying out loud—you don't mean Phil Delaunay's sister? Hey, Scipio—you ain't planning to tap *him* for the money, are you?"

"Damn right. He got it, ain't he?"

"Sure, but... but Phil Delaunay—he's a... a highmuck-amuck, a power broker. Him and his old man been manipulating this part of Massachusetts ever since James Michael Curley stepped down back in the 1940's."

"Ain't scared, are you?"

"Scipio, anybody who ain't scared of Phil Delaunay is soft as sponge cake. He owns judges, that guy. Got more influence in this state than the fucking governor. Which is why a cop showed up to dispose of the stiff. You can't put the screws on a honcho like that. He'll ship you to Walpole faster than you can zip your fly."

Gold chain bracelet scintillating like a ring of fire on his wrist, the pimp rapped the bar with the chunky knuckles of his right hand. "Shit! Delaunay can't hurt us none. He don't even know who we are, partner—and got no way of finding out, neither. Big-shot Delaunay! Fuck him. He going to have to pay just like anybody else who's got his nuts caught in the wringer. Believe it, pops. Otherwise his sweet little sister going to end up on the chicken farm out in Framingham."

Again the bartender materialized, and again the glass was filled with scotch and the money silently collected.

"I don't know," said Frederick Pomerantz, squirming on his stool. "Sounds like a doubtful proposition to me."

"Why? Them politicians all got deep pockets. One little telephone conversation, baby, and it'll start raining money. Don't you want to be rich? This here's the chance you been waiting for. We can bounce straight from the streets to the luxury suites."

"I don't know. Get-rich schemes, they can look simple and easy, but unanticipated things go wrong on you."

"Why you so worried? Ain't nothing risky 'bout this. Hell, all you got to do is make a anonymous call to the lady and tell her we wise to the whole evil business. Mention the guy's name—Harold Gilman. Yeah, and you better say we followed the Oldsmobile out of the parking lot and we know where the cold meat got unloaded. That ought to shake her good, put her in a generous frame of mind."

Fingering his walrus moustache, Pomerantz thought about the seventy-five hundred dollars he owed the loan shark, Alfie Jay, for his mistake with the video cassettes. "How could you handle the payoff, Scipio, without taking a lot of chances?"

"Easy. What we do is make her deliver the package—twenty K—to a apartment house in the project. Ain't no honky going to be able to follow her inside without us noticing him, 'cause all the folks there are stone black—see? She drop the money on the stairs on the second floor, and you be up above looking down on her. Then she leave and you just gather it in. I'll be standing in the entry there, to make damned sure she ain't companied by no police or nothing. But if she don't come alone, I give you a signal and you scoot out into the hall and depart through one of them other buildings. They all connected like a daisy chain. That's how we going to do it, partner."

How nice it would be if I didn't have to pay that fucking vigorish every week, Pomerantz thought, if I didn't have to worry about missing an installment and getting my jaw broken.

"Okay," he said hoarsely. "I'll go along with you."

"Solid," said the pimp in the fur coat, and drank his Chivas Regal.

19

A few days later Frankie Gates went again to the Symphony Road rooming house to see if he could squeeze more details of the parking lot shooting out of Ossie Peña, but the undersized thief wasn't home, nor could he find him at the Suds for Duds Laundromat when he drove over to Tremont Street.

From there the detective went downtown to Suffolk Superior Court to testify in a case involving the burglary of a Bay Village antique shop by a six-foot-four-inch fairy who somehow managed to hide in an armoire in the store shortly before the proprietor locked up and left for the day. When he returned the following morning the place was stripped. Gates's trip to the courthouse proved to be a total waste of time, though, since the A.D.A. never called him to the stand.

He was in a bad mood and very hungry as he walked briskly down Cambridge Street towards Giacomo's Cantina, where he hoped to enjoy a leisurely lunch of linguine with broccoli and anchovies before continuing his day's labors. Car horns were discordantly beeping and drivers complaining because of a minor traffic problem, but he paid no attention.

Suddenly, however, a battered Plymouth Volare made an unorthodox diagonal dash through the snarl of automobiles, and the tumult of protest rose to a crescendo. In spite of himself, Gates glanced around. He caught the tail end of this wild maneuver and recognized the reckless driver of the car as a Copley Square wino named Whitey Frainer. A moment later the Volare came to a herky-jerk stop next to a fire hydrant and the door opened, groaning and rasping. From out of the tenebrous interior three beer cans and an empty green wine bottle tumbled noisily into the gutter.

"Hey, Lieutenant! Could I talk to you a minute?" a shrill voice called above this racket.

Frainer, wearing a stained khaki army coat two sizes too big and badly scuffed down-at-heels cowboy boots, emerged into the light of day with a bewildered expression on his bearded face. He slammed the door vehemently, and great chips of caked mud and rust dropped off the dented fenders.

Advancing in hesitant hops and skips like a squirrel, he yelled, "Hi! Hi! Hi, Lieutenant. Been looking all over for you. Yeah, for more than a week now. Wanted to tell you what I seen."

Gates fixed a saturnine eye on the shabby man. Conversation with a speck bum was the last thing he desired at that moment. "What the hell kind of driving you call that, Whitey? I ought to run you in. One spin of your wheel and you almost converted a public thoroughfare into a fucking junkyard."

"Couldn't help it. I didn't mean to cause no trouble. I been looking all over for you, Lieutenant, ever since that night last week. So when I spotted you just now—"

"Okay, okay—what's on your mind?"

Frainer fell in step with him. "I want to tell you what I seen last week in this old house where I was sleeping with Samantha. Nobody lives there. It's by the Fenway, Lieutenant—and we was sleeping there, me and Samantha. What I seen was a guy's head in the fireplace. Yeah, I woke up—and cripes, was it hot! I thought the thermostat was too high. Then I heard noises and saw lights, so I crawled down the hall and looked through the floor in one of the rooms, and I seen this husky bozo—and he was the one who threw the head in the fireplace. Wearing a hat."

"That right, Whitey?" said Gates. "What kind of hat was the head wearing? A derby?"

"Not the head, Lieutenant—the husky guy. He was wearing the hat. Wasn't no derby. I don't know what you'd call it. But I seen it all. First he made this big fire, and then he threw the cut-off head on top of it... in a shopping bag with a lot of blood. The smell was terrible. Nobody lives in the house. It's by the Fens. Kind of creepy, but nice and warm on a cold night. Me and Samantha, we crawled in a cellar window."

"That's breaking and entering, Whitey."

"Why? Nobody lives there. The house is empty...by the Fenway. I seen the whole thing. It was like watching TV."

"I'll bet. And you saw it through the floor?"

"Yeah, ain't that funny? He kept pushing it around with a poker, the head. Guy like that got to be psycho, right?"

"Crazy as a coot," Gates agreed. "Must've been real exciting. Almost as exciting as that time you nearly got killed by the stampeding red buffalo down on the lower level of Park Street Station. Remember, Whitey?"

"I never said they was red," the wino protested, grinning idiotically. "Who told you they were red, Lieutenant? Not me. Only their eyes were red. The rest of them were gray—like rats, you know? Nobody believed me at the cuckoo hospital—at Bridgewater, there. I don't want to talk about them buffaloes, though. That happened a long time ago. This cut-off head thing only happened last week, in an empty house near the Fens. I could show it to you, Lieutenant. Got my car right here."

"Thanks, but I'm too busy now. Another time, maybe," Frankie Gates said, having drawn within a couple of yards of the cantina's fumed-oak front door. "Stay off the King Kong for a while, will you? That stuff can corrode your brain, Whitey."

After the detective disappeared in the restaurant, Frainer lingered on the sidewalk, scratching his shaggy head. Then he trudged dejectedly back to the beat-up Volare.

20

Bathed in the dull light from a pewter-gray sky, the capital's gold dome had less than its usual sheen. To Melissa Delaunay, waiting inside the warm taxi, it resembled the bottom of an old Chinese brass bowl, the stained, verdigris-spotted kind that elderly matrons tried to push on you at church jumble sales down at the Vineyard. Even the Bulfinch facade seemed drained of its elegance by the dreary illumination.

Once upon a time she loved the State House, but that was back in the glorious era of her father, Sunny Ned Delaunay, that tall and dignified, wise and handsome, bright and loving man who could almost always come up with slick solutions to her never-ending procession of petty, and not so petty, problems. But Sunny Ned was in his grave now. Only Philip stood between her and the hostile world—and Philip wasn't Daddy by a long shot.

Through transient openings in the Beacon Street traffic she saw her brother at the building's entrance, and watched him sedately descend the broad staircase nodding to people on either side of him like the queen of England. When he passed through the gate, Missy paid the cab driver and got out. Phil's mouth formed a rudimentary smile that was meant to be reassuring as he crossed between the red-light arrested automobiles, but she could clearly see the fear in his eyes even at that distance. Taking her by the arm, he led her past the Robert Gould Shaw Memorial and down the stone steps to the Common.

"Tell me everything," he said. "The exact words, if possible."

"Wasn't much of a conversation," she replied, her face half hidden by the collar of her coat. "He said, 'You shot Harold Gilman that Friday night, there in the South End. We watched you do it, Missy—saw the whole thing. And afterwards we followed your friend, the guy who drives the Olds, and saw where he dumped the body.' Then he told me to bring $20,000 to the second floor of some project house on Tremont Street. I wrote the number down. Wants it in tens, twenties, and fifties, packed up in a brown paper grocery bag."

"Did he mention photographs? Anything like that?"

"No, but I'm sure he knows about them. I'm sure it's all part of the same shitty scheme."

"What did you tell him?"

"Nothing, Phil. I hardly talked at all. I was shocked—tongue-tied."

"But how did you leave it, Melissa?" Delaunay asked impatiently.

"Well, I said okay to him. What else could I do? And

he said, 'I'll see you tomorrow. Be on time—and show up alone.'"

They walked in silence down the wide, inclined path. Above them the leafless trees converged to make a barrel arch, an arabesque vault inlaid with nacreous fragments of cloudy sky.

"Christ, what a mess! There's no end to it. What a catastrophe! How did this one sound?" Phil demanded of her. "His voice, I mean."

"Rough, gravelly—like he had a chest cold," she answered.

"Probably talking through a microphone. They have these machines now, disguise your voice. Commissioner McKeown was telling me about them. Wouldn't surprise me if the caller was one of my colleagues from across the road—an Everett Wheeler hatchet man. They're prepared to do anything to destroy my chances of getting the nomination."

"Phil, you said that the last time," Missy complained, as a sudden gust of wind wrapped spirals of yellow hair around her pouting mouth. "And it only turned out to be that jerk, Gilman. I figure he had an accomplice—somebody who was sitting in a car nearby. His wife Magda, I imagine."

"It wasn't a woman who phoned."

"She's got all kinds of people working for her."

"Why would the caller disguise his voice, if he didn't think you might recognize it?" her brother asked petulantly.

"I don't know—and what the hell difference does it make?" she retorted in a dispirited tone. "I'm never going to beat this thing. Magda Margolis is out to get me, Phil. She put her husband up to it. I'm positive. Got him to hire private detectives to take those pictures and all the rest."

"What does a woman like her want with more money? Sounds highly improbable to me," said Delaunay, the muscles of his square jaw tense. "Never mind. We'll fork over the twenty thousand and play for time. They'll squeeze us for more later, I'm sure, but by then Kevin Reedy will be back in action, and he'll soon discover who's pulling the strings."

"How?"

"The police have methods."

"Magda Margolis. She's the one he'd better check out. The whole plot is a conspiracy against me, Phil, not you," the sister said bitterly. "She hates my guts, just because her first husband fell for me. A beautiful kid, he was—sweet, kind, smart—a lot different than the other men I've known. Killed himself, the poor guy—but that wasn't my fault. It was hers. She was going to have him kicked out of Harvard."

"Please, Missy. I've heard the story before, and I don't have much time. I have to get to the bank and be back there by one."

"Magda Margolis won't be satisfied till I kill myself just like Gabriel did. She's a mean, miserable, heartless, conniving bitch."

"Nobody's going to hurt you. I'll see to that," Delaunay said, throwing his arm around her and giving her a little hug. "Don't get discouraged. Kevin will handle it."

Closing the neck of the beige polo coat with a brown kid-gloved hand, Missy declared in a voice devoid of inflection, "I think we ought to have her murdered, Phil. It's the only way. There's this guy I know—Stanley, a real criminal type. He could—"

"Are you out of your mind?" the politician exclaimed. "Jesus that's all we need—another corpse. You've got to get a grip on yourself, Missy—start acting like a rational, civilized human being." He grimaced. "Mother of God, can't you see that you've stirred up a lot of trouble already? Shooting Gilman was sheer insanity."

"You should've handled the negotiations yourself, brother dear," she taunted. "Everybody knows how terrific you are at dickering."

Delaunay tightened his matinee idol features into a mask of resignation and gazed off to his right at the bow-fronted brick houses that stood on the opposite side of Beacon Street. Sullen and silent, the two of them continued their leisurely pace beneath the bleached boughs of the tall trees. An adolescent of indeterminate sex, head swathed in knitted cap and muffler, sailed by them on a skateboard, tacking skillfully from one snowy verge of the asphalt lane to the other in a languorous voyage down the long hill.

"So what do you want me to do?" the blond woman inquired finally.

"I'll deliver the money to your apartment around three or three-thirty. Tomorrow morning, take it over there.

Follow his instructions and don't do anything heroic or stupid. Can you manage that?" Delaunay said moodily.

"I guess. Shouldn't be too large a bundle. Remember those neat bags of money Jeems Nugent used to drop off at the house every Sunday after mass, Phil?"

"Yes. White paper bags. Anyone would swear he was coming from the bakery with a dozen bulky rolls."

"Right, right. But Dad was always on the receiving end, wasn't he?"

"Don't kid yourself. He paid out plenty. That cash from Jeems trickled through a lot of fingers. You don't understand the mechanics of these things, Missy."

"Maybe not," she conceded, her voice dreamy. "I've been brooding about Dad lately, especially at night before I go to sleep. He used to tell me I was pure as a communion wafer, remember that? If he only knew. Couple of times I almost let the cat out of the bag, but I just didn't have the heart."

"How're you going to get home?" her brother asked as they drew near the Charles Street entrance to the Common.

"By taxi. Are you sure it's safe for me to go there alone tomorrow?"

"They're not going to hurt you. You're their money machine. I don't have anybody I can trust for a job like this. Kevin is still under the weather."

"Be funny if I got mugged by some fifteen-year-old snot nose in running shoes, wouldn't it? What a surprise he'd get when he opened the bag! Twenty thousand bucks. Poor kid would probably be dead of an O.D. by nightfall." Melissa giggled, but it was too shrill a sound to be pleasant. "See you later, Phil," she said, flagging down a Kenmore cab with a girlish wave of her gloved hand.

21

"Knew it was a heavy load because of the way the donkey engine was wheezing. Wendell, he called me—so I secured the winch and went aft," said Howie Osmund as he removed the dripping Red

Rose tea bag from his mug and deftly lobbed it into the dented galvanized bucket that served for a garbage pail. "A strange sight it was, him and those scallops. Then he swung the dredge on board and dumped the haul on the deck instead of the culling board. Even after Wendell cleaned him off a little, he still didn't hardly look real—not to me, leastways. Could've been one of those broken marble statues in a museum. The flesh was that white, you see. A big fellow, he must've been. It's a wonder the line didn't part from all that weight."

"Was it far from land, Howie?" the Boston Homicide detective, Jack Reinhardt asked.

"Four mile, maybe. Pretty danged stupid to sink him there, in my opinion—and Wendell, he agrees with me. Heck, everybody around here knows about the scalloping. Must've been a city person who done it—a summer resident."

"But this time of year there aren't any summer residents," said Reinhardt, tilting the rocking chair back until it touched a corner of the old-fashioned refrigerator.

Chuckling, the fisherman put a spoonful of powdered milk and three spoonfuls of sugar into the steaming mug. "That's my point," he declared happily. "If you only come to the Cape in summer, you ain't going to know about scalloping because we don't do none then. Season runs from the first of October to the thirtieth of March." Osmund stirred his tea noisily. "This fellow was probably familiar with the area, but he just never realized folks go out in the winter and dredge the bottom of the bay. If he did, he wouldn't have throwed the body there, would he? Stands to reason. Only had a small boat, I imagine—an inflatable, maybe, or a dink—so he couldn't travel too far, anyway. Pretty danged stupid, though."

He drank some tea, then cupped the mug in his chapped and calloused hands. Above his grizzled head a crude wooden crucifix hung on the wallpapered wall. The figure of Christ, though laboriously whittled, had no shoulders. The arms were separate pieces of wood that came straight out from the narrow, ribbed chest.

Frankie Gates, standing by the door of the furnished room, said, "Suppose it was a couple of people in a bigger boat? Suppose they came down here to dispose of the corpse? Came from Boston?"

"Have to be crazy to do it that way," said Howie Osmund, amused. "Why drop it in a bay near the land, if you got the whole wild ocean to use? No, sir—me and Wendell agree it was probably just one lubber in a dink. Heaved him overboard after dark. Tell you another thing, too. More than likely that same dink is setting in a shed not very distant from here—a shed alongside a cottage near Dennis or Barnstable or Brewster. Did I mention the bricks tied around the ankles? Tied with granny knots by a real landsman? Well, I'm prepared to bet a ten-dollar bill those bricks were baked in Andy Jepson's kiln over to Hyannis. That's my belief, mister—and if Wendell were awake and sober, like as not he'd tell you the same danged thing."

Biddle, the cop from Dennis, said appreciatively, "You should've been a detective, Howie. You got a good logical mind. We'll check on the bricks and poke around a few of the summer cottages. What about the head? You suppose he chucked that in the bay, too?"

"No, sir. Ain't probable. If it'd been me, I'd have buried that part of him in a cranberry bog. Why go to the trouble of cutting it off if you're only going to heave it in the same stretch of water as the carcass? Anyway, a head's easy to get rid of. Ain't like a body, is it?"

"You think a city guy could handle a boat out there in the middle of winter?" Reinhardt asked, rocking in his chair. "Must be cold, especially after the sun goes down."

"Cold? Cape Cod Bay?" Osmund offered them a toothless grin. "I wouldn't consider it so. Nothing like the open ocean up north. I spent twenty-two years fishing Georges Bank, and after I quit and came here it was like retiring to Florida. Back in '59 I was on the trawler *Ida Louise*. We lost a couple of young fellows in a dory up there. They went out to check the gear and got blowed away by a sudden squall. No more'n three hours later the mate spied them through his glass, bobbing on the swell off the port bow. Over we went to fetch them in. Well, sir, they were sitting there one behind the other, stiff as planks and white as snowmen. Had to break Eugene Rolfe's finger to free his hand from the gunwale when we hauled them aboard. All covered with glittery ice crystals they were, like hunks of frozen halibut."

"And they were dead?" asked Reinhardt.

"I should say so," the fishermen replied, his pale eyes as keen as a predatory bird's. "The cold made me give up that life. Took the strength out of my fingers, and most of the feeling, too. Couldn't gut fish anymore. To this day when I have a whiskey in a saloon, the fellow has to lay the change in my hand. If he puts it on the bar, I can't never pick it up. Yeah, mister, it's cold on Georges Bank—but Cape Cod Bay don't even get nippy in the wintertime." he gazed for a moment at the gnarled hands that held the mug, then added, "Of course, the fishing industry ain't what it used to be. The Russians are sweeping the oceans clean. Don't leave nothing for anybody else. And the Pope hurt us bad, too, when he allowed people to eat meat on Friday, except in Lent."

"You're a tough old guy." Reinhardt got up from the cushioned rocker. "Thanks for the help, Howie. Must've been a nuisance finding a corpse in your dredge like that, and being obliged to dump all those scallops back in the water."

Osmund's shaggy white eyebrows arched halfway to the line of his grizzled hair. "Didn't do no such thing. Why dump them?" he demanded to know, genuinely baffled. "It was the best catch of the day—almost the whole of them the legal size. Man'd have to be crazy to fling something back in the sea that he can sell for seven dollars a pound. Course, we threw a few buckets of ocean water on them before we sold them at the pier. Kept five or six dozen for myself, though." The mariner nodded towards the old-fashioned refrigerator. "Like to bring some home to the wife and kiddies, mister? Mighty tasty bay scallops are, if you eat them fresh."

Reinhardt glanced at Frankie Gates and rolled his eyes as he walked towards the door. "Er . . . no thanks, Howie. We won't be getting home till pretty late," he said, pretending disappointment. "Nice of you to make the offer, though."

The local cop, Biddle, waved good-bye, hopped in his cruiser and took off.

"Let's have lunch here, then head back," Gates suggested.

Jack Reinhardt, a tall man with a receding hairline and a pug nose, nodded and said, "Okay, Frank. I know a good steak house near Yarmouth. You going to bring the wife down?"

"Yeah, in the morning. But I'm positive it's Gilman. Same build, and he's got the mole on his arm and the hernia scar she told me about. Whoever killed the guy really did a job on him, didn't he?"

"Yeah, gave him the full treatment," said Reinhardt.

As they drove away Gates wondered if he was sorry about Harold's death. He decided he was only sorry for Magda. But who the hell would cut a man's head off? He seemed to recall a recent conversation about a cut-off head, but for the life of him he couldn't remember the circumstances or who it was he'd had the conversation with.

22

Hearing a sharp rat-a-tat on the glass, Stanley Gloag looked up from his newspaper and saw an ugly, pig-eyed face that sported a three-day growth of whiskers peering into the rented Skylark at him. Its lips were moving. Stanley leaned on the passenger seat and lowered the window.

"Yeah?" he said.

"Hey, bo, duke a couple of dollars on me, will you?" the face requested, although not in a very supplicatory tone.

"What for?" Stanley asked mildly.

"None of your fucking business, that's what for," came the unequivocal answer. "Just give me the deuce so I don't have to smash your headlights for you. And hurry it up. I ain't got all day, you cheap asshole."

Gloag bridled. "You touch my headlights and I'll call a cop," he said stiffly, playing the role of an irate citizen.

"There ain't no cops around, you dumb fuck. Think I'd be hustling herbies at ten in the morning if there was? Better make that five instead of two, since you want to act smart."

"I can't. Left my money home. I'm flat broke."

"Hey, what's the matter with you?" said the insolent beggar, who was dressed in a raggedy tweed coat with toggle buttons. "You want me to drag you the fuck out of there and kick your ass till your nose bleeds? Hand over the finif, Mister Charlie, and do it quick."

Feigning a nervous reluctance, Stanley tugged his wallet from an inside jacket pocket, opened it and withdrew a five-dollar bill. "Okay, don't get sore. Here," he said meekly, holding it in front of the window.

A soiled hairy paw snaked through the opening to snatch the greenback, but as it did, Stanley, eyes half-closed, seized it by the wrist with both hands and jerked it forward with such violence that the astonished beggar had neither the opportunity nor the strength to offer resistance. The upper part of his brutish face struck the automobile's roof, while the lower part gave voice to a bellow of pain and fury.

Not content with this result, Gloag grabbed the thumb of the hand, and yanking it like a stick shift, bent it back over the wrist until it softly popped. Uttering a second agonized wail, the beggar twisted free, jumped away from the car, and cowered on the sidewalk like a man with severe stomach cramps. On his forehead there was a purple welt, while the injured thumb dangled down from his wrist like a charm from a bracelet.

"Are you crazy?" he shrieked. "Why'd you bust my poor mitt for, you son of a bitch? Didn't have to do that. Only wanted a lousy couple bucks for a little muscatel, you miserable bastard."

Smiling genially, Gloag deliberately returned the five-dollar bill to his wallet and slipped the wallet inside his jacket again. But when his hand reappeared it held a switchblade knife—a large, finely made one with an olive-wood grip and bright brass fittings—which he snapped open and pointed at the wounded lazzarone. "If I have to climb out of the car, pig eyes," he said conversationally, "I'm going to slice your dick off and stuff it in your ear."

The beggar's face grew even uglier, though he retreated two more steps and performed an awkward turn. "Look at my thumb. It's broken, you fucking pervert," he whined, shambling down Tremont Street with the damaged hand extended out from his body. "Who's going to pay the hospital? Think I got Blue Cross?"

"I hope it gets infected, pal," said Stanley under his breath as the woeful figure vanished around a corner.

Laughing to himself, he depressed the knife's hilt to unlock the blade, folded the weapon up again, and tucked it in his pocket. Before he could resume reading the *Boston Globe*, however, an ITOA cab pulled into the curb alongside the housing project across the street and Missy Delaunay stepped out of it. A stiff breeze flattened the polo coat against her shapely body. She paid the driver and walked away. Several black teenagers offered her a few broad compliments as she hastened by the Ace Variety store, but none attempted to follow the woman when, carrying a paper grocery bag in the crook of her right arm, she entered the next to last apartment building.

Stanley went back to perusing the news story that had caught his eye just before the beggar's window-tapping interruption. It dealt with the grim discovery by a couple of fishermen in Cape Cod Bay of a headless and handless corpse. Despite the mutilations, a Brookline realtor named Magda Gilman had been able to identify the body as that of her husband by means of an abdominal scar.

Gloag raised his eyes from the paper and turned his head to cast a hooded glance at the doorway into which Missy had disappeared.

For the second time Frederick Pomerantz checked the door that led off the landing into the hall to make certain it wasn't locked. A flurry of frightening thoughts passed through his mind while he waited there for the Delaunay woman. He imagined the whole place suddenly crawling with cops, saw himself unable to reach the corridor, so that he had to flee to the roof and scramble down a fire escape, even envisioned getting shot to pieces by some trigger-happy rookie with a pump gun.

Yeah, but Scipio won't have any problems no matter what happens, he reflected enviously. He can duck into an apartment, fade into the background and become one more don't-know-nothin'-'bout-nothin' coon among the hundreds who live in this lousy dump. I must've been demented to listen to that tricky jig. They nail me and I'll spend the residue of my life at the Concord Reformatory.

At the bottom of the stairwell a door opened and closed. Pomerantz donned the black ski mask and said a silent prayer, peeking cautiously over the railing into the depths below. A kid-gloved hand moved up the banister in little leaps and bounds, accompanied by the hollow percussion of high-heeled footsteps on concrete. He caught a glimpse of a fashionably dressed young woman in a beret on the first landing. The sight of the brown paper bag clutched to her breast instantly banished his fears and quickened his hopes. When she arrived at the second floor she hesitated, then looked up.

Pomerantz pulled his head back. "Just put it down," he commanded. "Is it all there?"

"Twenty thousand, yeah," she answered coolly. "What're you giving me in exchange? That's what I'd like to know."

"Security. We're giving you security," he croaked through the mask.

"Funny, I don't feel secure. Twenty thousand is a lot. What about the photographs? You ought to a least hand those over to me."

Pomerantz was perplexed by this remark, but he didn't want to prolong the conversation by asking questions. His only desire was to collect the paper bag and get out of the building. "Never mind that. Leave the bundle and beat it. And don't try hanging around, either. If we have problems, you're going to have worse ones. Get moving."

"God!" Missy Delaunay said, but she set the bag on the floor.

As she retraced her steps, the investigator watched the descent of her gloved hand on the banister. A click-and-a-whoosh and a whoosh-and-a-click signaled the opening and the closing of the front door. He yanked the mask off, shoved it in his pocket, and crept down the stairs. Between the first two flights he heard another door open, however—this one close by—and his heart contracted with terror.

Cops, he thought frantically. It's a trap.

Nevertheless, he couldn't simply run away. He had to make sure, had to look over the railing one more time. Warily he stuck his head out, and there on the second-floor landing was a black girl in a skin-tight dress and a feathered purple boa. Like a bird of paradise she flew across his field of vision and vanished in a moment.

"Hey... hey, wait!" Pomerantz screamed after her, stumbling down the stairs as klaxons of alarm went off in his brain. "Come back here, Rubyjewel! What the hell you think you're doing? Come back!"

When he reached the landing the brown bag was gone. He raced through the fire door to the hall beyond and explored it in every direction, but the gaudy prostitute was nowhere to be seen.

Hunched down in the seat of the Skylark, Stanley observed the departure of Melissa Delaunay—watched her hail a Checker cab, climb in and get whisked away.

Five minutes later Frederick Pomerantz bolted out of the door of an apartment house towards the other end of the labyrinthine project, and though the day was far from warm, he appeared to be perspiring. Swabbing his brow, mouth, and moustache with a handkerchief, he stared up and down Tremont Street in a furtive manner before hurrying off.

"Good old Fritzie," Gloag said to himself. "Trying to promote a fast dollar. But where's the bundle? And how come he looks so unhappy?"

23

Riding the Allerton Arms elevator down to the garage, Frankie Gates Gates once again considered the very real possibility that Magda had murdered her husband. That morning while they were having breakfast together he had been strongly tempted to question her about it, but as usual he chickened out. His emotional involvement with the woman made him uncharacteristically timid in her presence. Besides, he wasn't entirely sure he wanted to hear what she might have to say.

Still, the detective couldn't help dwelling on the problem. It tantalized him and made him uneasy. With so much wealth and influence, Magda might well have assumed she could take the law into her own hands. She wouldn't have been the first, by any means. As for the man who had ditched the body, there were plenty of people around who'd do a job like that if the pay was right. Money bought everything, and Magda was a woman with all sorts of connections.

Jack Reinhardt, now in charge of the case at the Boston end, had questioned her for a couple of hours the evening after she identified the corpse. He seemed satisfied with her answers, though that didn't mean much.

The homicide man had interviewed Gates, as well, since a wife's lover is bound to be a suspect when the husband turns up dead, especially when the wife is rich. But luck had favored Frankie. On the night of the murder he had a perfect alibi. Detectives John Dolan and Herman Schilling could swear that he'd been in their company from seven P.M. Friday to two A.M. Saturday, at a hockey game and then two South Boston bars where they had done some heavy beer drinking.

Gates got off the elevator and walked down the garage aisle to his automobile.

At this point neither he nor Magda were under suspicion. Reinhardt's attention had been captured by Harold's gambling habits. Poker players and craps shooters were found floating in bays a little more frequently than the average citizen.

Gilman had been shot twice just beneath the right breast. One of the .25 caliber slugs had ricocheted off a rib and, traveling in an arc beneath the flesh, ended up on the opposite side of his body in a roll of fat above the hip. It was the other bullet that had done the real damage, though. After piercing a lung and severing an artery, it lodged in the spinal column. According to the M.E. there would have been considerable internal bleeding, but even so, the wound might not have been the cause of death. He had found the left lung full of blood, despite the fact that it hadn't suffered any injury, which aroused his suspicion that the victim had still been alive at the time of his decapitation. Blood in the lungs was a common condition of suicides who slit their throats.

Pretty weird, Gates reflected, driving out onto Beacon

Street. If that was true, then the woman hadn't actually killed Harold. The murder must have been done by the husky man in the course of erasing the victim's identity.

A saw-toothed instrument had inflicted the neck and wrist wounds. Whoever had performed these amputations was neither a surgeon nor a professional butcher, in the opinion of the lab man. While the precise time of death couldn't be determined because of the body's long immersion in the sea, he saw no reason to reject the Friday night of Gilman's disappearance as the probable period.

Both bullets were deformed, but the ballistic people felt they might still be matched with the murder gun, if it were recovered. Harvey Gunther at the Commonwealth Avenue lab had gone over the Audi a second time, though without finding anything new.

None of it sounded very promising, thought Gates. Even knowing what Ossie Peña had witnessed in the Laundromat parking lot didn't do much to clarify the mystery. Not that he had any intention of revealing the petty thief's testimony. If he spilled the beans now, the D.A. would want to know why he had waited so long—might even get hacked and hit him with a charge of suppressing evidence or obstructing justice or some damned thing.

This could happen later on, of course, but Frankie would have to take his chances. Come what may, he wasn't about to deliver Magda into Homicide's hands. While Jack Reinhardt had a reputation for brains and fairness, like most detectives he prided himself on his high batting average—the percentage of arrests to crimes, indictments to arrests, and convictions to indictments. Once a cop got the notion a person might be guilty of a felony, that person was in serious trouble. And a rich, prominent, good-looking woman like Magda Gilman would be in even greater danger than anybody else, because hordes of people would want to join in the prosecution, just to get a little exposure on the television screen or in the newspapers. Gates had to protect her. Whether or not he liked it, she meant far more to him than all the cops in Boston.

Before reporting in at the station house, he drove to Symphony Road—but if Osvaldo Peña was home, he didn't answer the door.

24

"A bad break. Cape Cod Bay—that's a big stretch of water," Reedy muttered, his tone defensive.

"Nothing seems to be going right, Kev." Worry lines marred the perfection of Delaunay's handsome face. "The whole wretched business is turning into a rat's nest."

"Just means we got to be more careful now. Those Homicide guys ain't dummies. With the newspapers starting to give the case a lot of ink, they'll investigate pretty thorough. If one of them gets lucky and picks up a thread someplace—well, that could be enough to hang us with."

"A comforting thought. Christ, you should've deep-sixed him in the cellar of that house of yours—or cremated the entire body."

"Maybe." Reedy rubbed the curved arm of the platform rocker with the palm of his hand as he gazed down at the diagonal bands of late afternoon sunlight that crossed his legs and stomach. He was bundled in a blue-plaid woolen bathrobe and had a king-size bed pillow under his head. "Thing is we got to stay cool, Phil—not lose our nerve. This hump you paid the money to—jeez, twenty thousand bucks—he must be somebody new. Otherwise he would've talked about them photos, especially after Missy brought up the subject. Probably ain't connected with Gilman at all. I guess he's the creep who swiped the radio out of the Audi."

"But even if he saw her in the parking lot, he didn't know who she was. How the hell did he find out?"

"He could've followed her back to her car, copied the license number and phoned the Registry the next day and got her address."

"I thought you can't do that anymore. Don't they have a password now?"

"Yeah, but it don't mean shit. You could try it right here, Phil. Call them up and say you're Officer Muldoon of the Traffic Squad. You need some information, only you can't remember the code word. The girl will make a joke and tell you anything you want. Happens all the time. We got to find the guy who copped the radio."

"Searching for a particular sneak thief in the South End must be like searching for a particular bedbug in a flophouse."

"Not necessarily. A little routine police work might turn him up, Phil," said Kevin Reedy with a reassuring smile that exposed his spaced-out teeth. "I got plenty of sources. Tomorrow, if I don't have a relapse, I'll go hunting for the slob. Shouldn't be too tough. And when I find the asshole, I'll work him over good. Slime like that you can terrify. What the hell—stealing car radios is a felony. I'll put the fear of God into him, and if we have any luck, that'll be the end of it."

"I hope you're right," the politician said fervently. He ran a manicured hand lightly through his razor-shaped hair, a distant and haunted look in his china-blue eyes. "This mess is beginning to dominate my whole life. Instead of concentrating on rustling up support for the nomination, I'm dithering around with a personal problem. My head is crammed with garbage—extortion demands, secret payoffs, criminals, dead bodies, police investigations. I'm out of my natural element, Kev."

"Leave everything to me, Phil. I'll be okay tomorrow."

"Christ Almighty, that sister of mine should be committed. You know what? She keeps needling me. Claims I don't know what I'm doing... that I'm not as smart as my father. Missy is obsessed with this crazy idea that Gilman's wife, a girl she went to school with years ago, is the mastermind behind the whole blackmail scheme."

"Yeah, she mentioned that to me the night I met her downtown."

"Did she mention that she wants to have the woman killed? Did she mention that she has a friend, some thug, who does assassinations at reasonable rates?"

Reedy shook his head in disgust and asked, "Is she serious?"

"Who the hell knows? But she's hired this character to follow Magda Gilman around, and now I'm shelling out money for his exorbitant fees."

"I hope to Christ she ain't confiding in him, Phil."

"She says she isn't. Says the guy isn't even interested in details, that he sticks strictly to the essentials of his own trade. Apparently he breaks the legs of welchers, and murders the more recalcitrant debtors. Can you believe that, Kev?"

"Sure, it's possible. Missy tell you his name?"

"No, she didn't."

"Chances are the guy's only bragging," replied the detective, his fleshy face contemplative. "But you better insist on her getting rid of him. Humps like that, they'll sell you for thirty pieces of stale bread. Got no morals at all."

Delaunay crossed one leg over the other and straightened out the crease in his charcoal serge trousers. "I'll read her the riot act," he said. "She's awfully hard to deal with, though. Always wants to run the show, do things her way. Of course, the kid's had to carry a lot of the load. She's the one who's had to deal with the bastards. But I *can't* get involved. Suppose somebody recognized me handing over packages to people in a South End housing project?" The politician's eyes grew dull with bewilderment. "So she gets sore, Kevin. Keeps saying that if Dad were alive, he would've squared the whole situation by now. Melissa just doesn't understand."

Yeah, Reedy thought. She's a headstrong, selfish little bitch. Got no brains, no decent instincts.

Then suddenly he remembered how feverishly hot her body had been in his embrace that night in her apartment, and blood flowed into his pale cheeks. To avoid her brother's eyes, he stared through the sun-filled gap in the drapes of the window at a corner of the back porch where half a cord of firewood was neatly stacked.

Standing up, Delaunay said, "You're absolutely right, buddy. I'll give her hell, see to it that she stops hanging around with this plug-ugly. But I've got to be off." He took his topcoat from the foot of the bed. "You hear Ruffing racing the engine out front? That's to remind me I have to be down the Parker House in about thirty minutes. Agnes's literary club is giving a tea, and I wouldn't want to miss a wingding like that, even though none of those damned Brahmins will ever cast a vote for me. It's great to see you up again. Don't try to do too much tomorrow, will you? And give me a call. So long, Kevin."

"Thanks for coming, Phil."

* * *

Feeling fatigued and vaguely dissatisfied, as though he had done a lot of hard work to no purpose, Reedy listened to the automobile drive away.

He gazed through the drapes again at the firewood on the back porch. Rita had stacked it there the previous fall. Mickey Conroy, a dumb son of a bitch if ever there was one, had dumped the whole load right in the middle of the yard, so Rita had to lug it up on the porch. The job was nearly finished by the time Reedy came home that night.

If he narrowed his eyes to slits and made a great effort, he could dimly recreate her image out there—see his darling girl carrying some of those quartered logs in a canvas sling.

It had been a cold, blustery day. Her hands had gotten badly chapped, but she never complained. Afterwards—after she went off on that visit to her mother and had the accident in Chelmsford—he saw her in the coffin at the funeral parlor down on Long Island, and her fingers were still cracked and rough. The sight of them broke his heart. He knelt there crying like a baby until her brother came and helped him back to a chair.

The diagonal bars of sunlight had risen to his chest. He rubbed the rounded arms of the platform rocker and moaned softly.

25

For a couple of seconds Frederick Pomerantz thought Scipio was going to try to slam the door in his face. Through the tiny windows of the black man's brown eyes he could see the gears and ratchets whirring and clicking inside his head, observe him weighing the options and making a quick decision to be friendly. The half-formed sneer changed to a deceitful grin, and the door opened wide.

"Expected you last night, Fritz. Come on in," the pimp said. "You never showed."

Pomerantz entered and looked around carefully. The

room was a small old-fashioned parlor, but the furnishings were modern and garish—chairs in glossy vinyl, tables of glass and stainless steel, a white leather pouf. Black satin curtains hid both windows, and there were a couple of imitation animal skins, fake heads and all, on the floor—one meant to be a tiger's and the other a leopard's.

"I did come yesterday—twice—only nobody answered the door."

"Yeah? Must've went someplace. I'm a busy dude. Grab a seat. I'll get you a drink. Want a little French Napoleon cognac?" Africanus said, shutting the door.

His hands deep in the pockets of his trench coat, Pomerantz shook his head negatively. "Only thing I want is my share of the score—my ten thousand dollars."

Scipio cocked his head. He wore a gray silk smoking jacket with white collar, lapels, and sash. "It ain't here," he said. "All them junkies in this neighborhood—shit, be stone simple to keep a roll like that in the house. Anyhow, the stuff got to be laundered. Some smooth people I know taking care of that."

"Laundered? What the fuck you talking about?"

"Those mother-rapers trying to be cute. They give us hot money, partner. All them bills has purple marks on them that shows up when the bank teller shove it under their machine. Try passing money like that and they going to catch your ass sooner or later. These friends of mine going to bleach the spots out so we don't get ourselfs burned. Extortion is a *hard* rap—and with that boss politician involved, they'll come down on us like a avalanche. So we got to be cool, pops. I did a nickel in the joint once, and I rather eat snake, drink muddy water, and sleep in a hollow log off in some *swamp* than sit behind them iron bars again."

Making a visible effort to control himself, Pomerantz said, "What is all this incomprehensible bullshit, Scipio? You must think you're moving a sucker."

"Ain't no bullshit, man, just telling you facts. We got to cover our ass, got to clean up that money. I'm giving you the right rundown so we—"

"You're giving me the fucking runaround, you mean," snarled Pomerantz. "You and me had a deal, and I handled my part of it nice and clean—did the work, took the chances. Now you're trying to stiff me. That dirtbag whore of yours snatched the payoff—and it wasn't supposed to be that way. Then—"

"We partners, ain't we? What difference do it make who collects the cash? We going to divvy it fair and square, Fritz."

"When? Next year? You think I'm mentally deficient? I want my ten K right this fucking minute—and don't insult my intelligence anymore with your purple spots. You try taking me off, Scipio, and you'll wind up in the trunk of your chartreuse pimpmobile with your eyes shot out."

"Hey, now don't go getting salty, pops," the black man said. "I might get miffed and strum your honky head for you. Ain't this *my* deal? Didn't the whole original scam belong to me? I mainly got the information, supplied the name of the fox in the Mustang, dreamed up the flim-flam. So you *lying* when you say you done everything. Ain't the truth, man. I only cut you in 'cause I needed—"

"A guy to take all the risks," interrupted Pomerantz, his homely face flushed almost to the point of incandescence. "A fucking patsy, in case things went wrong. Listen, you nigger fag, I want that money and I want it now."

Scipio's everted lips flexed in a cheerless smile. He started forward, but before he could advance more than a single long step, Pomerantz drew a black automatic from his trench-coat pocket and aimed it at the juncture of the pimp's white silk lapels.

The small room grew silent while the two conspirators glowered at each other. Finally Africanus turned his palms up as if to acknowledge his helplessness, and said, "Fritz, this is going too far. Hey, man, I'm only funning with you—just putting you on—and you taking me so *serious*. The money's right here." A broad smile divided his seal-brown face. "So shove that speaker back in your kick, 'fore we have us a accident. What is it, anyway? A .38? Look like a cannon out of a tough old Humphrey Bogart movie. Hey, you read in the newspaper how they found Gilman's body in the water down the Cape? That going to make them fuckers—"

"The money, the money," Pomerantz said impatiently. "Where is it?"

"Stashed in the clothes closet with my dope in the

other room," Scipio declared, and brazenly took another step forward.

The movement startled Pomerantz. Instinctively he backed up, but his heel came in contact with the open-mouthed head of the fake tiger on the floor behind him and he stumbled. The arm that supported the automatic swung off to the right. No longer threatened, Africanus pounced on the tottering man, took hold of his wrist, and smashed it against the sharp edge of a stainless-steel table. Pomerantz cried out in pain; the gun flew from his hand like a liberated starling, described an elegant arc in the air, and plopped softly on the vinyl sofa.

"That's better," the pimp grunted, and gripping his captive tightly by the throat, proceeded to box his ears. "Imagine you calling me a fag. I should bust you up good, leave you in the alley for the rats to nibble on, like they do the garbage. But I ain't mean, Fritz, 'cause I don't have to be. This is just to clear your mind, pops. Flashing a heater like Bogart—shit, that's funny. Guns ain't your trade, you simple-ass honky. I could see right off you don't know nothing about controlling yourself to pressure situations."

He shook the dazed man vigorously, as though he were a musty coat that needed airing, and then threw him down into a cushioned armchair. Next he retrieved the automatic and dropped it into the pocket of his exquisite smoking jacket. Then he faced Pomerantz again, pointed an umber-brown finger at him, and said, "Now here's how we going to play it," and went on to describe the manner in which the two of them would bleed money from the Delaunays during the coming weeks. In ten days they would hit them for another twenty thousand, and then follow up with a thirty-thousand bite a little later. After a month or so they would demand a final payment of a hundred thousand dollars, swearing that they'd never ask for any more. But once they collected the big lump, they could rest for a few weeks before starting all over again.

If the man in the chair was listening to this grandiose plan, he gave no indication of it. His face, except for a red welt on one cheek, was ashen gray. Against this deathly pallor his dyed eyebrows and moustache looked like recent additions to his visage, sketched there with a heavy hand by a comic artist with a black felt pen.

"But now we changing the split on account of that bonehead play you just made," Scipio rattled on, giving him a quizzical glance. "Your end going to be only a flat ten percent—hear? So alls I owe you is two K, but I ain't paying you till the next installment come in. Deal you four then, another three in a couple of weeks, and a fat ten thousand when we put the *big* squeeze on those suckers 'round about a month from now. That the new 'rangement, baby, and you in on it whether you like them numbers or not. Ain't bad pay just for jiving a lady on the telephone, anyway. But try walking out on me, Fritz, I'll peel you like a apple with my straight razor—dig? And don't go running to no police, neither, 'cause there ain't a thing to connect Scipio Africanus up with this pretty little hustle. I got me a cast-iron alibi for yesterday morning. Wasn't even in Boss-town. I'm out on the street a lot, pops, but that don't mean I fell off of a watermelon wagon." The black man laughed vibrantly. "Now get up and get going."

"You got to give me my gun," Pomerantz said hoarsely.

"I don't got to do *nothing*. Beat it, Fritz, before something fatal bad happens to you."

Like a sleepwalker the legal investigator made his way to the door. As he opened it and passed through to the hall, Scipio sang derisively, "Bye-bye, Bogart."

Back at his desk in his gloomy office Pomerantz poured himself a stiff shot of Canadian Club, gulped it and refilled the glass. The telephone rang and he picked it up.

"Pomerantz," he said in a monotone.

"Hi. This is Magda Gilman. I imagine you've heard the news, Frederick, about my husband's body being found in the ocean off the Cape."

"Yeah, yeah, I read about it and saw it on TV. Please accept my sincere condolences, Mrs. Gilman. A terrible tragedy."

"Thanks, that's kind of you. What about the Audi? Were you able to locate anyone who noticed it in that area or has any helpful information?"

"No luck so far," he lied. "Only thing I can tell you is that the detective—Frank Gates, your friend—was at the hockey game that Friday night. My confidential source at the station house passed me the word just this morning."

"Okay, Frederick," said Magda, who had learned of this the day before from Jack Reinhardt. "Send me a bill, since I won't be needing your services any longer. The police are finally taking the case seriously."

"All right," Pomerantz agreed, not caring much one way or the other. "I'll get it out to you. Thanks for using my professional services, Mrs. Gilman."

"You're welcome, Frederick. Good-bye."

He hung up, revolved his old oak chair 180 degrees, and gazed down at Tremont Street through the streaky window. It was growing dark, and most of the automobiles that sped by had their lights on. After several minutes he swung back to his desk, pulled a phone book from a drawer, looked up a number and dialed it. Stanley Gloag's grandmother answered and said he wasn't home. Pomerantz left his number. Then he replaced the receiver, noticed the second tot of whiskey sitting on the blotter, and lifting it in a hand that still trembled, drank it off.

For an hour he remained in the office, staring vacantly at the busy street below. Finally he got up and left.

In the toilet in the hallway he washed his face and carefully combed his dyed hair. The bruise on his cheek had turned an ugly bilious green.

26

A plastic sign suspended from two chains in the dirty front window said USED STOVES AND REFRIGERATORS, but when Reedy entered the place he saw only odds and ends of rubbish—thirty-year-old television sets, bald automobile tires, ramshackle furniture, rusty toilet bowls, an obviously broken air conditioner.

With a nervous smile on his wrinkled face, Jake Mints emerged from a little room at the back. His crooked spine gave him a slightly vulturine look. To keep from freezing in his frigid shop, he wore a knitted hat on his head and a thick colorful sweater on his bent body, an exotic cardigan that might have been cut from an old oriental rug or a Navajo horse blanket.

"You Jake?"

"Yeah," Mints answered, well aware he was talking to a policeman.

" I'm from Headquarters and I want to know who sells you your stolen car radios."

The shop owner's face assumed an expression of disbelief. "I don't buy stolen goods," he said. "This some kind of joke?"

"Do I look like a comedian, Jake? I asked you a straight question, and I'm waiting for a straight answer."

"Officer, I had a problem last year—okay? But it taught me a big lesson. I don't touch dubious merchandise no more."

Reedy strode past the bent-backed man to the tiny room at the rear, satisfied himself that it was empty, and then returned. "Let me explain you something," he said. "If I want, Jake, I can cause you serious grief. There must be ten easy ways at least of railroading a loser like you to the House of Numbers. If I search these premises, I'll find stolen property. I'll find it even if I have to plant it here. So be smart. I ain't interested in incriminating you. What I want is the names of your suppliers—the creeps who bring you radios ripped out of automobiles. Don't be a dumb fuck. Those scumbags wouldn't protect you, Jake, would they? I bet it was one of them turned you in the last time."

Mints kept silent, the network of wrinkles on his leathery countenance like a graph of a bankrupt life. Around the cluttered room his dull eyes roamed, hunting desperately among the rickety chairs and stained mattresses for an escape from his dilemma. Realizing at last that there wasn't any, he said in a subdued voice, "I know a nigger kid—Winston Huggins. Lives in Worcester Square, near the hospital. He likes breaking into cars. And there's a white guy—Tony Ross. Blond, five-ten about. Used to be in the Coast Guard. Wears a dark blue raincoat, usually. Tony swipes cars for a living, but he takes the radios out before he delivers them to the choppers. Has a little flat on St. Botolph Street."

"Who else?" Kevin Reedy demanded, copying the information into his notebook.

"Those are the only two I can—"

"Just two, huh? You sure you're not straining your milk

giving me such a long list?" the detective said sarcastically. "Come on, you asshole. Cut the shit. Cough up the rest of them."

Shoving his hands in the pockets of his outlandish cardigan, the crook-backed man surveyed the dismal shop. "Let me think, officer," he said, screwing up his dark face until it resembled a walnut shell. "There's this Spanish kid—Peña. He cops stuff like that, but I don't have no idea where he lives. A little shrimp—Artie Peña, or maybe it's Izzy Peña. I forget. Showed me a Blaupunkt a couple of weeks ago."

"You still got it, Jake?"

"No, no. I never bought that stereo," Mints said hastily, tilting his head to stare at his tormentor. "He wanted a hundred bucks, and this ain't a hundred-buck neighborhood. But I remember now where that kid works. Laundromat on Tremont Street, the same block as Karzulov's antique store, near Clarendon."

"Artie Peña," said Reedy under his breath, scribbling it down. "Keep 'em coming. I need more."

Mints slipped a grubby forefinger beneath his knitted hat and scratched the side of his head. "There ain't that many," he whined. "Only other one I can think of is Paxton, tall, black junkie from Columbia Point. Wears his hair slicked down with a lot of grease. Paxton—he tosses garbage cans through store windows and fills his pockets with the loot. But he breaks into cars, too. Paxton is his last name, that's all I ever heard him called. He'd steal a hot Franklin stove, that kid."

"Columbia Point, you say?"

"Yeah, the project out there. He's skinny, like a basketball player. He's the last one I got, officer. Don't know any other likely possibilities. Give you my word."

The detective treated him to a skeptical leer, but he closed his notebook and said, "Okay, Jake. This'll do for now. You keep thinkin', though, because if I don't find the punk I'm looking for, I'll be back here in a hurry."

"Sure, sure. I'll do that," said Mints, manifestly relieved.

"Christ, it's freezing in this dump. How the fuck can you stand it?" Reedy asked, flailing his arms across his stout body to generate some warmth.

"It ain't easy—and I'm in here ten, twelve hours a day," the wizened shopkeeper replied in a pitiable voice. "But the boiler downstairs is busted. If I turn on a couple of electric heaters, it don't really help that much—just costs a fortune at the end of the month."

He abruptly ceased his whimpering lament because his unwelcome visitor was halfway out the door.

Though he had already begun to tire, Reedy drove on to Tremont Street to have a look at the Laundromat. The place was busy. A dozen people of both sexes were in there folding clothes or turning the pages of tattered magazines. But he didn't see any small Hispanic attendant around. It was apparent from the layout of the store, however, that a person standing at the window at its rear would have a good view of the corner parking lot.

He got back in the warm Oldsmobile and returned home.

Mrs. Williams, the housekeeper, was just leaving when he arrived. She shook her head and said, "You don't look well to me, Mr. Reedy. No, sir—you never should've gone out. Stay home now and rest."

"Yeah," said Reedy, taking off his jacket. "That's what I planned on doing. Feel a little chilly. It don't pay to rush things."

"Well, raise the thermostat and put on a warm sweater," said the black woman. "I got to go along now to my sister's. She's having a birthday party tonight for her oldest girl, Donna Lou. But I'll be here early tomorrow, though. Should I sort them clothes?"

"Clothes? What clothes?" he asked, hanging the jacket in the closet.

"Miss Rita's. They're all getting so fusty and musty up in that wardrobe. Ought to be aired out good and packed away."

"Didn't I tell you to leave her belongings alone?" Reedy snapped as he turned to face her.

"Yeah, sure—but that was a couple of months ago. Can't just let coats and dresses hang on hangers forever. They're going to start losing their shape and—."

"Don't touch them," he broke in. "You hear what I'm saying? Keep your hands off my wife's things. Those clothes, they're her... her personal property, that she... she hung there herself. I don't want nobody rearranging it . . . nobody messing with her belongings. You understand me?"

Abashed, Mrs. Williams couldn't answer immediately. The detective looked strange to her—a little bit crazy—and the sight of the big gun on his belt added to her nervousness.

"Yes, sir," she said eventually. "Okay, Mr. Reedy. Don't matter none to me. I'll leave them alone, if that's the way you want it."

He nodded curtly and headed for the stairs.

27

He parked his Olds 98 near the station house on Warren Avenue and briskly walked south. The weather was cold, but not bitterly so. High in the sooty black heavens an almost round moon hovered like a Halloween jack-o'-lantern.

As he approached the Suds for Duds, a scruffy man with a seabag on his shoulder emerged from its door and slouched off in the opposite direction. Faint disco music drifted from the Grotto across the street, but nobody was hanging around outside the dimly lit barroom, and the whole area appeared deserted except for passing cars. He glanced at his watch, saw that it was 11:58, and entered the Laundromat.

Beyond the double row of washing machines a short, delicately built youth with curly black hair stopped shoving plastic clothes hampers under the tables to yell, "Hey, man, we're closed. Last wash is eleven o'clock."

"I ain't here to do my laundry," Reedy responded, flashing his badge. "You Artie Peña?"

"*Ossie*, not Artie."

"I'm looking for information. Go ahead and lock up, so we won't be interrupted."

"Yeah, sure," said Peña doubtfully. He walked towards him, a radio headset hanging from his scrawny neck. "I'm real beat, though, and I'd like to get the hell home."

"This ain't going to take long, kid. It's important."

"Okay," said Ossie, continuing on to the front of the shop, where he jammed the door bolt into its mortise. Then he returned, closing washer lids along the way. "What's it all about?"

"We have reason to believe a man was shot to death in the parking lot out back sometime around midnight a couple of weeks ago. I notice you got a window at the rear there," Reedy said, pointing with a hooked thumb. "Remember seeing anything suspicious through that window on a Friday night about then?"

"Two weeks? That's a long time." Peña frowned, as if delving deep into his memory. "Out in the parking lot? And you say a man got shot? Must've happened when I wasn't here. Every now and then this other guy fills in for me—takes the nightshift, so I don't go stir-crazy."

"You mean to tell me you can't remember if you was working in here the Friday before last?"

"Well, I guess I was—yeah. But I don't pay much attention to the parking lot. Too busy. And even if there was a shooting out there, I probably wouldn't hear it on account of the machines going."

"What are you talking about, Ossie? The machines are shut down by midnight. You trying to hand me a line of malarkey?"

"*Hombre!* Why would I do a thing like that?" said Peña, shrugging his slim shoulders. "The machines stop when the last customer leaves, and when the last customer leaves I go home. I don't stick around. I split."

"How?"

"What?"

"Do you leave by the front door or the rear door?" Reedy inquired with exaggerated patience.

"Oh. By the front. I always keep my car on the street, where I can see it. Around here the *moyetos* steal cars like they were sampling Oreo cookies in the supermarket. They clout everything. Snatch the contact lenses off your eyes, if you're too slow blinking."

"That's true enough, but they ain't the only grifters in the South End. How many times *you* been busted for larceny, kid?"

"Larceny? Never! Come *on*!" Peña's small body grew taut with outrage. "I work for a living. Used to be a jockey, before I fell off a mount. You police guys think all Hispanics are hustlers, and it just ain't so. I'm a hundred percent on the level, man—a hundred percent straight and honest."

"What *this* police guy thinks, Ossie, is that you're a hundred percent full of shit," the detective barked brutally. "Listen, you lying little prick, everybody knows you're a habitual crook. Jake Mints over on Chandler Street, he's getting rich off the crap you sell him. Stop talking like an asshole. I could probably roust you if I wanted to, but that ain't what I'm here for. All I want is for you to tell me what you saw in the parking lot that Friday night—the night you ripped the Blaupunkt out of that new BMW the dead man happened to be sitting in. And don't try feeding me any lies, because if you do I'll bust your fucking head for you."

The thief, as though propelled by a blast of gale-force wind, retreated several steps. Lambent glints of panic shone in his brown eyes. "Jake who? I don't know the person—and I don't know nothing about no dead man, either," he squawked, fingering the black wire of his Walkman as though he were telling the beads of a rosary. "Okay, a long time ago a cop picked me up for questioning, but it was all a big mistake. I thought they were throwing that snowblower out. *Sarito!* The thing was standing on the curb next to a garbage can."

Kevin Reedy gave him a frosty smile, turned, strolled unhurriedly to the rear of the store and began flipping light switches on the wall. Gloomier and gloomier the Laundromat became, until at last it was lit only by a wan sulfurous glow that filtered through the none too clean plate-glass window from a nearby streetlamp.

Suddenly Osvaldo Peña lost his composure completely, pivoted on his elevated heels, and fled towards the front door. Before he could throw the bolt, however, an iron hand encircled his neck, and a second later, grabbed by the seat of his pants as well, he found himself awkwardly hopping back into the deep, deep shadows of the elongate room.

Near the soap dispenser there were several folding chairs. Into one of these the detective shoved him, and said reprovingly, "Where the hell you running to, kid? Don't you like talking to me? Must be something on your mind. Ain't normal to get scared over nothing. What's the problem, jerk-off? How come you don't like me? Jeez, we only just met. Or maybe you know me from someplace else. Is that why you're so jumpy? Sure, you've seen me before—right?"

"No... *nunca*... never," whispered Peña emphatically, avoiding his tormentor's close scrutiny by looking past him to the row of GE dryers against the wall. "What are you roughing me up for? This ain't legal. We ain't in Russia. I want to phone a lawyer."

"No, you don't. It's too late, anyway. They're all in bed sleeping," Reedy declared, still studying the undersized youth's perturbed face. "What do you need a lawyer for? Unless you got something on your conscience. That it, Ossie? I think the best idea would be for you to start talking—get it off your chest. Jeez, kid, you're too fragile to be acting tough. I seen ten-year-old girls that was heftier than you are. If I slap you around even a little bit, you're liable to break in a million pieces. So what did you witness that night?"

"Nothing, nothing, I swear it on the head of my mother. I never stole no Blaupunkt from no Audi out there. *Hombre!* Somebody gave you the wrong information. Let me go home, will you?"

"A mocking smile returned to Reedy's broad Irish facc. "Audi? Who mentioned an Audi?"

"What? You did... before."

"Not me, sonny boy. I said the car was a BMW. It's a real old trick, but it still works with dumb fucks like you. Now the big question is—how did you know it was an Audi, if you never saw it?"

"*Coño!* Audi...BMW—both look the same to me. They're German, right? I can't *ever* tell which is which."

"Don't try bullshitting me, huh?" Reedy gently pinched the Laundromat attendant's soft brown cheek. "All I want from you is the answers to two little questions. One, what did you see that night? Two, who did you share the information with?"

"I swear to God, I never saw nothing," Peña pleaded movingly, a lachrymose film on his large eyes. "That's the truth. If I did, I'd tell you. Be crazy not to—ain't that right?"

Glaring at him, Reedy said, "You got any change, Ossie?"

"Change?"

"Yeah, quarters or dimes. Got any on you?"

"Sure. Always keep some for the machines," said Peña, puzzled. He dug in his blue-jeans pocket. "What do you want with change?"

The detective helped himself to four coins from the attendant's trembling hand. "Thanks, kid. I need it for a machine, too. I'm going to pop you in the dryer for a while, just to shake up your memory."

Peña's lower jaw fell an inch. "Hey, quit your kidding. *Mierda.* You're trying to scare me, right? Be impossible, man. I mean it's too . . . too *small.* I wouldn't fit."

"Of course you would. You're a fucking midget, Ossie. You could get lost in a gnat's ass. Anyway, if there's a problem, I can always break your legs to *make* you fit. Ain't that so? Come on."

Reedy jerked him from the chair by his sweater, hustled him across the narrow aisle, and threw him up against the bank of dryers. The impact of this collision dislodged the Walkman radio from the youth's belt, which dangled by its slender insulated lead for a few seconds before finally pulling the headset off his neck, whereupon they both crashed to the vinyl-tiled floor.

"I'm a human being. You can't stick no human being in a laundry dryer," Osvaldo protested through chattering teeth.

"Twenty-five cents for nine minutes," the cop recited, squinting at the instruction plate. "Jeez, that ain't expensive."

"Those things get hot as ovens. *Dios mio*, don't . . . don't do it . . . please. Have a heart. I'll be roasted alive."

"That's just a chance we'll have to take," said Reedy stoically. He opened the glass-paned door with one beefy hand and yanked his struggling prisoner towards it with the other. "See? Plenty of room. Get the fuck in there, you maggot."

Peña balked, shied and fought, but he was so overcome by terror that his efforts were too feeble to do more than delay the inevitable. When his palsied fingers lost their last grip on the doorjamb, he went flying into the hole headfirst. The shape of the drum forced him into a fetal position with his nose between his bent knees, while the thing's steel ridges dug into his back and buttocks.

"*Ay! Socorro!* Don't, don't," he squealed. "*Por favor!*"

Nevertheless, the round hatch slammed shut on him. Two quarters dropped into the coin slot with clicks and rattles, and the place of his close confinement slowly commenced to move.

Keeping the door shut with his hand, Kevin Reedy watched the huddled figure lazily rotate on the other side of the window. Over and over the youth went, like an acrobat on television. When a knocking noise developed in the machine, however, Reedy stooped to peek into the dark interior, but the cause of the racket was only a stacked heel loafer that had slipped off Peña's tiny foot and was now capriciously banging against the perforated walls of the cylinder. While it repeatedly struck its owner on the head and body, Ossie seemed quite oblivious to these gratuitous blows.

Indeed, he appeared to be withstanding the whole rigorous treatment surprisingly well. Hands clasped over his jackknifed legs, eyes wide open, mouth set in a firm line, he didn't look at all like someone suffering great pain or grave discomfort. As his body occupied every inch of available space he simply somersaulted around and around, without taking a battering.

After several minutes the burly detective opened the hatch, waited for the drum to halt its revolutionary motion, seized the attendant by his warm curly hair and pulled him halfway out of the hole.

"What did you see that night, kid?" he asked. "Tell me, so we can both go home."

But Peña was much too busy gulping air to answer him immediately. And, when at last he did speak, his words were hopelessly garbled by a tongue and mouth as dry as parchment.

"Sot...can bree...ahsay klor...no more...sot," he croaked, face flushed and delicate nostrils quivering.

"Talk sense," the detective snarled, shaking Ossie's head as if it were a gourd rattle. "What did you see that night, you stupid Spic? And who did you tell?"

"No more...sot...my trote...can bree...sot...don ...don," Peña gasped, blinking his eyes idiotically.

"Okay, be a smartass. Back in the space capsule you go," said Reedy, assuming the thief was faking his dazed condition and growing increasingly angry with him.

He slammed the round door on Peña again, stabbed the button to restart the dryer, and then strode to the front of the Laundromat, where he stopped in the shadows to stare moodily out at the dribble of late-night traffic on Tremont Street.

Just how much does the runt know? he wondered, suddenly feeling fatigued and even a bit giddy from his exertions. And who the hell is his partner, the blackmailer with the husky voice? Got to locate him, too. This fucking little greaseball, he must've seen everything. If I can get the name of the other guy and scare them both, maybe...

A cream-colored Chevy Impala gliding by out on the dark street caught the detective's eye and abruptly shattered his train of thought. The sleek car was virtually identical to the one he had bought for Rita at Campton Motors the previous summer, the one that smashed into the abutment on Route 495, instantly killing the woman.

Five thousand it had cost. Only a year old, with 11,000 on the odometer. Worse deal I ever made, he thought remorsefully. She always loved them light-colored jobs. Said they were highly visible on the road at night. Visibility ain't everything. The steering must've been shot. Yeah, a mechanical failure because Rita would never get behind the wheel if she'd been drinking. What was she doing up there in Chelmsford, though?

He began grappling with the whole mystery again, as he had done innumerable times before, and as before, no satisfactory explanation occurred to him. Not until the electric dryer startled Reedy by its sudden silence did he at last surface from his reverie.

Hastening back to the machine, he opened the hatch and hauled Peña out. "Shit!" he exclaimed, quickly dropping the limp youth to the floor. "You're a red-hot potato, Ossie. Guess it *is* like an oven in there. Hope you ain't too well-done. Get up, kid."

But the attendant lay motionless and silent on the grubby checkerboard vinyl tile, maintaining the same tight fetal position he had had to assume in the steel drum.

With the toe of his boot, Reedy roughly prodded him.

"Snap out of it, Sleeping Beauty. I ain't got all night. Tell me what you know," he barked, and then flipped him over.

Beneath his disheveled coal-black hair, Peña's face had an oddly pinched appearance—and it was as ruddy as a geranium.

"Holy Christ, the little hump really *does* look cooked," said the detective, alarmed.

He ran to the sink at the rear, found a plastic pail, filled it from the cold-water tap, rushed back and drenched the inert youth. Osvaldo Peña never stirred.

Cursing in an undertone, Reedy dragged him along the floor, hoisted him onto a Formica table, and slapped his morbidly rosy cheeks. But this effort failed to produce a pulse in the thin wrist, nor could Reedy detect the least murmur when he anxiously pressed an ear to the shallow chest.

Still unconvinced, he raised one of Peña's eyelids. What he saw shocked him. The pupil was hardly bigger than a pinhead, while all the rest of the eye had turned an ocherous brown. The whole orb had shrunk and shriveled, so that it now appeared grotesquely small for its socket.

"Jeez, the kid's really dead," he muttered, amazed, as he pushed the lid back down. "He croaked in there—dried up or something."

Reedy mopped his perplexed face with a handkerchief and retreated from the table. He felt very weak, worn out—and his stomach was churning painfully.

Why hadn't the little bastard kicked the door open if he was roasting? he asked himself. Would've stopped the thing from spinning—turned it off. Why hadn't he yelled the goddammed dummy? Shit! Now he's dead . . . and I'm responsible. Who the fuck would've figured a clothes dryer could get *that* hot? It's crazy.

Shaken and confused though he was, the detective realized he had to get away from there. But before he could do that, he had first to make a tour of the room and with his handkerchief wipe any surfaces he might have touched. This accomplished, he went to the back door and peered for a minute into the murky parking lot. When he was satisfied that there were no people in any of the cars he twisted the knob with a cloth-covered hand and let himself out.

Beneath the jack-o'-lantern moon Reedy hurried along the deserted streets. Violent spasms of trembling racked his chilled, sweaty body, and from time to time he mumbled under his breath.

28

Wearing her Cristobal Balenciaga no-waist black dress, Magda Gilman sat in the brocade-covered armchair and regarded the crowd of people in the room with tired eyes.

Now that my second husband has been reduced to ashes—all of him except his clumsy hands and poor impractical head—the relatives are rejoicing, she told herself resentfully. I know what they're thinking—Better Harold than me. And some of them are probably doing a little mental arithmetic, too, recalculating their chances of eventually getting a slice of the Margolis fortune. Human beings are vultures.

"It took them long enough to hand over his body," her sister Miriam said. "What did they find from the autopsy?"

"Nothing that helps," Magda answered, waving the kid from the caterers off as he approached with a tray of canapés.

"Harold led a funny life," said Miriam. She was seated on an articulated bridge chair. "Don't you think so?"

"All lives are funny."

"That's true—and very philosophical. But Harold consorted with underworld characters, Magda."

"How can you be a criminal lawyer, darling, and not associate with underworld characters?"

"He didn't *have* to be a criminal lawyer," said the sister, whose husband was a highly successful periodontist in Westport, Connecticut. "He could have joined the family business—become a broker, like you."

"Could he? He tried once, and Papa fired him. Remember?"

"Oh, that's right," Miriam said, helping herself to a cracker piled with caviar from the proffered tray. "Didn't Harold confide in you? I mean, don't you have any idea why he got...?"

"Killed and butchered?" Magda finished for her. "No, Mimi, I don't. You asked me the same question in the funeral parlor yesterday. I didn't know anything then, and I don't know anything now."

"Everybody's wondering."

"Yeah. They're all thinking my husband owed some gangster money and he got murdered because I was too cheap to pay off his debt. But they're wrong. Harold didn't have that problem. If he did, he wouldn't have hesitated to come to me for the funds he needed—and if he came to me, he would've gotten them."

"You don't have to tell me a thing like that, dear Nobody in this family thinks you're cheap," Miriam declared, scandalized. She was a woman of twenty-five with reddish-blond hair cut in bangs on her forehead and neatly styled around her ears so that everyone could enjoy an unobstructed view of her ruby-and-diamond stud earrings. "Magda, you're farmisht. People aren't blaming you for anything. We all know that Harold was a degenerate gambler."

"Big deal, Miriam. Who isn't a gambler these days Your Benny, for instance. He comes back from the Caribbean as pale as he went, because he spends every waking minute in those casinos."

"But he's not an addict. And when you play roulette or chemmy in Europe or down the islands, it's more of a social thing—*du rigueur.* Did I mention our trip to Monaco next month, by the way? That neighbor of ours, the mutual-fund director, is letting us use his gorgeous apartment in Monte Carlo for a couple of weeks because we lent him our house in Boca last winter. And by gorgeous, Magda, I mean genuinely old aristocratic European gorgeous. It's absolutely rococo. We saw pictures. Not only that, the condo is right near the palace, so we'll probably be bumping into the Prince and Caroline every time we step out the door. And we'll be able to catch the carnival at Nice, and hit all those scrumptious Michelin restaurants along the *côte.*"

"Lovely," said the widow, without enthusiasm.

"Who knows? Maybe if I get Benny in the right mood, he'll buy me a snazzy little *pied de terre* on one of those majestic cliffs overlooking the water. Wouldn't that be a dream? If it was up to me, I'd travel six months every year, but of course Benjamin has to maintain his practice to bring the money in. *Pierre qui roule n'amasse pas mouches*—a rolling stone gathers no moss, as the French say. If we get a place, Magda, you could stay there anytime."

"Thanks, but I prefer Tampa, where most of the people speak English."

"Well, you'd just have to do what I do. Take those Berlitz courses. A dozen lessons and you can talk just like a native."

After this glib piece of advice her sister finally left off chattering for a while, and Magda went back to brooding. She could recall her mother's post-funeral get-together almost twenty years earlier, could recreate the whole scene with her father sitting next to the fireplace, his face like a weathered chunk of granite. At the time she'd only been eight years old, yet she had been filled with guilt feelings because she couldn't cry, couldn't generate a single tear, much as she adored her mother. The poor woman had been operated on for an ovarian cyst and died of an embolism on the table. Even the top surgeon at Beth Israel couldn't save her.

Then, almost a lifetime later—or so it seemed—there had been Gabriel's traumatic end. Magda hadn't even wanted a gathering of relatives after that service. Throughout the ordeal she'd been unable to think, talk, eat, sleep. Nonetheless the affair was arranged, and she had spent the whole long night misty-eyed and silent, passionately wishing that she, too, were dead.

When her father passed away she handled things better. He was so old, and his death had been expected. Yet it caused her considerable sadness all the same, since she'd been much closer to the elderly man than had her sister or anyone else. Their relationship had always been a near perfect blend of love and respect, probably because the two of them were so similar in temperament.

Now Harold, too, had perished. Was it possible? Poor, poor man! And what had they done to him? How much pain had he suffered? While she couldn't grieve for him with the same abandon as she had for her first husband, the sensation of loss and emptiness was almost the same, surprisingly.

So much death, Magda thought. Perhaps I attract it. Or maybe I'll be the next to go, the next absent guest at one of these dismal, macabre parties.

She shuddered, dipped two fingers in her glass of iced Perrier, and dabbed the cold water on her feverish temples. Whose klutzy idea had it been to build a fire in the fireplace? she wondered. It's like a sauna in here.

Harold's mother's brother, a nice old gentleman who manufactured ladies' lingerie in New York, stopped by her chair and murmured some kind words of condolence and encouragement. Then, after patting her shoulder and squeezing her hand, he tottered off shaking his bald head.

Magda stood up and said, "I'm going to my bedroom and make a phone call. If you see the kid from the caterer, tell him to serve more drinks. Everybody's standing around with an empty glass in his hand."

"Okay, Mag. He's being kind of chintzy with the caviar, too," Miriam replied.

"So tell him . . . tell him, darling."

"No, I just came in the door. I was at the club, playing racquetball," Frankie Gates said, in reply to her question. "How is everything going?"

"All right, but I'm dead on my feet," she answered. "These family assemblies are just too much. I'll be glad when they all leave. Have you heard any news from that Reinhardt?"

"Nothing. He's been questioning Harold's gambling buddies—the poker players and craps shooters—but none of those guys thinks your husband wrote up any big markers. They say he wasn't a real plunger."

"That's true, I guess," said Magda, carrying the phone to the bed, where she sat down next to somebody's blond sable coat. "Harold was never a smart gambler, but he did know when to quit."

"Jack still thinks his card playing is the key to the case, though."

"What about Harold's clients—all those crooks? Isn't he checking on them?"

"Yeah, but he's drawing blanks," said Gates. "A lot of them are behind bars, Magda."

"Listen, Frankie, something else occurred to me just tonight. Do you remember a couple of weeks ago—maybe a little more—we were sitting in the living-room and Harold's phone started ringing? And we heard him pick it up? You asked me if his being around bothered me, and I said it didn't. Remember?"

"Yeah, why?"

"Because unintentionally I happened to overhear part of his conversation that night. I was getting a Kleenex from the table by the double door, and I stood there listening for a minute. It was a peculiar phone call. Sounded like he was threatening somebody."

"Threatening in what way, Mag?"

"Harold said it was strictly a business deal, but that there wouldn't be any second chance if the person he was talking to crossed him up. Then he dropped hints about giving what he had to the media."

"Blackmail," Gates said, a strain of suppressed excitement in his voice. "Can you remember any more of the conversation?"

"No, that's it for the moment," said Magda. "But blackmail could be the answer, I suppose. It ties in with all that nonsense he was spouting just before he disappeared—that talk about landing a big political job and having his picture in the newspapers. Maybe Harold had the goods on one of the wheels at the State House, or one of the bosses at City Hall, and he was trying to use it as a lever to get what he wanted. The man had that kind of devious mind."

"Yeah, but evidently he tried it on the wrong guy. Did he mention any names while he was talking? Either on the phone or when he did his bragging?"

"No, not that I can recall. I'll keep prodding my memory, though, Frankie, and see if I can't stir up some more details. Look, why don't we discuss it tomorrow over a nice dinner? I need my spirits lifted."

"You're asking the right party. I'd rather lift your

spirits than do anything else in the world," said Gates gallantly.

"Aren't you sweet," she responded, pleased. "But you may have your work cut out for you, lover. I'm so weary and neurasthenic—even paranoid. This afternoon I imagined a guy was following me from Chestnut Hill. Crazy, huh?"

"You sure it was only your imagination, Magda?"

"Yes. Don't you start, darling. I turned off Beacon and sat there watching as he whizzed by in his Skylark—and he kept right on going, straight down past Coolidge Corner."

"Did you get a look at him?"

"Not really. He was just some ordinary man in a peaked cap. But if I see that tan car again, I'll recognize it."

They arranged to meet in town the next evening at seven o'clock, and after several more minutes conversation, said good-bye.

Feeling better, Magda returned to her guests.

29

At six-thirty the next morning the owner of the Suds for Duds discovered Osvaldo Peña's lifeless body on the Formica folding table. The police, once they arrived, had no trouble guessing what had happened when they saw the dessicated condition of the corpse and found the other shoe in the dryer.

"A new form of murder," the Eyewitness News announcer labeled it two hours later, as the television screen flashed shadowy pictures of the owner in his Laundromat, the fatal electric dryer, and the childlike body being carted away on a gurney.

Watching the newscast while eating his breakfast in South Boston, Gates was shaken. Later at the stationhouse he asked questions about the bizarre killing, but the Homicide cops had little solid information to offer. Peña's wallet was still in his pocket and none of the machines had been tampered with, so the motive hadn't been robbery.

One old-timer—a twenty-year veteran who'd been a friend of Gates's Uncle Dinny at Division 11—said with a certain amount of relish, "Lot of psychos cruise Tremont Street that hour of night, Frankie. Some guy probably just flipped him in there for fun, like that Swedish lady down Rutland Square who fried all those cats in her microwave oven. People get funny ideas in that part of town."

Gates had trouble believing it was a casual murder. Of the city's teeming thousands, why should Ossie—a witness to a homicide—be the one to get bumped? Maybe I should've told Reinhardt the kid's story earlier on, he thought, but I'll look real bad if I try to tell him now. And he'd probably go after Magda like a hungry hawk, because he's stymied.

30

Thinking that it was good to be doing something positive again, Frederick Pomerantz turned down Blagden Street and pulled into the curb alongside the Boston Public Library. As he switched the engine off he spied Gloag approaching through the smoked windshield, recognizing him immediately in the darkness, though his face was half hidden by the bill of his cap.

"He even walks like an animal," the investigator whispered to himself.

The door opened and Stanley climbed in. "Nice car, Fritz. What kind is it?" he said, removing his mittens and unzippering his corduroy jacket.

"An Omni. Not expensive, but for my type of work you can't drive something real ostentatious. You like the tinted windows? Nice, huh? I can park outside a subject's domicile all night long and the prowl cars don't even know somebody's in the vehicle."

"Not bad, not bad."

"It don't have excessive chrome, either, no whitewalls, no bumper stickers, no eye-catching emblems or decals. Anonymous, that's what you have to be. And I unscrew all the light bulbs—in the ceiling, the instrument panel, the radio. I can sit in one spot for hours, and the cops never notice. Starts real quiet, too."

"Beautiful. Got a CB radio also, huh?" said Gloag appreciatively. "The latest equipment."

"Absolutely. You have to, Stan. See this here? That's a rheostat for my headlights. Regulates the width of the beam—so, if I'm tailing a guy at night, I can make him think it's a different car every few miles just by twirling that knob."

"No fooling? Pretty nifty. I should get stuff like this myself."

"These days you got to be scientific in everything," said Pomerantz weightily. "You should see the photographic gear I have home—zoom lenses, infrared film, low-light movie cameras. This business ain't like it was formerly, when all you needed was a few hundred bucks for a license and the money to post a bond. You got to keep up with the competition—with the big agencies. And everything is so costly. Even a lousy Browning automatic can set you back four bills—and that's on sale out at Ivanhoe's in Watertown."

"I know what you mean, Fritzie. We got too much inflation in this country. Month ago I bought a switchblade. Three hundred and twenty-five dollars. Would you believe it? Never thought I'd have to spend that much for a knife. Of course, it's custom-made out of molybdenum stainless steel from Germany. They harden the blade with ice, temper it, then do all the grinding and polishing by hand. Gives you a good sharp edge, like an old-fashioned straight razor. And the button and the spring work real nice—a precision mechanism. But three and a quarter is a lot of dough for a shank. Used to be a guy down in Somers—twenty years he was doing for raping babies—who would make you a pretty reliable one for a pack of cigarettes."

"Yeah, it's crazy. And clients complain about my fees, or don't want to pay the expenses."

"So shove your Browning into their faces, Fritz. Can't beat a loaded gun when it comes to winning an argument. But you don't walk around carrying, do you?"

"Nah, nah. I ain't really much for firearms. I leave it

home in the safe, unless I'm out on a tricky assignment." Pomerantz smiled wistfully. "If I was good with guns, Stanley, I wouldn't have asked you over here tonight."

Gloag's droopy eyelids flickered. "Who is this guy? The one you want me to kill," he said, in the same tone of voice he used while discussing inflation.

The legal investigator opened his shearling car coat, made himself more comfortable on the seat, and said, "A smartass nigger down the South End. What would the price be? And remember, I'm an old friend from the neighborhood."

"Is he a big guy?"

"Kind of tall, yeah."

"What does he weigh?"

"Shit, I don't know. Two hundred, maybe. But you can handle him, Stanley. You're a professional. What's it going to cost me?"

Gloag pushed the peak of his cap up. "If I take the job, it'll run you four thousand. Usually I charge five."

"Wow. He's only a boogie."

"Yeah, but a big boogie. You have to go into the ghetto to bag a jig, and that increases the difficulties. And I guarantee my work, Fritzie. If he don't die, you don't pay."

"Sure, Stan. I ain't haggling," said the other man, averting his eyes. "If the price is four, four is what I'll pay. But there's one minor problem. I can't deliver the up-front money for a couple of days. By that time I'll have collected this fat fee I got coming to me, and when I do I'll call you and we'll arrange another meet. Okay? Speed is kind of important. I want the son of a bitch dead. He ripped me off on a deal. I guess I better finger him for you. They all look alike, and we don't want to make a mistake, do we?" A coarse laugh rattled in Pomerantz's throat.

"I never did the wrong guy in my life. That'd be as bad as a dentist yanking the wrong molar." Gloag folded and unfolded the heavy mittens in his lap, a meager smile on his thin lips. "But I'm not sure I can handle this for you, Fritz. At the moment I'm working on something else, and there's no way I can fill both contracts simultaneously."

"Shit. Well, I suppose a day or two ain't going to make all that much difference. Unless you want to do mine first. You know I'm good for the money."

"It wouldn't be right. My policy is, first come first served."

"Okay. Bump my guy after you bump his."

"Sounds logical, but it's impossible," said Stanley, continuing to watch his companion from under his drooping eyelids. "The situation is unusual. If I carry out the first contract, I won't be able to carry out the second."

Mystified, Pomerantz squinted at him. "Why not?"

"There's a conflict of interest involved. That's what you'd have to call it, I guess."

"I don't get it. How the hell can there be? We're talking about two totally differentiated transactions here."

"Well..." Gloag let the enigmatic syllable hang unsupported in the close warm air of the automobile for several seconds, before adding, "the thing is complicated."

"Sounds simple enough to me. Just a matter of priority, ain't it? I don't want to be inquisitive, Stan, but is this other guy you have to scrag somebody I know or what?"

"You know him, yeah. Funny coincidence, isn't it? The other murder contract is on you, Fritzie. So after I hit you, who's going to pay me for hitting the big dinge?"

The investigator's mouth jerked open. For a moment he stared at Gloag in disbelief, then he grinned and said, "Stanley, you got a weird sense of humor. But you always did, even back in the old days. A contract on *me*, for crying out loud. That's a good one. No more jokes, though, huh? I'm very serious about this thing."

"So am I," said the man in the cap. "It's no joke. I was going to go looking for you tomorrow, then you called me up and saved me some trouble."

The smile on Pomerantz's face gradually melted into a simper. "Jesus Christ! Come *on*, Stan. Quit kidding around," he implored.

His plea brought no reply, however. Evidently embarrassed, Gloag had ceased gazing at him. He continued to fold and unfold the leather mittens in his lap.

"Nobody's got a *reason* to want me killed. The only guy I owe is Alfie Jay, and he's been getting his dough right on time—like dividends from Smith Barney," said Pomerantz defiantly. "I don't have no enemies. I'm legitimate. I ain't even screwing somebody else's wife—so what the fuck are you *talking* about, Stanley?"

"You must've made a mistake somewhere along the line," Gloag said in a sympathetic voice, his eyelids masking the upper part of his eyes. "Give it a little thought, Fritz. Maybe it'll come to you."

"Holy Christ!" Pomerantz blurted out. "Delaunay!"

"Right—the whole story in a nutshell. Delaunay. You were seen in the wrong place at the wrong time, pal."

"Hey, Stan—*listen*. I got sucked into that deal. It wasn't my idea, I swear to God. This woman hired me to find her missing husband, so I started canvassing.... But you saw her—that day in the sub sandwich shop, when I bumped into you. Remember? The broad with the big boobs."

"Sure, I remember. Actually I'd been following the lady for a couple of hours, which is how I happened to be there. But I don't have time to listen to any long stories."

"I was just interrogating people in the neighborhood and—"

"Who cares, Fritzie? It's not important now. I've been paid to do you, and do you is what I'm going to do. For a minute there I did consider rearranging things—kill the dinge first, collect for the job, and then kill you—only it's too complicated. Besides, the Delaunays will probably reimburse me the extra four thousand when I explain how I'm saving them a lot more money. That fat fee you were talking about a little while ago—you were going to extort it out of them, weren't you? Sure. The boogie robbed you of the first shakedown payment, so you figured to collect another one in a couple of days. I'm really surprised you let yourself get mixed up in a grift like this. Why'd you do it?"

"My obligation to Alfie. That fucking vigorish was keeping me a pauper," Pomerantz answered huskily, as he scanned the dark street through the smoked windshield. There were neither pedestrians nor cars in sight, however. The public rarely used this tucked-away route, since it wasn't a shortcut to anywhere, which was why he had chosen the spot in the first place. "For chrissake, Stanley—I know you thirty years."

"This is the one I was telling you about," Gloag declared, producing a switchblade from within his corduroy jacket. "Three-hundred-twenty-five dollars. Cost almost as much as that Browning you didn't bring with you. But the grip is special, see? Genuine olive wood. The guy in the store said it comes from trees that grow out in the middle of the desert, said you need very dry conditions to get those beautiful black streaks in the grain. You want to recite a quick Our Father or anything, Fritz?"

"Thirty years. You slept over my house... we used to go to the movies together in Harvard Square every Saturday. You remember that? To the Uni—the old University Theater. We saw Pinocchio there. Remember, Stan? And you liked the part where all the little kids turned into donkeys and started—"

"Hey, snap out of it. Thirty years ago got nothing to do with this. You trying to con me?"

The investigator's eyes, teary and desperate, were fixed on the latch of the door.

Tonelessly Gloag said, "Don't even think about it. I'm too fast for you. Pin you to the seat before you ever got it open. As long as we're remembering, remember how I used to catch flies out of the air? See one buzzing by, and just grab it? I was the only kid in the neighborhood who could catch them between my thumb and my finger. You wouldn't stand a chance, Fritz." He pressed the button on his knife. It clicked smartly, and the long, thin, pointed blade leaped up from his fist like a jet of silver flame. "Everybody dies sooner or later."

"Listen, *listen.* I'll triple their price, Stan... give you fifteen K. Day after tomorrow I'll have it... or tomorrow night, if you're in a hurry," Pomerantz babbled, his lips glistening with saliva.

"I can't do that. Wouldn't be ethical. My reputation for reliability would suffer. You can't double cross your customers."

"Be reasonable, Stanley—*please.* Fifteen thousand. You can return their money, give them an excuse. Nobody's going to report you to the Better Business Bureau."

"Impossible. We're wasting time. You're in a no-parking zone here. Any minute a cop might come along and tell you to move, and that could cause me unnecessary headaches."

"I'll make it an even twenty thousand. How's that? Twenty thousand. Why should you... I mean we're old friends... from the Clay Pits in North Cambridge... it ain't right... and those fucking Delaunays... they're strangers... don't mean nothing to you. Why don't we become partners, Stanley? How about that? Hey, we could really shake them for a bundle, milk them...."

"No, we couldn't. I'm no blackmailer, Fritzie. You know that. And I can't let you off, either."

Pomerantz licked his lips, then wiped his mouth with the back of a hand. "Okay... okay. So don't let me off. Break my arm... my leg... break my jaw. But for chrissake don't kill me, Stanley. You don't have to—"

"What are you talking about? That's what they hired me for, and I accepted their money. You're getting delirious, pal. In my profession you got to maintain high standards, because there's a lot at stake—matters of life and death, right? Stop acting hysterical. You got nothing to be scared of. I'm an expert. Twenty minutes I spent sharpening this thing on my diamond blade-sharpener. The point's like a needle, and both edges have been honed as fine as a razor. You won't hardly notice you're being cut. Think of it as a kind of surgery. Or acupuncture, maybe. Good-bye, Fritzie."

"Break my leg!" Pomerantz wailed hoarsely, shrinking down in the seat.

But the hand that held the dagger had already begun its deadly journey. In a short horizontal arc it swung, passed between the unzippered flaps of the shearling coat and banged against the investigator's chest with a loud thump. Though it struck a rib, the custom-made knife glanced off that rounded surface and penetrated to the hilt. A gasp burst from the stricken man's gaping mouth.

Stanley Gloag calmly watched his victim's eyes snap shut and his moustached head fall forward, felt him shudder and collapse, saw the plump pale hand slip lazily from the steering wheel.

"Now that didn't hurt, did it? Went straight into your heart, Fritz," the assassin said, and released a pent-up breath.

He drew the blood-drenched weapon from the dying Pomerantz—it scraped softly against the rib—and paused warily to listen to a distant sound. Someone was coming. Crouching, he turned his head and saw two well-dressed men approaching on foot from the direction of Copley

Square, advancing at a leisurely pace and conversing in a cadent undertone.

Gloag froze, holding the dripping knife between his legs to keep the blood off his clothing. His face was empty, but his cowled eyes gleamed like embers in the darkness.

The interlopers drew near. He could see them quite distinctly—one in a gray topcoat with the collar up, the other in a fashionable suede jacket.

"...how she ever keeps that beautiful figure, because she eats like a pig," the closer of the two was saying in a clear crisp voice. "I took her to the DuBarry over on Newbury Street and the bill came to ninety-seven dollars. She ate everything but the tablecloth, and guzzled a whole bottle of sparkling Burgundy. The girl must've fasted for a week before that meal, but I still don't know..."

The words faded as the strollers, having passed the parked Omni without so much as a casual glance at it, moved farther away.

"Thank God for the tinted windows," Stanley whispered as he wiped his switchblade clean on Frederick Pomerantz's flannel trousers. Then he closed it up, stuck it back in his pocket, donned his mittens, opened the car door and got out.

31

When the patrolman who had been writing up parking violations in the Copley Square area that morning peeped through the tinted glass window of the Dodge Omni and spied the crumpled figure with the mahogany-brown blot on its shirt front, he growled an oath, slammed his ticket book shut, tucked it in his trouser pocket, and wondered bitterly why these things always happened when he was about to go off to Dunkin Donuts for his second breakfast. Yet being a dutiful public servant, he called headquarters on his walkie-talkie and then stood around stamping his feet in the cold wind while waiting for the experts to show up.

Within ten minutes a Homicide unit of two detectives,

one photographer, and one forensic technician arrived, and a small crowd gathered as they went to work hunting clues. Nothing of value was found, though—no fingerprints, strands of hair, cigarette butts, or tell-tale personal belongings. A gangland killing, that was the off-the-cuff conclusion drawn by this team of violent death specialists—an opinion that received additional support when it was later learned that the victim knew a number of Cambridge and Somerville hoodlums and owed a pile of money to a North End loan shark.

Gates and his colleagues in the Burglary Squad heard all about this crime, but since Frankie didn't know of any connection between the Gilmans and the murdered private detective, Pomerantz's death held no significance for him.

What occupied his mind as he drove away from the station house to see a complainant that morning was the phone conversation Magda had overheard weeks before—the conversation in which Harold seemed to be threatening somebody. Remembering those papers the murderess had been looking at just before she pulled the gun, he couldn't help but think that they were the reason for the killing. Could they have been photographs? He should have asked Ossie more questions when he had the chance. Maybe Magda should mention the blackmail call to Reinhardt. It wouldn't do any harm, and it might put him on the right track.

Gates had begun to get leery about the whole business. Peña's brutal slaying—his lungs, the Medical Examiner said, were so dry they were like leather pouches—nagged at him. Aside from everything else, the kid probably confessed to his tormentor—told him all that he had witnessed and how he had passed the information along to a detective named Gates.

I'll have to watch my ass, Frankie thought as he parked his Mercury on Fayette Street. The murderess and the husky guy who helped her might be getting desperate. A pity I can't tell Homicide Peña's story, but with him dead now, they'd come down on me pretty hard. I'd end up back in uniform. And the bastards would still go after Magda. She and I ought to search Harold's apartment, see if we can't find that blackmail evidence and turn it over to Reinhardt. Jack could use some fresh clues.

The complainant, a waitress named Lily Spritzer, lived on Cortes Street. He knocked at the door of her ground-floor flat, and she opened it promptly and greeted him with an arch smile.

"Sweet of you to come over so fast, officer," said the plump blonde in a flowery housecoat that didn't quite extend to her bare knees. "This is the third time. I really hate to bother you fellows, but what else can I do?"

High heels clattering on the worn, carpeted floor, she guided him along a hall to a disordered living room. Gates cast a swift professional glance at the clothing dumped on the drab sectional sofa, the jimmied suitcase and the tipped-over standard lamp with the dented cardboard shade.

"Lose much?" he asked.

"My twelve-inch TV, my steam iron, my hair dryer, clock radio, costume jewelry. Took a pair of new shoes, too—and, oh yeah, three bottles of Gordon's gin. It's those winos from the alley out back, like I told you the last time. They hop up on a garbage can, climb the fire escape, and sneak in that bedroom window."

"Was it locked?"

"Sure, but the wood is rotten. That lock ain't worth a damn."

"I thought you were going to have an iron grill installed?"

"Yeah, well I was—only the sharpy there on Berkeley Street wants sixty bucks to do the job. Cash. Jesus, Detective Gates, it's cheaper to get burglarized. Anyway, they took the best stuff the first time. I ain't got too much to lose these days. Come here, let me show you," she said, grabbing his arm and pulling him into the adjoining room. "See? Those are the thieves right there, so why can't you guys get rid of them?"

Frankie looked out the uncurtained window and saw a half-dozen grubby individuals clustered around a fire in a perforated ashcan on the pavement of the building's wide-open backyard. He nodded, shrugged his shoulders and said he would ask the uniformed men who worked that sector to cruise the alley a few times a day, to chase the bums and discourage them from gathering there.

While he was speaking, a noisy quarrel suddenly developed among the coterie of derelicts below. Four or five of the group had surrounded a bearded man in a sort of imitation cowboy hat and were shoving and poking him in a manifestly hostile manner. The target of this aggression put up a vigorous defense, however, and soon the whole assembly collapsed on the littered asphalt in a wriggling tangle of arms, heads, and legs.

"I'd better go down there," said Gates unenthusiastically. "Otherwise somebody's liable to get a fractured skull."

Lily Spritzer thanked him for coming, showed him to the door, and returned to the window to watch the comedy.

Reaching the alley by means of the cellar exit, he found the battle proceeding at a fast and furious clip. Grunts and curses filled the air, and now and then a bleary-eyed face, unshaven and wine-red in color, would stare out from the knot of writhing bodies.

"Break it up, you fucking grease bags. This isn't the Boston Garden," the detective snarled, kicking a broad rump in dirty denim which projected from the slithering heaving huddle.

The recipient of this boot, a roly-poly vagabond, tore himself from the melee, and giving Gates a why-don't-you-mind-your-own-business glare, waddled off in the direction of the street. The other combatants paid him no heed, however, and he was obliged to kick several more backsides before the lacework of thrashing limbs finally unraveled and the scrimmage came to its inconclusive and inglorious end.

The winos skulked away—all of them, that is, except the bearded individual who had been at the bottom of the pile. Apparently uninjured, he rose to his feet in an unhurried manner and said cheerfully, "Thanks, Lieutenant, you saved my life. Them bozos wanted to steal my seven dollars, and I wasn't going to give it up to them unless they killed me."

Only then did Gates recognize the bearded warrior as Whitey Frainer, though this recognition brought him no joy. "Can't you stay out of trouble?" he said crankily. "I keep bumping into you. Why don't you hop a freight and go to California for the winter?"

"Why should I hop a freight? I got an automobile."

Whitey dusted himself off, picked up his tawdry cowboy hat, wiped the wide brim on the sleeve of his khaki coat, and jammed it down on his shaggy crown. "If I got a car, why should I hop a freight?"

"Listen, somebody in your social circle has been robbing apartments in that building over there—committing burglaries to pay for his Zinfandel—so now none of you Boy Scouts can camp out here anymore. Pass the word, Whitey."

"Wasn't me, Lieutenant. I don't steal. I only spare-change people—you know, lean on my crutch and buzz the nine-to-fivers. Today the heater in my car is busted and I got no place to go because the library don't open till twelve."

"Tough shit."

"Maybe I can sneak in that empty house over by the Fens, the spooky dump where I seen that bozo throw the cut-off head in the fire. Or maybe I can hang around the bus station for a while, if that tough security guard ain't—"

"Wait a minute. What cut-off head?"

"The one I told you about—on Cambridge Street that day. Don't you remember, Lieutenant? But the new security guard down the Greyhound station is a rough customer. Last time I went there—"

"When was it that you saw this guy throw the head in the fire?"

"When? I don't know, two, three weeks back. Me and Samantha had a little party in this empty house by the Fens, drank a bottle Cossack and some peppermint schnapps. Later on I woke up because it was so hot. Figured Samantha turned the thermostat too—"

"You were probably dreaming. You sure it was a human head?"

Frainer stroked his matted beard. "I seen it as clear as I see you, Lieutenant. Guy chucked it in the fireplace...along with the cut-off hands. A big bozo, he was, wearing a white sweater and a fedora hat."

"And you weren't hallucinating, Whitey? Weren't tripping on acid or having the jimjams, like with the red buffaloes?"

"They weren't red. They was gray, like rats."

"I want you to show me that house," said the detective,

pulling him away from the warmth and comfort of the ashcan. "We'll go there right now."

"Yeah, okay," Frainer answered submissively, looking even more dazed and muddled than he did normally.

Hoping to dilute the bum's distinctive personal aroma with some fresh air, Gates drove with the windows open. It was a cold journey, but thankfully not a long one. Whitey unhesitatingly directed him to a three-story brownstone building, set back behind an ancient cast-iron paling and a dense overgrown hedge of hawthorn and not too far from the Museum of Fine Arts. With its ivy-covered walls and tall windows masked by weathered sheets of plywood, it could have been the set for a low-budget horror movie, Frankie thought wryly.

A rusty chain and padlock secured the front gate, but a driveway ran through a tunnel of bushes on one side of the property, which led to a small clearing at the back. There they parked and got out. Beyond a stand of sumac trees and shrubbery the ice-filmed waters of the Fen were visible. They proceeded to enter the enclosed area through a gap in the iron palisade—a gap created by the corrosion-induced collapse of a ten-foot section.

"Spooky, ain't it?" said Frainer. "And it's worse at night."

"How did you ever find this mausoleum?"

"Accidental, that's how. Me and another fellow were having a nice conversation on the other side there by the Victory Garden—we was popping phenies and chugging Gallo—and I guess I sort of blacked out. It was in the summertime, over by the Garden. Anyway, when I woke up I was in this crazy house laying on a pile of broken plaster and wallpaper and stuff. Don't remember how I got there, but it must've been through the cellar window. See it, Lieutenant? The little window . . . under the bush."

Gates looked in the direction the wino was pointing and saw a horizontal casement set in the granite foundation. There were others—three more, at least—on that side of the house, but this was the only one that hadn't been boarded up.

Frainer said, "So after that I started coming here—especially in the winter—because it was better than sleeping in a hot doorway or on a vent. But I never left no bottles around or nothing. I'll show you how we can crawl inside. It's real easy. I'll show you."

"I'm tempted," said Gates. "But officers of the law are supposed to do things legally, and I don't have a search warrant."

'Oh. What do you need a thing like that for? You're a policeman."

"Never mind, Whitey. It's too complicated to explain. Let's take a quick look around the outside, though."

For ten minutes they circled the old brownstone, checking the front entrance, the back porch, and the two outbuildings. Gates made several efforts to peek through the cracks that bordered the plywood shields, but could discover nothing of interest in the gloomy, dilapidated rooms.

They returned to town. He dropped the aromatic Frainer off at the public library and went on to West Newton Street to interview a shopkeeper who had been held up at gunpoint the night before.

After that he telephoned the Real Estate Assessment Office at City Hall and was informed by a helpful woman that the residence at 987 The Fenway belonged to Timothy K. Dunn of 868 Rodney Street in Brighton. He copied the address down and went to have his lunch at a delicatessen on Massachusetts Avenue.

Then Gates checked in at the station house, where he did some paperwork and ran through the Master Name Index file. Timothy K. Dunn was not listed. While he was busy at his desk, Pete Grandi, who was handling the Peña murder case, showed up, and the two of them talked for a while over a cup of coffee.

At four o'clock he drove to 868 Rodney Street, which turned out to be a triple-decker house badly in need of new shingles and a fresh coat of paint. The hall and the stairway had a rancid smell. Names and initials were scratched on the plaster walls, and the rickety banister was missing a lot of its balusters. Timothy K. Dunn lived on the top floor, but no one came to the door, despite Frankie's repeated knocking.

32

Missy Delaunay, smelling strongly of musk, shook a cigarette out of her pack of Benson & Hedges, thrust it in her mouth, lit it with a throwaway lighter, and said, "Who's the gink up there, Stan?"

Gloag followed her gaze to a framed sepia print that hung over the back of the bar. "Nikolai Lenin," he said. "Founder of Russian Communism. Don't you recognize him?"

"No, why should I? What kind of joint is this, anyway?"

"It's a place where a lot of revolutionaries and freethinkers congregate. I kind of like it." Gloag nodded at the plastic Lord & Taylor bag and asked, "Is the whole ten there?"

"Sure. Do you think I'd shortchange you?" She smiled at him sweetly. "I'm beginning to feel like a bank messenger, carrying cash all over the damned city. To raise this tidy sum, I had to sell three hundred shares of Raytheon stock my father gave me ages ago."

"You wanted the job done, didn't you?"

"Yeah, only I didn't expect to have to fork over an extra five thousand. Explain that part to me again, Stanley."

"The guy asked me to snuff this jig for him, and to pay for the contract he was going to squeeze another twenty out of you. But I rejected the deal, girlie, which saved you all that loot. Turning him down, though, cost me five grand, so it's only fair you reimburse me, right?"

"I guess."

"You're still fifteen thousand ahead. Why make faces?"

"I'm not making faces, you savage. Did you remember to ask him about the photos?"

"I was going to, but then he started doing a lot of sentimental rambling and I forgot. Slipped my mind. Was it important?"

"My brother thought so," said Missy, blowing smoke in the general direction of Lenin. "However, Phil didn't help with the financial arrangements, so to hell with him. All that's important as far as I'm concerned is that that sleazeball private detective is dead. I can hardly believe you did it, Stan. The papers say you jabbed him only once. Why'd you let him off so easy?"

"Hey, Missy, you're talking a little loud—and in my business it doesn't pay to advertise," Gloag warned her softly. "The hit was nice and clean. Did you want me to slice him to ribbons?"

"Yeah, would've been terrific," she answered, imitating his sepulchral drawl.

"I'd've had to charge you extra for that—especially since he was an old friend of mine."

"Ha, ha! Getting soft-hearted, Stanley Gloag?" Doffing her beret, she tossed it on the seat of the booth. "An old friend—that's a riot." She straightened the lengths of her ropy hair into rough parallels, drank a mouthful of vodka and tonic, puffed on the cigarette, and continued in her mildly railing tone, "How come you weren't able to recover any of the blackmail money from that sneaky rat, your old friend? Did you check his wallet?"

A scowl of revulsion deformed Gloag's spare mouth. "Of course not. You think I steal from the dead? That I'm a ghoul? Besides, the man was broke. Didn't I just get done explaining that he was going to extort more dough from you so he could pay my fee for hitting the dinge? The way I figure it, he didn't get to keep the money you handed over to him in that housing project. The dinge must've seen what was happening there, and afterwards muscled poor Fritz out of the paper bag—which is why Fritz wanted him whacked. Last night I noticed a bruise on his cheek, the kind of lump you get when you've been mugged."

"Serves him right, but it would've been nice to retrieve some of that twenty thousand. When are you going to do the other one?"

"Soon. She's not alone very often, and that makes it more of a problem. The opportunity will come, though," said Stanley, noisily opening a bag of potato chips. "You like this place?"

Missy sucked on the Benson & Hedges and looked around. The other customers were a shabby lot—serious, long-haired types, hunched over steins of flat beer in the unpretentious wooden booths. "It's okay, I guess. Everybody here looks as if they're plotting to overthrow the government."

"They probably are—and why not?" said Gloag, offering her the potato chips. "I'm thinking of overthrowing it myself."

"You?"

"Yes, girlie—me. Know how I'd do it?"

"Can't imagine, Stanley. Tell me."

Gloag lifted his stein and drank some beer, wiped his mouth with a paper napkin and explained, "First, I'd set up a jailbreak on a large scale—spring all the cons at Walpole. Then, using these guys as troops, I'd storm the other prisons here in the Northeast—Thomaston, Cranston, the Concord Reformatory, Somers, Ossining, Attica—start a chain reaction. In a month I'd have an enormous army, an army of real hard, ruthless people, an army of experts in crime, gunmen, bomb makers, counterfeiters, drug dealers, burglars, forgers, knife fighters, poisoners, arsonists, conmen, safecrackers—"

"The crème de la crème," Missy said, chewing a potato chip.

"Exactly. And we'd have representatives of the straight professions, too. Plenty of lawyers in the can, and doctors, bankers, social workers, politicians, stockbrokers, clergymen, business executives, engineers." A faint impish grin formed on Gloag's pallid face. "Eventually we'd crack every jug in the country. Picture it, Missy—a whole army of convicts. Be like the movie *Spartacus*. No fooling. And after, we'd invade Canada and Mexico and South America and Europe—set all the prisoners free in those countries, too."

"And you'd be the leader?"

"Right. Field Marshal Stanley Gloag."

"Lovely—and you'd establish a world government of crooks and gangsters. But how would that be different from the kind of governments we have now, Spartacus?"

"Well, our guys wouldn't be a bunch of lying hypocrites, for one thing. We'd be honest chiselers. All the corruption would be up front and out in the open. I believe the common man is ready for that sort of government. They've always had a lot of secret admiration and respect for bona fide bandits, hustlers like Robin Hood,

Jesse James, Al Capone, Bonnie and Clyde, John Dillinger."

"I suppose you'd steal from the rich and give to the poor."

"You think so, Missy? I don't know. We'd steal from the rich, all right, because they happen to be the ginks with the money, but I doubt if we'd hand over any of the boodle to the poor. Wouldn't be a realistic economic policy. If you give it to the have-nots, they become the haves, and you have to swipe the money a second time. My legislature would never go for an idea like that. After all, when you stop and consider it, what have the poor ever done for anybody?"

"That's true, Stan. You're not as crazy as you sound," the blond woman declared, pressing the glass of vodka and tonic to her hard-painted lips.

Gloag watched her out of half-closed eyes. "Pretty good plan, huh? I'd be King of the World."

"Sure. And now that we have these space ships and everything, you might even become Emperor of the Universe."

"Why not? What I meet I master—because I never give in, never give out, and—"

"Never give up," she finished for him, giggling. "I take it back about your not being crazy. You're a twenty-four-karat cuckoo, Stanley Gloag."

"That's what they said about Genghis Khan when he first started raiding," he replied, smiling inscrutably. "Hey, why don't we go over to my house in Cambridge and have some fun?"

"Your house? Really? What about your poor old granny?" Missy asked, snuffing her cigarette in a tinfoil ashtray.

"No problem. She sleeps on the top floor and doesn't hear too well," said Gloag, slipping his hand under the table to caress his companion's warm thigh. "Anyhow, we'll go down the cellar, where I have this little room all fixed up."

"The cellar?"

"Sure. You'll love it. Kind of weird, if you know what I mean."

"Do I ever," she said, her blue eyes growing rounder and brighter."Off to Grandmother's house. I feel like little Red Riding Hood. And you, you loony—you must be the hungry wolf."

"Why not?" Gloag retorted, signaling the waiter for his check.

33

Each morning after her breakfast Magda Gilman looked at the *Boston Globe,* but she only read the front page, the entertainment section, and the business news, therefore she never came across the small article dealing with the sudden demise of Frederick Pomerantz. Even if she had, however, it's unlikely that she would have connected that murder with the one of her husband.

Two nights later, she and Gates dined at Locke-Ober's, and afterwards they wandered off to the financial district, ending up in a vulgar little café where they danced and drank until one in the morning.

Since the funeral party the widow had been unusually cheerful, and on this occasion she seemed gayer than ever. Her delighted escort was favored with frequent hugs and kisses, and all his remarks and jokes were laughed at whether they were funny or not.

Gates, the more sober of the pair, did the driving when they returned to Brookline. They had used her Cadillac because his Mercury still reeked of Whitey Frainer's pungent spoor. The detective hadn't mentioned the house in the Fens to her because he hadn't spoken to the owner yet. For the moment the wino's revelation remained only a possibility—and a long-shot possibility at that.

"I need Perrier, darling," Magda declared when they were a block from the Allerton Arms. "Stop at the store on the corner there, like a good boy, and buy me a couple of chilled bottles so I shouldn't have to drink that chlorinated tap water."

He veered left and double-parked. "Go on ahead. I'll meet you in the garage," he said.

"Okay, lover. don't be long," she answered, and kissed him on his rugged chin.

He responded manfully by running his hand over her

breast, but she pushed him away with a laugh, and he got out of the automobile.

The convenience store was virtually empty, so Gates required only a minute to accomplish his mission. Walking briskly, he crossed the street and entered the towering building's underground parking area by the pedestrian side door. The place was warm and quiet. Before he had gone more than a few steps, though, the stillness abruptly exploded in a clamor of shattering glass.

At once the detective's flinty gray eyes swiveled in all directions, and when they lit on the convex ceiling mirror that warned of cars emerging from the hidden aisle angling off to the right, he saw a strange scene reflected there in curved miniature. The Gilman Cadillac was parked in its usual spot, but next to it stood a slender man in a peaked cap who was busily smashing one of its side windows.

Gates set his bottles of Perrier on the floor and raced around the bend. Grabbing the brazen vandal by his raised arm, he flung him violently against the garage wall and yelled, "What the fuck are you doing?"

"What does it look like I'm doing?" countered Stanley Gloag, annoyed by this rough and unexpected interruption.

From within the damaged automobile, Magda called shrilly, "He's got a knife, Frankie!"

"You asshole!" Gates roared, lunging at him.

But in his anger he failed to perceive the connecting rod in the slender man's fist, and now this heavy implement came slashing down on the detective's onrushing skull. Only good instinctive reflexes saved him from destruction. At the last millisecond Gates ducked and the bludgeon glanced off his left shoulder, sending a streak of pain the length of his arm.

Gloag smiled grimly and came forward to attack again. Dodging and feinting, Gates retreated until the automobile brought him to a halt. The connecting rod whizzed past his ear and bashed an irregular basin in the gleaming surface of the Cadillac's hood. Behind him Magda screamed.

Fumbling to unbutton his topcoat in order to draw the Colt .38 Special on his hip, Frankie crouched low and tried to escape to a less constricted area, but the third blow came in on him almost horizontally, missing him only because he lurched frantically to one side and shrank gainst the car door. This time, however, his overanxious ssailant swung too hard, lost his balance for an instant, nd left himself open to retaliation. Frankie whacked him n the rib cage with a roundhouse right.

Gasping softly, Gloag, his heavy-lidded eyes aglint with genuine appreciation, rasped, "Nice move, pal."

Gates succeeded in unbuttoning the lower part of his opcoat, jerked the revolver out, aimed and pulled the rigger. But as the hammer fell on the cartridge, the onnecting rod struck the gun's short barrel. Well wide of ts mark, the slug hit the garage wall and spit chips of oncrete. Almost simultaneously the Colt Special sailed off nto the shadowy region behind the Cadillac.

"Hey, you're a cop," said Stanley Gloag, surprised.

Without bothering to affirm or deny this, Gates kicked him in the shin. While the slender man was still grimacing, e seized his wrist and shoved him backwards, knocking the ron bludgeon from his hand by savagely smashing it against he concrete wall. It fell to the floor with a hollow clank.

Pivoting, Gloag did his best to ram his knee into the etective's groin. When this failed because of an interposed high, he drove his head into the other battler's snarling, raggy face. Gates saw stars, but didn't give an inch.

Locked together in a tight embrace, the two men anced along the wall, each seeking to gain an edge. Fists nd elbows flailed, striking cartilage, flesh, teeth, bone. For moment Frankie had a good grip on his opponent's hroat, but a thumb thrust in his eye caused him such earing anguish that he finally had to let go. Capitalizing n this momentary advantage, Gloag ground the heel of is palm into the detective's already bleeding nose.

They lost their footing and toppled over. Gloag's peaked ap cartwheeled into the darkness. Thrashing about on he hard floor like epileptic Siamese twins, they tore at ach other's skin and clothing.

Twice Gates felt sure he had his adversary pinned, and wice he found he was mistaken, the second time after eceiving a crocodilian bite on the forearm. This new njury, added to the bashed nose, near-blinded eye, and apidly stiffening left shoulder, caused him to wonder if e was overmatched. There was something inhuman about he wiry man—inhuman or superhuman or subhuman.

Earlier in the evening the detective had happily consumed seven or eight Johnnie Walker Blacks, and now this aged alcohol had begun to exact a toll on him. His lungs were on fire and he couldn't suck in enough air to cool them off because of his blood-clogged nostrils.

Back and forth they rolled on the grimy concrete. Then, with his remaining good eye, Gates glimpsed the white convenience-store bag no more than a yard away, sitting exactly where he had left it an eon ago. If he could just wrap his fingers around the neck of one of those Perrier bottles, he would bring the brawl to a satisfactory end in a hurry.

Breaking loose, he scrambled towards the paper sack—but swift as he was, he wasn't swift enough. Gloag overtook him like a mongoose, and now in his hand he held a double-edged stiletto—sharp as a razor, bright as a laser.

Frankie only had time to flop over on his back and grab the fist that clutched the knife. Seized by the hair, forcibly twisted to one side, he could see little more than Gloag's triumphant countenance. But somehow he knew that the point of the steel blade was beneath his chin at no considerable distance from his throat.

"You're dead," Stanley declared, grinning down at him.

"You're full of shit," said Gates defiantly, through gritted teeth.

Nevertheless, his confidence had begun to ebb with his strength. To keep the knife from his Adam's apple he had the use of only one hand, since the other, his left, had gotten tangled and snared in the loose flap of his topcoat. And while Gloag wasn't any better off in this respect, he could at least bring his body weight to bear on the single hand that held the weapon. Still the detective refused to quit, and the stalemate persisted for a minute that seemed like half an hour. Then, remembering Magda helpless in the Cadillac, he summoned his final reserves of energy and gradually compelled the fist and dagger to deviate an inch or two from its lethal path.

Stanley Gloag, the sinews of his neck grotesquely enlarged by his mighty exertions, released his opponent's hair and brought this other hand up to reinforce the one already clutching the switchblade. Suddenly the knife straightened out again—and an instant later, it resumed ts slow yet inexorable descent.

But Gates, his head free, now had more slack for naneuver. In desperation he twisted his body violently ınd heaved like a bucking horse. Taken by surprise, Gloag vas thrown in the air—and as he came down again, Frankie shoved him aside, and nimbly crawled on top of he knife wielder. Their situations were suddenly reversed. Now it was Stanley who lay supine on the concrete floor, vhile his intended victim sat astride him with a mad leer of exultation on his rough, mantled face. Moreover, the letective still had a grip on Gloag's fist and, when he rought his left hand up to assist his right, he improved nis position even further. Though he himself didn't hold he dagger, he now had some control of its use.

Staring fixedly into his foe's hooded eyes, he promptly et about redirecting the deadly weapon's orientation. Little by little he forced its twinkling tip to turn. Like a hin accusing finger of doom, and slow as the minute ıand of a clock, the blade rotated around and down until t pointed at a spot in the middle of its owner's smooth erspiring brow.

Four inches from annihilation, Gloag grinned confidently. I never lose, pal," he said, and proceeded to make yet nother strenuous attempt to regain possession of his ustom-crafted stiletto.

For tense moments the knife hung in a state of perfect quilibrium between the two straining antagonists. Then apidly weakening and unable to continue the struggle eyond another few seconds, the final driblet of Stanley Gloag's formidable physical prowess abruptly drained away.

The long bright blade fell, piercing his forehead with o more difficulty than if it had been a ripe casaba and nking straight in up to its S-shaped hilt. He did not utter sound, but his eyes widened malevolently. Then the rown irises rolled diagonally down towards the bridge of is nose, leaving the rest of the socket filled with white.

Gates, the breath rattling in his scalded lungs, drew his naking hands back and contemplated the dead man's allid cross-eyed face. "Dumb son of a bitch," he muttered onelessly.

The grin faded from Gloag's thin lips. Then his hands,

too, relaxed and slipped off the olive-wood handle of the weapon. Down his cheeks they glided and onto the zippered front of his corduroy jacket—but they stayed there fleetingly for flexed muscles in the arms slowly wrenched them apart. Not until the limp fingers touched his shoulders did they at last come to rest.

To Frankie Gates it looked as if his savage enemy were making the sign of the cross. He shuddered and got drunkenly to his feet. Staggering to the Cadillac, he saw that Magda was gone. Above the rasp of his labored breathing he heard the low sound of sobbing, however and soon discovered the woman behind the automobile on her hands and knees.

"What are you doing?"

"The gun . . . I'm looking for that damned gun, you Irish schlump," she answered brokenly, tears streaming down her face. "Did you think I was putting air in the tires?"

He lifted the woman up and held her to him.

"I was halfway out of the car . . . he came at me with that . . . that bayonet," she whimpered. "My God, my God He wanted to kill me, I could see it in his eyes, Frankie And there was nobody else around . . . not a soul. So jumped back inside and locked the door . . . and he got a . . . an iron tool or something and started smashing the window. Frankie, I couldn't run . . . I couldn't move . . . couldn even scream. I was petrified, Frankie."

"Yeah, Mag—but everything's okay now," said Gates gently, wiping the tears from her cheeks with a bloody hand. "Guy's dead. That knife . . . it went right in his brain Died instantly. There's nothing to worry about now, Magda Come on. I've got to phone the Brookline police."

They entered the office and there found the garage attendant under his metal desk. The dark blood had already begun to coagulate on his mouth and chin, and two knife wounds were plainly visible in the vicinity of his hear

Later the investigating detectives came across a pair of lead-weighted leather mittens on the workbench and examined them with interest.

"A good job that punk didn't have them on," commente one. "If he had, the Boston guy would be the stiff going the freezer now."

34

The black headline was sprawled across three columns in the upper right-hand corner of the *Globe's* Metro/Region page.

DETECTIVE KILLS THUG WITH
OWN KNIFE IN BROOKLINE

The moment she saw it, Missy intuitively comprehended what it meant, but she read on, and her face wrinkled. Halfway through the article she crushed the newspaper between her hands and flung it down into her brother's lap.

"Shit, shit, shit!"

Phil Delaunay said rancorously, "You knew about it, didn't you? Even though I gave you strict instructions not to, you went ahead and arranged this... this piece of insanity."

"That bitch, Magda. First Gabriel, now Stanley. She's trying to destroy me. I hate her guts. She won't be satisfied till I kill myself. And all you can talk about is your instructions."

"Did you pay him?"

She swept the snakelocks of blond hair away from her unhappy face and wiped her eyes with the knuckles of both hands like a child. "Somebody had to do something, Phil."

"You're a maniac, Missy. That woman isn't a blackmailer. Even Kevin says so. She's rich as Croesus. Did you make out a check to this gangster? Did you put anything in writing? A letter? Note? Phone number?"

"No," she answered. Her wet eyes shone with malice. "But I've been seen with him. We went around together, and met lots of people we both knew. I suppose the cops will dig that up."

"Wonderful, Melissa. Icing on the cake," Delaunay exclaimed, rising suddenly to his feet and sending the *Globe* catapulting across the floor. "What's wrong with you? There's one homicide investigation going on already.

Jesus, Mary, and Joseph, do you have a death wish?"

"Maybe, Phil." She slipped a cigarette in her mouth. "Maybe."

"Well, leave me out of it. Last week I heard that Everett Wheeler's playing the bloodhound, too." Delaunay's handsome face was ravaged by anxiety. "He's got two eager Harvard Law students poking into my private affairs—searching records, newspaper files, checking my fund-raising activities, my real estate transactions, interviewing my worst enemies. An Achilles' heel is what they're after. This morning Al Pinelli called me to say that one of the dirty little bastards—a kid named Travis Trumbull—tried to obtain copies of my Federal Income Tax returns from him. Claimed he had a right to them under the Freedom of Information Act. Thank God Al is no ninny. He tossed the guy out the front door."

Missy pulled the cigarette from between her pale lips. "If you're so worried about Everett Wheeler, you'll never be able to defeat him. Might as well quit now, Phil, let him have the nomination."

"Quit? I will like hell! I'm going to clobber that skunk, Melissa—no matter what unprincipled extralegal tricks he employs to libel and slander me. I'm going to cream the son of a bitch. I'll get that nomination. And I'm going to win and go to Washington." Delaunay didn't look as confident as he sounded, however. "We have to be very circumspect, use our heads, not take foolish chances. That Trumbull even phoned Agnes the other day—wanted to know if we still owned the building on Fairfield Street—Heywood Hall. Of course, she hung up on him. All the same..."

Missy wandered to the window and contemplated the cars crawling by on Storrow Drive eight floors below. "What can Wheeler find?" she inquired, smoke seeping from her shapely nose.

"The photographs and the negatives, perhaps, or this connection of yours with a professional murderer."

"That bitch is the only person who could possible have those pictures. Harold was her husband, wasn't he? Don't be such a thickhead, Phil. Have Kevin kill her, and your worries will be over."

"Missy, I'm not a murderer. I'm a civilized human being."

"You'd do it, if you weren't afraid."

"It's not a question of... of bravery. It's a question of common sense. Look what happened to your chum there." Delaunay pointed the toe of his black, pebble-grained oxford at the rumpled newspaper. "Even a vicious, sleazy hoodlum like him—"

"Don't go bad-mouthing Stanley Gloag. I had real tender feelings for that man. Only a couple of nights ago we were together... at his house."

"Ain't love grand. Well, if the police come around and ask you about him, I hope—"

"Stanley was very brave—a better man than you are, Phil. Better in every way."

"—I hope you'll be smart enough to tell them you hardly knew the guy, and that you never suspected he was a criminal."

Exhaling smoke at the windowpane, she said, "Maybe I will... and maybe I won't."

"I sometimes think you've gone soft in the head, Melissa, you talk such irrational drivel," Delaunay snapped, matching the venom in her voice with a few drops of his own. "Those expensive shrinks never did you any good. Neither did all that booze you drank, the greenies you popped, and the coke you snorted. Stuff fried your brain, and now you're getting schizoid."

"Go fuck yourself, Phil," she replied, her blond head wreathed in white smoke.

The politician opened his mouth to answer, then thought better of it and shrugged. He picked up the newspaper, folded it tight and tucked it in his coat pocket. "Well, there's nothing to be gained by quarreling, is there? Kevin Reedy is healthy again, and he'll try to find the photographs. Perhaps I'll jerk a few strings and have him transferred to Homicide, put in charge of the Gilman case. That should provide us with some protection." He glanced at the banjo clock. "I have to be on my way. I'm meeting the mayor at the Parkman House."

"Give him my regards," said his sister sarcastically.

"If the police turn up and start acting tough, call Matty Fogarty. He knows how to handle those birds. I'll be in touch."

"Swell," Missy murmured.

After her brother let himself out, she began weeping quietly. Then the telephone rang.

Picking it up, she said, "Yeah?"

"Hi, Missy. This is Kevin," the instrument blared. "Can I talk to Phil?"

"You just missed him. He left a couple of minutes ago."

"Hell. Are you going to see him again today?"

"I might. Why?"

"Because a couple of guys just paid me a visit—young punks who work for Everett Wheeler. They wanted to interview me," said Reedy, obviously indignant. "I ain't used to pushy people like that. Almost lost my temper. But I got rid of the bastards, finally."

She dried her eyes with a handkerchief, and said, "How do you know they were working for Wheeler?"

"They told me, for chrissake. One of them even gave me his card with an address and a phone number—in case I want to turn stool pigeon. Wait a minute—here it is: *Travis L. Trumbull*—that's his name. And underneath it says *Massachusetts Coalition for Progress*. Mean anything to you?"

"No, but it might to Phil. I'll have him call you," she said, dinching her cigarette in an ashtray. "Listen, did you find out who's been bothering us yet?"

Reedy hesitated, and when he answered he sounded wary. "There's nothing I can tell you right now. I ain't been idle, but I don't want to go into any details."

"Why don't you talk to that rich bitch in Brookline: Harold's wife. She's the key to the whole thing."

"Yeah? I've been reading about her in the morning paper. Was that your boyfriend who got zapped? Pretty stupid," he said disgustedly. "I thought Phil told you not to—"

"Kevin, do me a favor. Check the woman out," she broke in, her voice as sharp as a scalpel. "She's responsible for everything. Long as Magda's alive, none of us are safe."

"You got any evidence to support this theory?"

"She hired a detective, a private detective, and he was the guy I gave the money to in the housing project."

"Yeah? Nobody told me nothing about that. What's his name?"

"His name doesn't matter now."

"Why not?"

"Because he's dead," she retorted, and then giggled nervously.

"Don't tell me any more. You got to watch what you talk about on a phone."

"I'm asking you to do me a favor, Kev. Go and put some pressure on Magda. She's got the rest of the pictures. I'm sure of it. Please. I did *you* a favor, didn't I? Couple of weeks ago? On the couch?"

"That was a favor to *me*? Jeez, I never thought of it that way."

"Didn't you? Well, maybe my brother will think of it that way, if I happen to mention it to him."

"Missy, you're really something. If you don't start acting like a grown-up pretty soon, you and me and Phil are going to be through, finished forever. Give him my message. I'll see you."

The phone went dead, and she cursed softly. Then Melissa noticed the teal bruise on the inside of her arm, touched it tenderly, and began to cry again.

35

Two days after the battle in the garage Frankie's nose was still swollen and his eye still black, but otherwise the detective had made a good recovery. It was Magda who had sustained the more lasting injuries, psychological ones that kept her awake at night and jittery and skittish during the day. The Valium she took couldn't block out memories.

At Gates's suggestion the two of them went into Harold's apartment and searched it thoroughly, but they found no tapes of conversations, no photos or reels of film, and no copies of confidential letters or memos. Disappointed, they returned to Magda's flat, where he poured two tall drinks.

"And you're sure there's nothing in his office?" Frankie asked.

"Absolutely." Magda's eyes were dark with fatigue. "It was a mishmash down there. Harold and his secretary were both disorganized people. They had no safe and they never locked the files. If Harold had a top-secret document, he would've left it lying around on a table like *The Purloined Letter.*"

"Like the what, Mag?"

She sighed soundlessly. "It's a story by Edgar Allan Poe," she explained. "But that conversation I overheard—maybe I misinterpreted it, Frankie. Maybe there isn't a blackmail scheme."

"People don't kill unless they have a good reason," he said, sitting on the sofa. "Now they're after you, so they must figure you have something or know something."

"Well, they're wrong." She placed her glass on a coaster, looked at him intently for a moment, and then added, "This week I'm flying to Tampa. My nerves are frayed. I need sunshine . . . a whole change of scene. I can't even go into that damned garage anymore. Have to park out on the street, I'm such a coward. I can't think straight, and one careless blunder might cost me millions."

"Am I invited?"

"To Tampa? Please, darling." She kicked her shoes off, stretched her shapely legs and critically inspected her pedicure. "I'm in desperate need of solitude and rest. I just want to forget the past few weeks—want to take long siestas, swim a little, bake on the beach, clear my head. We'll go together next trip, okay?"

"You said the same thing last November, Magda. This *is* the next trip."

"Did I? So much has happened lately. Oh, don't be a kvetch, Frankie. What about this police inquiry? Won't you have to appear?"

"It's not for a couple of weeks," Gates replied, his voice subdued. "Traveling by yourself could be risky. You should have a bodyguard. I know a real good one. Guard your body like it was his own. It won't cost you anything, either."

"I'm only going to be gone for a few days, lover. No one but my most trusted business associates will be told about it. I'll be safer there than I am here. I positively have to be alone for a while." Raising her eyes, she saw the poignant look of rejection on Gates's banged-up features. "Does it bother you that much?" she asked, mildly amused.

"Yeah," he admitted.

"Why, Frankie? Tell Momma what gives."

"Because the thought of not being with you for a week—not having you around—it sort of drives me nuts."

"That's nice. I never realized you were such a sentimentalist. I'm glad you like me, sweetheart. I'm crazy about you, too."

"Are you? I doubt it. Anyhow, that's not exactly what I meant," Gates said gravely. "I don't like you, Mag—I love you."

They exchanged glances. In his there was a shadow of fear; in hers there lurked a trace of skepticism.

Then Magda Gilman arched her eyebrows and commented gently, "This business of personal feelings, Frankie—you can't let them run wild. We're not teenagers, right? Adults, like you and me, have to exercise a little self-control."

"Good advice. Comes too late, though. Three or four months ago you should've warned me."

Her hands opened palms upward in her lap. "I never considered it necessary. You've always been such a worldly, practical kind of guy. Maybe this trip out of town is the best thing I can do, under the circumstances."

"Not as far as I'm concerned. I get pretty miserable when I don't see you for a couple of days. It's real dopey, like being sick. Never happened to me before." He stared off into space, evidently stunned by the idea. "I never figured I'd fall in love at this age. And certainly not with a Jewish girl."

"Come on, Frankie. It's probably just a phase, darling. Something hormonal. After I return from Florida we'll discuss it further, all right? Maybe by then you'll have recovered, and you won't be so romantic," she said, laughing lightly to soften the impact of her words. "You want to watch some television now? Isn't there a hockey game or a basketball match on?"

"What I want to do is marry you," said Gates, a distinct note of longing in his low voice.

Magda leaned back in the armchair and rolled her brown eyes towards the ceiling. "This conversation is becoming a little heavy, Frankie, and I'm in no condition to bear any more emotional burdens. Give me a break, will you? We'll talk about it when I get back."

"Is that your answer to my marriage proposal?" he asked, still gazing abstractedly into the dark fireplace.

"It's not an answer to anything. It's a reasonable request for a postponement of the discussion."

"Then you're going to consider it, Mag?"

The woman wriggled in the chair, and the green silk of her loose gown rippled sinuously. "What I'm going to do is go to Tampa and relax. Stop hassling me."

"You're turning me down," the detective told her, looking doubly forlorn because of his tumid nose and black eye. "You like me okay as a boyfriend, but you'd never seriously think of marrying me. Am I right or am I wrong about that?"

She sighed and shrugged.

"I'm not interested in your money, you know," he went on gruffly.

"I believe you," Magda said. "But..."

"But what?"

Wearily she put her hand to her throat, kept it there a moment, then let it fall gracefully to her lap. "I just recently lost my second husband. He died within the past month."

"I know, Mag. I know. I'm not trying to rush you. I'm willing to wait."

"That's considerate," she answered, a hint of irony in her voice. "I only wish you could've waited a while before bringing up the whole subject."

"I *have* been waiting," he blurted out plaintively. "That's not really the point, though, is it? You don't want to be my wife. I caught you by surprise, popping the question like that. The idea of marrying me never even occurred to you, did it?"

"Darling, I just never thought your intentions were honorable."

"That supposed to be a joke, Mag?"

"Listen, Frankie—I've got all these relatives, all these ethnic and religious and social ties. I'm part of a Jewish family, which is like belonging to the Mafia. You can't simply resign from it. You're committed. My life isn't entirely my own. It's a highly complicated structure, a Jewish family. Being a Gentile, you don't understand. My sister Miriam, in Westport—do you have any idea what she'd say if I married an Irish policeman? Hysterical paroxysms, she'd suffer. She'd think I was a mental case meshuga. Probably come around one day with a legal order, a psychiatrist, and a couple of nurses with a straitjacket."

"Who cares about your sister? You're a grown woman. It's not like I'm asking you to give up your family," he said sullenly.

"Never mind what you're asking me. It's what they're going to ask me. And even if I'm convinced you love me for myself alone, Frankie, there's an awful lot of gelt involved just the same. Suppose we have children? Does my half of the kid become a millionaire and your half go on Welfare? You can't begin to appreciate the way my sister and her husband—all my relatives, in fact—the way they view matrimony and inheritances and so forth. To them, getting married is a ten-times more serious business than dropping dead. And you definitely don't do it with somebody who isn't Jewish."

"Okay," said Gates. he finished his drink, set the tumbler down and stood. "I guess that answers my question."

"Now you're sore at me? Why?" she asked, genuinely curious. "I've always been honest with you, Frankie. I'm well aware that you saved my life the other night, that I'd be—"

"What the hell kind of remark is that to make, Magda?" His cheeks flushed.

"I'm just saying—"

"You're just saying I'm a cheap conniver, the kind of miserable bastard who'd try to capitalize on a thing like that to get you to marry him. Jesus, you've got a great opinion of me."

"Sit down, you stupid Mick. I didn't mean it that way at all," the woman replied calmly, her tired eyes dark with sadness.

"No, thanks. I'm going."

"All right, sorehead. Call me tomorrow."

"I'll call you after you come back from Florida…maybe."

"But I'm not leaving till the end of the week," she said in a conciliatory tone as he stalked from the room.

The wooden hangers in the foyer closet clicked and scraped. Shaking her head, Magda Gilman heard him struggling into his coat. After that the door opened and closed and Gates was gone.

36

Though he spoke to Phil Delaunay twice on the phone, Reedy never mentioned Ossie Peña's bizarre death. There seemed to be no reason to burden his friend, who was jittery enough already, with yet another piece of bad news. Moreover, Reedy was ashamed of what he had done that night in the Laundromat and hated to think about it. His reckless behavior had only made things worse. He was going to have to find the blackmailer with the raspy voice, get him to hand over the photographs—and it had to be done fast, too.

Reedy, however, wasn't feeling particularly strong or confident. While he had recovered from his strep throat, his stomach still caused him constant pain, and no amount of milk or Maalox brought him relief. Nor was his mental health very good. Unable to sleep at night, he did a great deal of brooding.

I can't think straight no more, he told himself—ain't right in the head or something. I been making dumb mistakes. They never would've found Gilman if I had buried him like Phil said. And the little Spic, I must've been dopey from the penicillin to shove him in that dryer. He was our only lead. Now we got nothing. Of course, there's the rich wife. Missy's a flake, but maybe the Jewish broad does have some information that would help.

Reedy didn't think Magda Gilman was actually a party to the extortion plot. Why would a millionairess shake anybody down for a lousy twenty grand? But the dirty pictures might be in her home somewhere. The husband might've stuck them under his shirts in a bureau drawer. It was even possible that the woman could provide a clue about the guy with the raspy voice who had phoned Missy and collected the money.

Phil had told the detective that he was going to have him put in charge of the Gilman homicide, and when that happened Reedy could interview the wife. He'd be able to investigate out in the open.

And even if she proved to be a dead end, the blackmailer was bound to call Missy up again and ask for another installment. He might be scared because of the Spic kid's death, but he'd do it anyway.

And that's when I'll grab the son of a bitch—nail him when he shows up for the payoff, Reedy decided. The important thing, though, is not to make any more dumb fucking mistakes.

37

When Gates came back down from the top floor of 868 Rodney Street he saw a man in an electric wheelchair sitting outside an apartment on the last landing. He had crew-cut gray hair and a gray toothbrush moustache.

"Looking for Tim Dunn?" the man asked, his manner almost accusatory.

"That's right." What time does he usually get home?"

"Ha! Won't be home till next week. Tim's in Mexico—Acapulco." The cripple studied him shrewdly. He had broad shoulders and a full chest, but the lower part of his body had atrophied into narrow hips and skinny legs. "You a cop?"

"Yeah."

"Plainclothesman or deek?"

"I'm a detective," said Gates brusquely.

"Oh. That's nice. What grade?"

"Third. And I take a size eleven shoe and I have a scar on my ass where a Doberman bit me one day down Castle Island."

The man in the wheelchair chuckled. "Hey, don't mind me. I'm all alone, you know? So I get awful bored. I don't have anybody to talk to, not since my wife left me a couple of years ago. So what do you want with Tim?"

Ordinarily Gates would have rebuffed the nosy man with another sharp retort, but since Dunn was going to be gone for a week, he decided to act more friendly. Maybe he'd learn something useful. Busybodies were good sources of information.

Therefore he said in a more amiable tone, "Nothing important. He owns a house in town near the Fenway. There's a whole lot of garbage piled up in his backyard. Some people must be using it as a dump and the next-door neighbor is complaining. Says the garbage attracts rats. I went over to the house, only nobody's living there."

"They don't usually send a detective to handle a thing like that, do they?"

Gates smiled ruefully. "No, they don't. This neighbor happens to be a close relation of the precinct captain, and generally speaking, it's a good idea to do what the captain tells you," he lied confidingly, winking a gray eye. "Dunn must be pretty well-off. From what I hear, the property values there in the Back Bay have shot right through the roof."

"Tim Dunn well-off? Ha! Every month I have to chase that lousy deadbeat to collect my rent from him. Only reason he can go to Acapulco is because his stupid girlfriend is footing the bills. Funny how some guys can live off women, isn't it? Don't have any character. Of course, Dunn gets a disability check from the city. Pulled one of those 'wrenched back' compensation swindles years ago, when he had a job with the Public Works Department over on Western Avenue. He's a nobody—an ignorant loafer, a crook, a nothing."

"I must have the wrong name, then. Those girls in the Assessment Office must've—"

"No, no—they gave you the correct information. Dunn *is* listed as the owner of that piece of real estate, but that's only because he's helping to perpetrate a flimflam. One night when he and his jerk of a girlfriend got zonked on port wine he told me the whole disgusting story. It seems Tim has a cousin who's a great pal of Philip Delaunay—the big politico from Brighton here?—and this cousin bought that house in the Fens for back taxes. Get the picture? A place probably worth a quarter of a million and Delaunay's crony was able to buy it for something like thirty-five-hundred dollars. Nice, huh? What's known as a 'sweetheart deal.'"

"And they stuck Dunn's name on the deed?" Gates asked.

"Of course. They like to hide these rip-offs from the taxpayers. The way the papers are written, Dunn can't sell the property or make any money from it. He's nothing—just a cat's paw for his cousin."

Flipping levers and pushing buttons on the arm of his mobile throne, the cripple swiveled the vehicle back and forth to express his agitation. The battery-driven motor accompanied these movements with short bursts of bombination.

"So it's the cousin who actually owns the building," said Gates, affecting nonchalance. "What's his name?"

"I'm not sure. I think his name is Reilly—but it might be Rooney. Has a house in Jamaica Plain someplace. Kenneth Reilly—I'm pretty sure that's it. Hey, maybe you know him. He's a Boston Police detective, too. A husky guy with a boozy red complexion—came here once to see Tim.

"Delaunay and this other chiseler have been buddies for years. Tim Dunn told me his cousin was dirt-poor as a kid, used to have holes in his shoes and wear hand-me-down rags. The family lived in Hanoville. You know that weird little section in Allston? Near Union Square. But some relative felt sorry for him, I guess, and paid to put the ragamuffin in St. Columbkille's—that's where he met Phil Delaunay. If his name isn't Reilly, it might be Ratty—Kenneth Ratty. Supposed to be a rough jaboney, so don't mention where you got your lead on him. I don't want any hassles. Have more than my share already."

"Hassles? Over what? Garbage in a backyard?" Gates said depreciatingly.

"You think I believe that fairy tale? Ha!" the disabled man said, affronted. "They'd never send a detective to serve a lousy summons for a misdemeanor. I wasn't born yesterday. There's an article in this morning's *Herald-American* about Delaunay's real estate shenanigans. I know what's what—and that's why I'm giving you this information. If you can send that miserable Tim Dunn to jail for a few years, you'll be doing me a big favor. God knows, he deserves it. And if you can ship his girlfriend along with him, it would be even better. I could tell you one or two juicy stories about her, also. Know the lady well. She used to be my wife. Still is, legally. But after I had my accident there on Mystic Avenue, that rotten little bitch went and—"

Abruptly the paraplegic stopped talking. His tongue licked away the bubbly froth that had formed on his quivering lips, while the light in his eyes, which had been shining with an acetylene brilliance, swiftly faded.

The wheelchair ceased its erratic swiveling, veered off to the right, and without pausing sped straight into the apartment. When the door slammed it sounded like the blast of a shotgun.

"Thanks for the help," Gates called, turning to leave.

As he walked thoughtfully towards his automobile, the whole picture began coming into focus. An influential politician like Phil Delaunay was a perfect target for a shakedown. And hadn't Gilman bragged to Magda about getting a big political appointment? Harold wanted power, not money. The lawyer was a conniver. He wanted to be put in charge of some government agency so he could wheel and deal.

But who the hell was the woman in the car? Delaunay's wife? Or his sister, maybe. Sure, sure—the girl with the psychological problems that Magda knew in school, the dippy one who stole her first husband. Gilman probably had something on *her,* and was using it to squeeze Delaunay. And when the sister met him to talk it over, she must've flipped and shot the guy. Then she phoned an old dependable friend of the family, the husky detective, and he raced to Tremont Street and took the body away. Except Harold was still living, and didn't actually die till this Reilly or Ratty sawed his head off in that house near the Fens.

Yeah, it's all pretty logical, he thought. Where does Stanley Gloag fit in, though? Maybe they think Magda had a part in the blackmail scheme, and because of that and the threat posed by the murder, they hired the punk to kill her. As for Ossie Peña, one of them must've noticed him staring out the window, so they went after him, too. There were some loose ends, but not many.

"I'd better have a long talk with Jack Reinhardt," Gates muttered to himself, a half smile on his rugged face.

38

A locker door banged in the adjoining room, and a waggish voice said, "Hey,

Aram, you know that kid you nabbed on Columbus Ave? The one who was raping all the nurses in the dormitory there?"

"Poindexter? Yeah, what about him?" a second voice responded against the background radio noise of rub-a-dub disco music.

"This morning the little bastard escaped from Charles Street—that's what about him. Didn't they tell you out front?"

"You serious, Grady? They let him get away? Poindexter escaped? How the hell did he do that?"

"It was easy for him, Aram. He just screwed the lock off his cell door."

Discordant laughter greeted this reply, and a third voice boomed, "Got you that time, rookie!"

In the Arrest Room next door Kevin Reedy bared his teeth in a crooked grin and remarked, "Jeez, that joke was old when I first came on the job twenty years ago."

Reinhardt nodded, the fluorescent light glinting off the bald forepart of his head. "Yeah, I must've heard it a million times," he declared, replacing the rubber band on the folder. "Everything's in the file, Kev—the interviews with his family, his friends, his secretary, his legal associates, the scalloper down the Cape. And the lab reports are there, too. Read it over. Maybe you'll pick up on something I missed. I wish you the best of luck."

"Thanks, Jack. And you think he got bumped because he owed a loan shark money? Even though his wife is rich?"

"She's rich, all right—only she doesn't throw it around. One of Gilman's gambling buddies, a ginzo from Revere, said the lady is so tight that her ass squeaks when she walks. Gilman might've been scared to tell her about his debts." Reinhardt shoved the folder towards his colleague. "And the guy's head and hands were lopped off. Somebody went to a lot of trouble—probably that creep Gloag, who was a professional bill collector. He worked for Max Goukas, Alfie Jay, Vito Bandello, Bernie Mulcahy—all those back-alley bankers."

Reedy considered Reinhardt's remarks, staring vacantly at the sign over the blackboard that said: PRISONERS NOT TO BE LEFT UNATTENDED AT ANYTIME IN THE ARREST

PROCESSING ROOM. "But how come this Gloag tried to zap the wife? I don't get that."

"My theory is they were after her to pay what Harold owed, and she wouldn't do it. Of course, she denies anybody bothered her for money. You can't pressure wealthy people like her. The best lawyers in this city work for Magda Gilman."

"You mean to tell me she didn't give all that expensive legal business to her husband?" said Reedy, grinning slyly.

"Nah, she knew what a hopeless bastard he was. They used to say Gilman was the kind of lawyer Jesus of Nazareth had," Reinhardt retorted, a rudimentary smile on his pug-nosed face. "God, Harold was an awful defender. Everybody here loved him, naturally. He could boost our conviction rate ten, fifteen percent, just by himself. The dumbest A.D.A.'s used to beat him, Kev. As a matter of fact the widow's theory is that he was killed by one of his former clients—some mug whose case he fumbled."

"She figures the guy got out of the slammer and then cut off his attorney's head for malpractice? Jeez, it's an idea. But they start murdering all the incompetent lawyers in Boston and we're going to have a fucking crime wave on our hands, Jack, ain't we?"

Before the Homicide detective could answer, his phone jangled and he snatched it up and barked, "Reinhardt."

Kevin Reedy left his chair, went to the water fountain and took a drink.

In the other room an Irish tenor shouted, "Hey, Aram! You ever hear that story about the cannibal butcher shop?"

"Sounds a little familiar, O'Brien, but lay it on me," said the voice of Aram in a guarded tone.

"Well, this lady goes in and asks the price of the meat. So the butcher says, 'German meat, a dollar a pound. Italian meat, a dollar a pound. French meat, a dollar a pound. Armenian meat, six dollars a pound.' And the customer says, 'Hey, why is Armenian meat so expensive?' And the butcher says, 'Lady, have you ever had to *clean* an Armenian?' "

Reverberant hoots of laughter drowned the measured beat of the disco music for at least a minute, but when the merriment finally subsided Aram could be heard saying, "Not bad, O'Brien. You know something? I just happened to remember a story about that same butcher shop. Want to hear it?"

"Why not?" said the tenor patronizingly.

"A different lady goes in there one day, and says, 'I'd like to buy some brains. How do the prices run?' And the cannibal butcher says, 'Well, we got English brains, a dollar a pound. German brains, a dollar a pound. Armenian brains, a dollar a pound. Irish brains, ten dollars a pound.' And the lady looks at him, and says, 'Ten dollars a pound! Why are Irish brains so expensive?' And the butcher says, 'Lady, do you know how many Irishmen we have to kill to get a pound of brains?'"

This anecdote provoked the loudest and most hilarious reaction of all, which continued unabated until an authoritative bellow brought it to an abrupt end. "Come on, you guys," roared the commanding voice. "What is this? Saturday Night Live? Get out to muster. The lieutenant's waiting."

In the grumbling drone that followed, someone with a brogue said plaintively, "I didn't think that joke was so funny, Obie—did you?"

"No, Callahan, I didn't," the Irish tenor replied. "I thought it was in very bad taste—absolutely uncalled for. They're just not recruiting the same class of officers anymore. You can't walk into the station house these days without finding yourself ass deep in vulgarity."

"Move it," yelled the authoritarian.

Listening at the open door, Kevin Reedy chuckled. Then he wandered back to the Arrest Room where Reinhardt, having finished his phone conversation, was now talking to a lean, rough-featured man who had a black eye.

The Homicide detective introduced them to each other, and Reedy said, "Hey, I know you. You're the guy who saved the Gilman woman there in Brookline."

Frankie Gates, studying the florid face of his new acquaintance, nodded curtly. "Jack was just telling me you're taking over that investigation."

"Yeah, been reassigned. Only I ain't so sure there's much of a case left. Probably this hump you shanked—this Gloag character—is the one who did the lawyer. Wanted to knock off the two of them for some reason."

"Could be," said Reinhardt. "But what bothers me

about that, Kev, is the M.O. Everybody I talked to claims Stanley never used anything except a knife, always told people he wouldn't carry a firearm because it was against the law."

"Must've been a real comedian—but it's a good point," Reedy answered, taking the rubber-banded file from the desk. "You wouldn't be related to Dinny Gates from Southie, would you?"

"He was my uncle—my father's brother," said Gates.

"No shit? Jeez, me and Dinny were great pals. We worked Dorchester together, years ago—old District 11. And I had him for a supervisor in the Tactical Patrol Force. Dinny was one helluva good cop—and very loyal, you know what I mean?"

"Sure. He was a helluva good uncle, too—the best."

"Absolutely," Reedy said, and tucked the folder under his arm. "Okay, I better get my ass in gear. Nice meeting you, Frank. I'll be in touch with you, all right? I'll be needing information about the Gilmans. Be nice if I could clear this case—start off with a bang, show everybody I ain't rusty. Okay, Jack. Thanks for the help. Take it easy."

With a wave of his hand, the burly detective turned and headed for the stairs.

Gates had planned to tell Reinhardt about Whitey Frainer and the house in the Fens, but as soon as he arrived the Homicide man had informed him that the Gilman investigation had been turned over to somebody else. Even so, he might have given what he knew to Reedy if Reinhardt hadn't mentioned in an undertone that "this guy has political pull. Been on the tit for years." The remark set off alarm bells in his brain, and when he saw that the new investigator was a husky man with a boozy red complexion, he instantly decided to keep his mouth shut for a little while longer.

"Funny, him knowing my uncle Dinny. Where'd he work before he was transferred here?"

"Kevin had a special assignment—ran errands for Phil Delaunay. They're old friends," answered Reinhardt, with a cynical smile. "But the guy has plenty of experience. Ten years back he and Tom Traubel broke the Lummis case—that young couple who got murdered in their Beacon Hill apartment by those three assholes from Wollaston. Kev and Tom traced them through a matchbook cover they found at the scene. Came from a dump on Morrissey Boulevard that featured nude exotic dancing."

"If he had a soft job, why'd he transfer back to Homicide?"

"He told me he was tired of listening to bullshit—tired of ward bosses and favor seekers. So he got Phil D. to have him reassigned. Always nice to have a friend in power. But Phil Delaunay isn't as sharp as his old man was, from what I hear. That Sunny Ned—politicians like him don't come along too often. Jesus, he was a shrewd bastard. Whenever he campaigned in the North End or Easta Bost, he'd have the announcer introduce him as Edward DeLeone. Yeah. And if he talked at some French-Canadian club, the accent would go on the last syllable. Then with the Wasps it got a very refined English pronunciation—Day-*Lawn*-ay. And for the Irish, of course, it was always Delaney. That son of a gun never missed a trick."

"Didn't he have a daughter, too?"

"Yeah, but she's the black sheep of the family, a kook, completely gonzo. I know a guy—I won't mention his name—who said he slipped her the eel once in the back of his station wagon, after a Saint Patty's day party at the Emerald Society. The word is she's a real nympho." Reinhardt shoved his chair out from the desk and said, "But enough of this high society gossip. I got to beat it. Have to see a deputy super at headquarters about my new case—some suspicious—deaths at an old ladies' nursing home. Sounds like it's going to be a real pain in the ass. See you, Frankie."

"Yeah, Jack. Take it easy."

Gates dropped into the still-warm chair, picked up the phone and called the Personnel Office. After a five-minute wait he learned that there were no Kenneth Reillys, Kenneth Rooneys, or Kenneth Rattys currently employed by the Boston Police Department.

The name that cripple out in Brighton couldn't think of has to be Kevin Reedy, the elated cop told himself. How am I going to handle it, though? With Ossie Peña dead, the only witness I got is a stumblebum wino with a history of mental problems. And this son of a bitch Reedy has powerful political friends. But there must be evidence in the house. Will I be able to get a warrant to search the place? Maybe I should talk to somebody in Internal Affairs.

Pondering the dilemma, he went off to perform his regular duties.

39

Kevin Reedy, too, had been giving thought to the problem of obtaining a search warrant, one that would enable him to examine the Gilman premises at the Allerton Arms.

From the police station he had gone home to Jamaica Plain, where he spent the next two hours poring over the file. Convinced at last that there was nothing there that might pose a danger to the Delaunays or himself, he returned the stack of papers to its folder with relief. Still, he hadn't discovered any clues as to the whereabouts of the photographs, either, which made him all the more anxious to rummage through Harold's personal belongings.

Shortly before noon he telephoned Magda Gilman, explained that he was now in charge of her husband's homicide, and asked to see her. She balked at first, spoke of having several important appointments, but eventually gave in to his arguments and told him to come over at two.

Hungry and a bit tired, Reedy ate a quick lunch of an American cheese sandwich, a bran muffin smeared with butter, and a glass of warm milk, then he dozed in a chair for an hour before getting up again and washing his face with cold water.

Large fluffy snowflakes were beginning to fall from the ashen sky as he left the house. He reached his destination fifteen minutes later and parked diagonally on Beacon Street.

Magda herself, wearing a skirt and blouse and a double string of pearls, opened the apartment door, and afte closely inspecting his identification, invited him in. Although they had met briefly ten years earlier at th Delaunay house, she recognized neither his name nor hi face. But Reedy had no difficulty seeing Missy's teenage friend in the mature woman who stood before him.

They went to her office. His questions for the most part were routine, and having answered them during previous interviews, Magda soon grew restless and curt. After a quarter hour of this he offhandedly requested permission to visit Harold's apartment—to "take a look around"—and she point-blank refused to grant it.

"Why?" he asked blandly, annoyed, but careful not to show it.

"Oh, come on. Would you like a stranger to enter your home and search it?" Magda countered. "I cherish my privacy as much as anybody else, and that apartment of Harold's belongs to me. Anyway, Frank Gates and I went over the whole place last Sunday, after that nightmare in the garage, and we couldn't find a single thing that was remotely suspicious."

Reedy restrained himself for a moment to conceal his eagerness, then inquired, "What exactly were you looking for, Mrs. Gilman?"

Thus Magda was inadvertently obliged to relate the whole story of the overheard phone conversation and of her notion that Harold might have been trying to pressure someone into doing him a favor.

"You mean he could have been blackmailing somebody?" asked the detective, without a trace of censure in his voice.

"From the way he spoke, I considered that a possibility."

"But you ain't got any proof. Didn't he mention names? Or say what he had that he was holding over this person's head?"

"No, he didn't. His part of the conversation consisted almost entirely of vague threats, just as I told you. And there was nothing helpful in his flat—no tapes, documents, pictures, letters." She paused and fingered her pearls. "Of course, I could be wrong about what I heard, too. I wasn't paying much attention at the time; I didn't even recall the incident until recently."

Kevin Reedy's face assumed a pensive expression. He gazed past the woman and out the wide clear window. Through a flickering veil of snowflakes he could see the tall buildings of downtown Boston hovering in the cold gray air like the turreted walls of a fortress. Swinging his eyes back to her again, he said, "What about your husband's business office?"

"His secretary and I searched it from top to bottom and we didn't find a thing of interest."

"Well, Mrs. Gilman, if it ain't in any of those places, he must've hid it in a safe-deposit box."

"Assuming there was something to hide."

"Do you know if he rented a box?"

Magda shook her head and glanced deliberately at her wristwatch. "Years ago we shared one. He might still have had a key to that."

"What bank?"

"Boston Guarantee Trust, the branch in Kenmore Square."

Once more the detective's ruddy features took on a thoughtful cast. Then he said earnestly, "Jeez, I know you're terrible busy, Mrs. Gilman, but could we just run down there and go through that box?" His lips widened in an ingratiating smile. "I'm very concerned because I received information this morning about some photographs, see? One of Harold's gambling buddies told me that your husband told him he had a bunch of pictures that would embarrass a certain person."

"Who's the certain person?" she demanded.

"The guy didn't know, so I don't, either. But if Harold stuck them in that safe-deposit box, we could find ou pretty quick."

She looked at her watch again, and said, "I have a appointment at four-thirty. Why don't we go tomorrow? then she grimaced. "No, I can't do it tomorrow. I'm takin a short vacation, and I have to pack. Is there a big hurry?

He shrugged his broad shoulders. "Last week some body tried to murder you, Mrs. Gilman."

"Okay. We'll dash down and dash back. Let me get th key."

They used Reedy's car, and when they arrived, he accom panied her into the bank. But as soon as they entered th lower level where the vault was located, an officious platinum haired lady in rimless spectacles refused to let him ad vance beyond the reception area even though he flashe his badge. Only box owners were allowed in the steel-lined adytum. Magda walked through an iron gate and vanished behind an opaque glass door.

Sitting on a leather sofa, Reedy waited. An elderly man in a homburg came tottering down the marble stairs a few minutes later, and without formality entered the inner crypt. As the glass door swung open to admit him, the detective caught a glimpse of Magda Gilman reflected in its shiny black pane. Fleeting as this sight was, he could see quite clearly what she was doing—examining a handful of 8 × 10 color photographs at a stand-up table.

When she reemerged, one end of a brown envelope projected from her leather bag. "I found something," she said laconically.

"Terrific," he responded, and they went back upstairs.

Snow had begun to accumulate on the sidewalk, and the fluffy flakes were coming down faster than ever. He took her elbow so she wouldn't slip, then held the car door open for her.

"Can I see what you got?" Kevin Reedy asked once they were settled in the Olds.

"Not yet. I think I'd better speak to a lawyer about it first," she answered in a firm voice.

"But it's evidence in a homicide case, Mrs. Gilman. I'll have to bring it into headquarters."

"Do you have a court order?"

"Nah. Never thought I'd need a thing like that."

"Then what's in this envelope belongs to me, until a judge says otherwise."

"Sure, sure," Reedy replied, appearing to accept his defeat graciously, though his heart was full of cold panic.

Into Kenmore Square he drove, but instead of turning, he continued on towards downtown.

"You're going in the wrong direction, aren't you?" she said mildly, after a couple of blocks.

"We'll swing around when we hit Mass Ave and return by way of Huntington and Longwood. My house is over near the Museum of Art, and I've got a mug shot there I'd like you to look at. Won't take more than a couple of minutes. Do you mind? It could be important. This guy is a professional poker player, and he used to be a pal of Stanley Gloag's. Claims he don't know a Harold Gilman, but maybe you saw him with your husband someplace sometime."

"That's unlikely," said Magda. She clicked her tongue in annoyance, and glanced again at her watch. "I rarely met his gambling friends."

"Don't worry. I'll have you back home by a quarter after three," he assured her. "Miserable weather, ain't it?"

At the juncture of Commonwealth and Massachusetts the traffic slowed because of a couple of stalled cars, but Reedy put his siren on and skillfully wormed his way through to Boylston Street. Along the Fens they traveled, past acres of dead Japanese bamboo and leafless willow trees stippled with perfectly white snow. Then suddenly they were on the weed-choked driveway and the noise of the other automobiles faded and died in the backwoods silence.

"Who's your gardener?" Magda wisecracked, though there was a hint of uneasiness in her eyes.

"I'm having work done on the entrance," he explained glibly, "so I got to use this side road. But the place is going to look great when it's finished."

At the little clearing he stopped the car. The dark stone bulk of the old house was visible through bare branches and falling snow. It had a ghostly appearance everything unnaturally stark, like a scene from a 1930' black-and-white movie.

"How come you want to bring them photos to you lawyer, Mrs. Gilman?" Reedy asked, staring through th snow-speckled windshield.

"Who said they were photos?" she countered.

"Ain't that what we were after? Besides, when that ol guy went in the vault, I happened to see your reflectio on the glass door."

"I want legal advice because what's in this envelop might be connected with the death of my husband. I'm businessperson, and I do things in a businesslike manner She tapped her wristwatch with a forefinger. "Let's g moving. I can't afford to be late for my appointment."

"Sure," he answered agreeably, and opened the doo But then he hesitated and turned to confront her agai "Only I still don't understand, Mrs. Gilman. Did yo notice something suspicious in the pictures? That why you won't hand them over?"

Eyelids flickering nervously, Magda met his gaze. "Suspicious? Like what?"

"Like a familiar face."

"And if I did, what difference would that make to you?" she snapped. "Sounds like you're trying to hit me up for a schmear."

"Nah, I just want to see them photographs," the detective said, smiling uncertainly. He felt strange—as if he were being forced to play a role, as if he no longer had full command of his mind and body. "I'll give them back when I'm done looking, Mrs. Gilman—honest to God."

"Nothing doing," she replied adamantly.

"Jeez, you ain't being reasonable."

"Until my lawyer says it's okay, nobody's going to get a peek at them. Now stop wasting my time. Do what you came here for and then drive me the hell home."

With surprising swiftness Kevin Reedy's broad countenance darkened into a coppery red. "Yeah, I'll do what I came here for."

When he lunged at her Magda screamed, but neither loudly nor long—and his hands on her throat prevented her from uttering a second cry.

40

After a long night of bad dreams about Magda, Stanley Gloag, a headless phantom, and even Osvaldo Peña roasting in a microwave oven. Frank Gates felt depressed and weary. He regretted having argued with his lady friend, and before the day was over had decided to pocket his pride and offer her an abject apology. Late that afternoon, therefore, he drove to the Allerton Arms, and when no one answered the door, let himself in with his own key and sat down to wait in the empty apartment.

Shortly after five o'clock someone from the Boston Redevelopment Authority phoned, asking for Mrs. Gilman.

He explained that she was not at home and he didn't know where she could be reached. Angrily the caller said that she was thirty-five minutes late for a vitally important meeting and that all the participants were growing impatient, especially the two city councilmen, who were not accustomed to being treated in such a high-handed manner. Gates soothed the BRA man, took his number, and promised to find the woman if he could.

This news disturbed him, since Magda was a stickler for punctuality. Dialing the lobby on the intercom, he soon learned from the doorman that Mrs. Gilman had gone out at two-thirty.

"Alone?"

"No, sir. She went with a policeman. He came at two, and they left together around a half an hour later."

"A cop? How do you know he was a cop?"

"Saw his shield. Hold on a minute. I got his name in the log book. Here we are. Detective Reedy, Boston Police."

"Reedy," Gates echoed softly. "Did they mention where they were going?"

"No, sir, but Mrs. Gilman said she wouldn't be gone long."

"And that was two-and-a-half hours ago."

"Just about."

Definitely worried now, Gates called the station house. The desk sergeant informed him that Kevin Reedy wasn't there, then provided him with the man's home number, which Frankie dialed. The unanswered phone rang fifteen times. Gates hung up, muttered a curse, and put his coat back on.

Because of the curtain of falling snow, the slippery pavement and the hulking orange plows on every other block, the few cars on the road were obliged to move at a snail's pace and it took Gates twenty-five minutes to travel the three or four miles to the old brownstone house in the Fens. He had a tough time locating the entrance to the narrow driveway because of the uniform whiteness of the hedge.

Off the street he found himself in another world. The ground, the bushes, and the overhead boughs were lavishly caked with sparkling snow. Down this alabaster tunnel he rolled and into the small clearing, where he saw the

Oldsmobile sitting under a silvery blanket. It was a sight that did nothing to relieve his mounting anxiety.

Acutely conscious that Reedy carried a gun, he got out of the car as quietly as possible. The dry snow squeaked beneath his shoes as he strode through the gap in the iron paling. He spied a basement door at the bottom of three granite steps, descended, turned the porcelain knob, felt the door give, and slipped inside.

Darkness engulfed him. Blind and disoriented he dared not move until his eyes, dazzled by the winter landscape, adjusted to the thick gloom. He waited and listened. Only a vague background murmur—a whispery echo, impossible to analyze—reached his straining ears. When an opening in the whitewashed wall appeared, Frankie made for it. Under his feet were round pebbles that grated and scraped on the uneven floor. Squatting down, he picked one up. In a sliver of light that seeped through a crack at the edge of the door, he gazed at the tiny stone for several seconds before realizing it was a pearl. He dropped it in his pocket, shook his head, drew his revolver and continued on to the next room.

Almost immediately he perceived someone sitting on a chair or box in a far corner of this murky chamber. Gates drew back instinctively, but the figure made no threatening move. Another three steps enabled him to distinguish that the sitter was a woman in a flowery white blouse. Despite the awkwardness of her pose, he knew it to be Magda.

She's unconscious, he thought, or tied and gagged. If I could see her face, but it's hidden in the shadows...

Softly calling her name, he advanced.

Frankie Gates groaned. It was a low poignant sound, the kind of hopeless cry a mortally wounded animal might utter.

For it was clear to him now that the figure had no head. The woman's neck terminated in a glistening black stump. What he had taken for flowers on her blouse were actually splashes of blood and gore.

"No... no... no. Magda, no," he whispered in anguish, his face contracting like a clenched fist while his broad shoulders began to tremble. "Magda, no... no... no."

With the tips of his fingers he caressed her arm. The

flesh was cool, yet soft as in life. Then he noticed that the hands were gone as well; the two tattered wrists lay in a dark shallow pool in the lap of her skirt.

"I'll kill the son of a bitch, Mag—I swear to Christ I will." He choked on the words as if they were chunks of hot metal. "I'll kill him. I'll get him, Magda. I'll kill him, I swear."

Abruptly he turned away from the headless corpse, moving in an oddly mechanical fashion. His gray eyes gleamed in his tortured face. Gun in hand he resumed his stealthy advance, climbed the steps, attained the top and entered a corridor alive with flickering light.

Like a disco, he thought irrelevantly.

At the same time he became aware of a crackling noise and the acrid smell of smoke. No more than a dozen feet from where he lingered a wide and pointed arch interrupted the opposite wall. Out of it came the mercurial beams that eerily illumined the otherwise dim passageway. Gates cautiously approached the opening and furtively peered around its near edge.

What he then beheld was a fair-sized room in a state of decrepit deterioration. Its walls were broken, and from their crumbling surfaces long shreds of mildewed wallpaper limply fell like dead lianas. Great gaps in the leprous plaster exposed the inner grill of ancient laths and scantlings. The ceiling was gone completely, of the floor there was little left beyond an ill-matched assortment of warped and rotten planks and the front of the room contained two boarded-up bay windows. The only sign of life in this cavern of decay was the sprightly fire in the large and curiously undamaged fireplace. It leaped, it swooped, it shimmered—driving the resident shadows off into distant corners.

On top of this blaze sat an odd object—a big ball of crumpled newspapers. One by one the pages of the irregular sphere were burning away in graceful curlicues of golden radiance. Like someone in a cataleptic trance Gates watched, until the final flimsy paper wrapping disintegrated into powdery ash. Then, as he had feared it might, a human head came into view amidst the writhing smoke and reeling sparks. Upright, though tilted to the left, it faced forward. The face was that of Magda Gilman.

A chilling grief flooded his pounding heart. To view those so familiar features in such a setting—disembodied, surrounded by a corona of orange flame—almost made him doubt his sanity. And as he stared, even more bizarre things commenced to happen. Stirred by the fiery draft, the head's brown hair began drifting sinuously about her slightly flushed cheeks, while tiny wrinkles appeared at the corners of her mouth. Gradually the full lips parted. Between them he could see her white teeth.

Stunned, Gates leaned against the doorpost. "Jesus, she's going to talk," he whispered in anguish.

No audible sound emanated from the head, however—no human voice disturbed the roaring fire's cackle. Like a sleeper deep in blissful dreams, Magda grinned.

That smiling mouth—how many times have I kissed it? Can she be dead? Is she really gone forever?

As if in response to these questions, the woman's eyelids twitched and fluttered, then tremulously opened. She gazed across the room at him, her lovely face alive, natural, happy.

"Magda, Magda," he mourned, in an undertone taut with yearning.

But the illusion endured for only seconds. The heat of the blaze, the seething fluids and gases in the roasting skull, soon induced even more grotesque physiognomic changes. The pretty eyes took on a sly and evil look, and from one of them a gout of blood dribbled like a ruby tear. Swiftly the cheerful grin became a nasty simper, and the nose wrinkled up like an angry dog's. The floating hair caught fire, and in an instant became a glaring sunburst of yellow flame. Darkening to an umber hue, the skin cracked and shriveled, while an ear turned into a bit of twisted charcoal.

Gates closed his eyes and his shoulders slumped. Then suddenly something hard jabbed him in the nape of the neck. A harsh voice growled, "Drop it or I'll blow your fucking brains out."

Involuntarily he flinched, and the muzzle of the gun dug deeper into his flesh.

"You ain't got a chance, Frank. Let go of it or you're gone."

Gates opened his hand, and heard his Colt .38 hit the floor with a hollow thump.

"Jeez. Good thing you didn't have it cocked," said Kevin Reedy. "One of us could've got a slug in the leg, or in the nuts, for that matter. Take three slow steps forward, Frankie, and don't try nothing cute, huh?"

Gates did as he was told. From the noises behind him, he sensed that Reedy had stooped and retrieved the fallen revolver. "The doorman at the apartment house—he told you I went out with her, right? But how the fuck did you locate this place? It ain't even registered in my name."

"What difference does that make?" said Gates stonily.

"Makes a big difference. Maybe you told somebody you was coming here. Did you?"

"Go fuck yourself," Gates retorted, and waited for the gun at his head to click and fire.

Reedy chuckled, then said, "You're a hard-nosed dude—a real tough rooster, Frankie. But I ain't surprised. So was Dinny, your uncle. I admired that man, no bullshit. He saved my ass a couple of times. Anyhow, I guess you didn't tell nobody. If you did, you'd try to stall instead of giving me guff. Listen, Frank, listen. You don't have to die, you know. Let me explain what's happening here, because I think I can trust you to understand the situation. I got this friend, see, a guy I've known all my life... like a brother, he is. And he was being shaken down by a shit-heel—that lady's husband. So my friend asked me to help him out. What do you do in a case like that? No way you can refuse... turn your back on him. Not if you're a decent person. If a man ain't loyal to his closest pal, he ain't nothing but a fucking piker—a piece of dirt, a guy with no pride or morals. Am I right or am I wrong?"

Gates, grimly staring at Magda's disintegrating face, said, "When you kill innocent people, you got to be wrong."

"What innocent people? Blackmailers? Besides, Frank, I didn't really want to hurt any of them. It all happened kind of accidental. I ain't no murderer... no criminal, honest to Jesus," Reedy blurted out irritably. "But never mind that. Listen, will you? This friend, my buddy, he's a bigwig. Shit, he's got wires that run straight into the governor's office, even down to Washington, D.C. He can smooth this over. All *you* got to do is dummy up—yeah, and I'll see that you collect a nice hunk of cash, enough to buy yourself a little summer house there on the Cape. And after, you'll have an in at City Hall—a rabbi who'll take care of you, get you plenty of quick promos. Ain't that better than a bullet in the brain? For chrissake, I don't want to whack no cop—especially if it's Dinny Gates's nephew. Be reasonable, Frankie. You're a young guy—and I'm only asking you to keep your mouth shut. Don't be a fucking jerk. What do those rich sheenies mean to a couple of Boston Micks like me and you? Both of us are on the force, too—remember that."

A plaintive note of supplication had crept into the man's gruff voice.

But Gates, his whole mind in a turmoil of wrath and hatred, was unable even to fake such a dishonorable agreement. Scornfully he snarled, "I don't do deals with scumbags, Reedy."

Stillness followed this short reply, a deathly quiet disrupted only by the crepitation of the fire. The detective with the revolver sighed wearily, and at almost the same instant, something extraordinary happened. A flashing, tumbling object of indeterminate size and shape came hurtling down from the upper reaches of the room, landed on the hearthstone like a grenade, and loudly shattered into a hundred scintillating fragments. An odor of alcohol pervaded the musty air.

Gates wasted no time in idle speculation about this reeking bolt from the blue, however. Spinning on the sole of his left foot, he rammed his right fist into Kevin Reedy's stomach.

The burly man grunted in pain and stumbled back. Grabbing his wrist in both hands, Frankie bent it earthward. The short-barreled gun went off with a booming detonation, harmlessly sending a bullet into the moldering baseboard. Then, by wielding the arm as if it were a whipstock, Gates flung his foe against the wall and nimbly followed through by driving a shoulder into his throat.

Loose plaster showered down on them as Frankie desperately tried to bow the wrist between his hands, hoping to snap it like a stalk. Before this could happen, however, Reedy cried, "Shit!" and released the revolver. It fell, clunked heavily on the floor and skittered away into the surrounding gloom.

Somewhere high above the wrestling combatants an eerie voice yelled, "Bust him one! Bust him in the nose!"

Momentarily distracted, Gates raised his head and received a knuckle in the eye—the same eye Stanley Gloag had blackened the week before. And while he was bemused by the galaxy of stars this blow engendered, Reedy wriggled loose and went lumbering down the hall.

Gates started after him. But then, remembering the man had a second revolver—the Colt—he returned to search for the other gun on the floor.

"That bozo's run down the cellar, Lieutenant," cried the ghostly voice aloft. "I seen him. You better hurry or he's going to skedaddle on you."

Crawling about in the flame-dappled shadows, Gates finally found the ebony-handled weapon and jumped to his feet. A quick dash through the arch and along the corridor brought him to the wooden stairs, but as he descended them he heard the Oldsmobile's powerful engine bellow, and by the time he reached the outer door, after a couple of false turns in the dark labyrinthine basement, the only sign of Reedy's car was the tire tracks—two cinereous parallel lines in the snow that curved around the clearing and vanished down the white tunnel of the driveway.

"Where the hell you running to, you stupid asshole?" he shouted hoarsely. "Where do you think you're going to hide, Reedy?"

The Mercury, still warm, started up easily—too easily, in fact. Its wheels spun, and then mired in slush and ice. Cursing, Gates made a more deliberate effort, rolled out of the tire troughs and steered for the narrow lane, but the car skidded, slewed sideways, and slit deep in a clump of bushes. Shifting desperately into reverse, he tried to back out. As the front wheels had gone down a small declivity, however, the task proved hopeless.

"Goddammit!" he snarled, throwing the door open.

There was no handy shovel leaning against a wall, no toolshed in sight. What he saw instead was a woebegone figure in a shabby, scruffy khaki overcoat and a bogus cowboy hat shambling through the snow near the iron palisade.

"Did he escape, Lieutenant?" Whitey Frainer called sympathetically. "Cripes, I chucked my bottle of Cossack at him, only I missed. Almost full it was, but I got scared. Figured he was going to shoot you and chop off your head. He's a crazy bozo, ain't he. Must be possessed with that idea—cutting heads off. Yeah, nearly full, the jug was. Didn't have time for more than a few sips, when I heard him talking. Funny how he likes chopping off heads. Takes all kinds, don't it? Too bad I missed him with that brand new, almost full bottle of Cossack, Lieutenant. Sure made a noise though, didn't it?"

Half mad from sorrow and frustration, Gates glared, but after a moment he managed a pained, uneven smile. "Thanks for saving my life, Whitey. I won't forget it," he said, sounding a little embarrassed. "And don't worry about that vodka. I'll buy you a case of it—all you can drink. Now help me get this fucking car out of the woods, will you?"

41

Night had fallen, but because of the thick layer of sugary snow draped over the world there wasn't much real darkness. The flakes were still tumbling down.

Reedy swung off the street and ploughed the heavy Olds through a two-foot drift on his driveway. Clutching the envelope in one hand, he climbed out and made his slow and difficult journey to the porch.

Within the house all was silent, gray, and cool. He shut the door, flipped on the light, and stamped the snow off his shoes and trousers and onto the mat, sending hollow thumps reverberating through the high-ceilinged rooms like the rhythmic beats of a bass drum in an armory. His face was frozen in stony desperation.

Upstairs he hit more light switches, tossed the envelope and Gates's Colt on the double bed, and stripped off his jacket. He then retrieved twelve hundred-dollar bills from the underside of a dresser drawer—emergency money he had taped there years ago—and shoved them in his pocket. Into a Samsonite bag from the closet he hurriedly stuffed shirts, socks, and underwear, but while he was doing this he noticed that some of the colored photographs had spilled out of the envelope onto the chenille counterpane.

"What the hell!" he exclaimed, startled by what he saw.

The naked, sweating blonde in the topmost picture was obviously Melissa Delaunay. And the man lying beside her, though his handsome features were more difficult to distinguish in the less-than-perfect print, was just as certainly her brother Phil.

Kevin Reedy's countenance registered disbelief, but by perceptible degrees this skepticism soon faded into a troubled stupefaction. He frowned, bowed his head, licked his lips and wiped his mouth with the back of a hand.

"That's incest," he muttered indistinctly. "Him and her."

With a forefinger he pushed aside the incredible photo to uncover a second shot of the same couple, this one an even sharper delineation of the scene.

How could he do a thing like that—screw his own sister? Reedy wondered, bewildered. Incest is a crime against nature. It ain't . . . ain't *normal*, for chrissake. The two of them are perverts—degenerates. That's why Phil couldn't let Missy turn herself in. If the story came out he'd be finished. That's why I had to get rid of the guy she shot. That's why Phil was so worried—why he was scared of Everett Wheeler. That's why I had to commit murders.

Kevin Reedy struggled to comprehend the whole sordid business, but he couldn't do it. The thing was too monstrous.

Suddenly infuriated, he snatched up the envelope and hurled it against the wall. At once pictures and negatives came floating down onto the wide expanse of the bed like variegated autumn leaves. And among them he caught a glimpse of yet another familiar face.

"Rita!" he whispered.

Plucking the colored sheet from the counterpane, he held it an inch from his nose and saw the only two people he had ever loved in his life locked in a rapturous embrace. Their mouths were agape, their eyes shut, their nude limbs taut with passion. The camera had captured it all.

"My Rita," the detective said in a grating voice. "And Phil."

He crumpled the glossy print in his hands and let it fall to the bed—but even as he did, he spotted a second graphic photo of the pair.

From deep in Reedy's throat a painful gagging sound arose. As if he were strangling, he staggered backwards until his legs touched the platform rocker. His bulky body sagged, yet he didn't sit down in the chair.

"Jeez...jeez. The day she died...that's where she was—up there seeing him," he croaked distractedly. "My best friend. My...my *pal*." He closed his right hand into a maul-like fist and punched the side of his head. "Why? Why? Why? I never hurt either of them—never."

For some minutes, swaying like a grief-racked mourner at a wake, Reedy stood there. Over his unseeing eyes a glaze settled, and his mouth hung open in a ghastly burlesque of a smile. Where he had struck himself on the temple, a coral blotch bruised his flesh, an irregular stain that seeped off under the line of his gray-streaked hair.

Then the soft winter silence was shattered by the labored rattling of a snowplow as it drove its iron blade into a drift out on the street. Reedy woke from his syncope of tormented brooding and blinked like an owl.

He went to the bed and calmly commenced to gather up all the photographs and slip them back in the large envelope. Even the picture he had crushed in his rage was carefully flattened and returned to the pile. Finished, he carried the thin packet into the next room and sealed the flap with some Scotch tape from the reproduction Governor Winthrop desk Rita had bought several years earlier at a country auction in Lee. Though his fingers trembled a little, he made a neat job of it.

Next Kevin Reedy groped in one of the pigeon holes, found the small white calling card he was looking for, and propped it up against a stapler. In embossed black letters it read:

Travis L. Trumbull
Massachusetts Coalition for Progress
1845 Court St.
Boston, Ma. 02204

He copied this name and address on the brown envelope with a felt-tipped pen, and all but surrounded it with twenty-two-cents postage stamps from a roll that he fished out of the desk's center drawer.

Wearing neither hat nor coat, Reedy left the house braving a rising wind as keen as a scythe as he plodded through knee-deep snow to reach the mailbox a half block away. If the raw weather bothered him, he gave no indication of it. His eyes were empty, his face a stolid mask. Once the envelope was safely deposited in the chute, he waded back to the house in the same unflinching manner.

The front door securely locked, Reedy walked leisurel into the kitchen and poured himself a tumbler of milk. This he carried along with him to the second floor, where he went again to the Winthrop desk and sat down. At measured rate, like a sideshow automaton, he drank his chilled milk in small sips, until he heard the screech of car brake outside.

Reanimated by the sound, he drew a pad from pigeon hole and began scribbling on it with the felt pen producing a crude, fuzzy black script that soon covere the smooth white paper.

A second automobile arrived, and shortly thereafter third. But the detective paid no attention. When he ha decorated several pages with the thick though legible cursive characters, he got up from the desk, returned t the bedroom and tossed the pad on his pillow.

Down below, somebody rang the doorbell, and a moment later a gruff voice called out, "Hey, Kev!"

Reedy took the Colt .38 from the bed and examined with a professional eye. His expression softened somewhat. He snapped the cylinder open, saw that every chamber held a cartridge, and snapped it closed again.

"Feels strange," he said, grinning absentmindedl "Fucking thing probably don't even shoot straight."

Looking around for a likely target, he spied Rita's blu cotton nightdress hanging on the closet door, aimed quick and sent a bullet into it just beneath the frilly collar. While the sudden noise of the shot echoed through the big old house, the flimsy blue gown floated languidly to the floor.

The shriek of splintering wood came from downstairs, as somebody's shoulder hit the front door.

Reedy's grin widened. Sticking the hot muzzle of the revolver in his gap-toothed mouth, he squeezed the trigger with his thumb.

42

"The poor man was a loony. Why is everybody making such a fuss over nothing?" said Melissa Delaunay, glowering at them from behind the corkscrew drapery of her blond hair.

Detective Petey Capodichino smiled engagingly. "All I know is what they told me at headquarters, miss. Your friend wrote a confession, and in it he implicated you and your brother. Why would he do a thing like that if it wasn't true?"

"Because he was out of his mind, that's why. Didn't he commit suicide, for God's sake? Anyway, Kevin Reedy wasn't my friend. He was Phil's buddy. I hardly knew the guy."

The other Homicide man, Dave Corcoran, shook his head sadly. "But there's a lot of evidence that lends credence to his story—like that photograph of you and your brother that we found under Reedy's bed yesterday."

Missy Delaunay flushed, then treated him to a contemptuous glance. "I'll bet you liked looking at that," she said nastily. "Trick photography is all it is—it doesn't mean shit. I'm not acquainted with any of these people who got killed. Never even heard of them."

"You went to school with Magda Gilman, didn't you?" Corcoran said, almost apologetically.

"Yeah, yeah, but that was a million years ago, and her name wasn't Gilman then." She straightened her hat in the mirror over the couch. "I shouldn't even be talking to you bastards. My lawyer would have a fit. That's why you didn't call up and warn me in advance, right? So he couldn't be here to protect me."

"Nobody's trying to pull a fast one on you, Miss Delaunay. We read you your rights, didn't we?" Capodichino said suavely. "The reason they issued the warrant was because Kevin put down a lot of verifiable details—about like where he threw the pieces of the derringer on Route 3 and so forth. And you had a license for a derringer, didn't you?"

"Did I? I'm through blabbing, fellows. Let's go," Missy said, her pretty face marred by a scowl. "Should I bring a toothbrush? Oh, fuck it. Matty Fogarty will have me out of there in a couple of hours at most." From the coffee table she scooped up her pack of cigarettes, then added, "This is all just a load of political bullshit."

Capodichino shrugged. "I don't know about *that*, Miss Delaunay," he remarked, turning to follow her. "Your brother's taking it very seriously. Dave here tells me he's already offering to P.B."

"Yeah. Wants to plea bargain," said Corcoran, opening the door.

"Phil? You're lying," she snapped petulantly, though a twitch of fear distorted her painted mouth. "Phil won't cop any plea. Jesus, if my father were still alive he'd have your badge and pension before you got back to headquarters."

As they entered the elevator a distant telephone rang.

"That's mine," Melissa said, and made an attempt to return to the landing.

But the detectives blocked her way and refused to budge.

"Don't worry. They'll probably try again later, after you come home," said Petey Capodichino ironically as the doors slid closed.

The caller, Rubyjewel, did try again. Indeed, she kept the phone ringing for the rest of that day and well into the night, but the lady from whom she expected to score another bag of money never came back to the apartment.

Not until the next afternoon did she and Scipio Africanus discover what had happened. Spread across the front pages of the newspapers were pictures of Kevin Reedy and both Delaunays. And when the pimp read the stories that accompanied them, he realized at once his dream scam had hopped a twig—that it was stone cold dead, and as good as buried. An evil mood took possession of him for the remainder of that week.

43

From behind a snowbank on the other side of Beacon Street, Frankie Gates watched the two Homicide detectives escort Missy Delaunay to their car. Seeing the maroon beret and beige polo coat the woman wore, he recalled Ossie Peña's description of her.

But she doesn't have the same build as Magda, not at all, he reflected sadly. I should've asked the kid more questions. It might have made a difference. Should've kept after him. If I'd known for sure that it wasn't Magda he saw, I probably would have told Reinhardt the whole story and she'd still be alive. Only Peña never got a good look at her body because of the coat. Maybe I should've believed in her more—but then a big shot like Delaunay might've railroaded her to prison. Did I handle it wrong? I did what I thought was right.

The car drove off. For a while Gates remained standing there on the sidewalk, a tall uncertain figure starkly outlined against the dazzling white snow. At last he walked slowly back to his Mercury, his lips moving soundlessly as he continued to ponder the question of his guilt or innocence.

44

In the garish lobby of the Montevideo Motel on Route 3A outside Nashua, New Hampshire, Mr. Ortega stared at the wrinkled page of the *Boston Globe*, shrugged his eyebrows and said, "It could be anybody. Gilman isn't such an unusual name."

"Oh, *mon Dieu*—it's him, *absolument*," said Nathalie, jiggling her carpet sweeper. "The mouth, the eyes, the funny wavy hair—he is certainly the brother of Ludy who came here two months ago. Now he also is dead, and his rich wife, too—their heads chopped off like with the guillotine. *Quelle horreur*!"

"The guy who came that day didn't look like a millionaire to me."

"Did he not drive a Cadillac?"

"Cadillacs don't mean anything, Nathalie. My cousin has one, and he's been unemployed for over a year and owes me four thousand bucks," said the motel owner, dropping the paper on his desk.

"About faces, Mr. Ortega, I have a memory *extraordinaire*. It is him," said the maid unequivocally. "And they are all of them dead—the two brothers and the young rich wife. What a tragedy, eh?" She struck a dramatic pose and recited feelingly:

"La vie est vaine,
Un peu d'espoir,
Un peu de haine,
Et puis, Bonsoir."

Mr. Ortega glanced at her quizzically, and said, "I don't speak French, Nathalie."

"*Quel dommage*. That is a little poem by Alfred de Musset—a thing I learn when I am small at school in Rimouski," she replied, a wistful note in her voice. "It means only that life is good for nothing. A little hope, a little hate—and then, good night. Very sad, *n'est-ce pas*?"

Before the motel owner could answer, however, his telephone rang and he picked it up.

Nathalie sighed, and resumed sweeping the wall-to-wall electric-blue broadloom.